"Why don't we get married?" Tessa declared.

They'd be here all afternoon if she waited on Shane to decipher her hints. "We already know each other. Sort of. And you said it yourself before. We each have something the other needs." Before he could speak, she rushed ahead. "No one could take the place of your first wife, I'm sure."

Something flashed across his face, an emotion she couldn't read. "I wouldn't expect anyone to."

"It's what you said," Tessa went on, relieved they were finally speaking on the same topic. "Things are different out West. Marriages are arranged for practical reasons. We're simply being practical."

"I just want to get this straight," he said, not appearing at all eager. "You're saying we ought to get married? You and me?"

Her enthusiasm deflated, and she pressed two fingers against her temple. This had seemed much more logical back in the marshal's office. Sitting here before Shane, trying to think of a good way to convince him that she was the perfect choice for a bride, nothing seemed clear.

Covering her unease, she snapped. "Of ___ rse you and me!"

Now that th ___ ed.

Sherri Shackelford is an award-winning author of inspirational books featuring ordinary people discovering extraordinary love. A reformed pessimist, Sherri has a passion for storytelling. Her books are fast-paced and heartfelt with a generous dose of humor. She loves to hear from readers at sherri@sherrishackelford.com. Visit her website at sherrishackelford.com.

Books by Sherri Shackelford

Love Inspired Historical

Visit the Author Profile page at Harlequin.com.

SHERRI SHACKELFORD

The Rancher's Christmas Proposal

HARLEQUIN® LOVE INSPIRED® HISTORICAL

Recycling programs
for this product may
not exist in your area.

 LOVE INSPIRED BOOKS

ISBN-13: 978-0-373-28335-4

The Rancher's Christmas Proposal

www.Harlequin.com

Printed in U.S.A.

Being confident of this very thing, that he which hath begun a good work in you will perform it until the day of Jesus Christ.
—*Philippians* 1:6

To my editor, Tina James,
because she can work miracles with even the most
disjointed manuscripts. Even though I'm convinced
that each book I turn in will end my career,
she always manages to dig out a little magic.
And sometimes she has to dig really, really deep.

Chapter One

❧

Train Depot, Wichita, Kansas, 1886

For one brief, idyllic interlude, Tessa Spencer had believed her days of living on the run were behind her.

That time was over.

Perched on her steamer trunk, she considered the list of cities chalked across the destination board, searching for inspiration. Her hasty exit had left her with few options and even less money.

Earlier that morning, a member of the notorious Fulton Gang had been asking some very pointed questions about her at the Harvey House café where she worked serving tables. She'd packed her belongings and set off for the train station before the outlaw's coffee had cooled. Since her regular shift began with the dinner service, she had until this evening before Dead Eye Dan Fulton discovered she'd flown the coop.

Her stomach pitched. Time was slipping away at an alarming rate.

"Ball," a small voice said.

She searched for the source of the interruption.

"Ball."

She glanced down.

A bright-eyed toddler with shiny blond hair smiled up at her. The boy was smartly dressed in a sky blue sailor shirt tied with a red scarf, his feet encased in gleaming black patent leather shoes.

Tessa frowned. "Where are your parents, little fellow?"

"Ball."

The wooden sphere he proudly displayed was obviously well loved, the painted stripes faded.

"Yes," Tessa replied. "That's quite lovely. Except you've gone and gotten yourself lost, haven't you?"

Most likely the boy's frantic parents had already begun their search. Keeping an eye out for stray members of the Fulton Gang, she studied the passengers milling beneath the awning of the train station, seeking any sign of a disturbance.

The boy tugged on her apricot-colored skirts. "Ga."

"You'd best be careful," she admonished gently. "Being lost is a lonely business."

The toddler extended his chubby hand, offering up his most prized possession.

Tessa waved off his gift. "Oh no, I couldn't possibly take your toy. Although I thank you kindly for the offer."

The boy grinned. He clambered onto the trunk, and she instinctively aided his ascent. He perched beside her and scooted close, pressing the warmth of his small body against her side.

"Best to stay put when you're lost," she said. "Or you only become more lost. That's what my dad always told me."

The boy tilted his head and stared at her. "Da-da."

"Yes, Emmett is my da-da." Tessa rolled her eyes. "He's a bit of a rogue. Not that he thinks of himself that way. Oh no. Emmett fancies himself a righter of wrongs, earning his living playing cards with folks who can afford to lose. Except lawmen don't appreciate that fine moral distinction, do they? And now he's run afoul of Dead Eye Dan and the Fulton Gang, which is even worse—I'll tell you that."

Heedless of her startling confession, the boy merrily kicked his heels against the trunk. She braced her hands on her knees and locked her elbows straight. Yep. She'd gone loopy, all right. At least talking to this little fellow was better than talking to herself, and she'd done plenty of that since Emmett's disastrous attempt at robbing a bank. He'd been tasked with concealing himself inside and letting the others in after closing. Except the bank vault had already been emptied when the Fultons arrived, leaving Emmett the only suspect.

"As you can imagine," she continued, "Dead Eye Dan is fit to be tied if he's come looking for me. I don't know where Emmett is hiding any more than he does, but I'm not sticking around to argue the point."

Obviously Dead Eye didn't know about her falling out with Emmett. Her throat tightened. She hadn't realized until recently how gloriously unsuited she was to a solitary life. The longing to see Emmett once more had become an almost physical ache. His love had been negligent, but as she'd learned over these past months, a slipshod sort of affection was better than nothing at all.

A nearby commotion snagged her attention. A towering gentleman in a cowboy hat and boots held a crying toddler—a girl, about the same age as the boy who'd taken up residence beside her. Though handsome, everything about the man was slightly askew. His hat sat at an angle, his collar was bent on one side, and the hem of his trouser legs was partially snagged on the stitching of his boot. He frowned and studied the area immediately surrounding his feet.

Tessa reluctantly stood. Though the boy's conversation was limited, he'd been a welcome diversion from her own difficulties. "Come along little fellow. I believe your da-da has discovered your absence. You will be my good deed for the day."

The boy eagerly took her hand. "Ga."

The distinctive word was obviously all encompassing. "*Ga* to you as well."

The gentleman's back was turned, although the woman beside him noticed the boy soon enough. From her sharp chin to the pointed tips of her black boots, she was about as welcoming as a barbed wire fence.

Her lips pinched, the woman extended her arm toward them, palm up. "The child is safe. There's no need to fuss."

Tessa narrowed her gaze and scrutinized the details. Emmett always said a good lookout needed to know who belonged where and why. Folks tended to pair up by status and temperament, and these two were opposites in both, meaning they were clearly not husband and wife.

The man whipped around. At the sight of the boy, his face flooded with relief.

He crouched and balanced on the balls of his feet. "Owen. You gave me a fright."

His obvious affection touched something kindred in Tessa, and she blinked rapidly. With her hopes of ever seeing Emmett again growing dimmer by the day, the sight was all the more poignant.

Everyone should have at least one person in their life who minded when they were lost.

The woman slanted a glance down the blunt edge of her nose. "Don't reward the boy. He'll only run off again."

Her tone pricked Tessa like a nettle. Memories from the year following her mother's death came rushing back. Only eight at the time, she'd been sent to live with distant relatives who begrudged having another child underfoot. Unaware of their simmering resentment, Emmett had arrived for a visit some months later. He'd discovered her huddled on the front porch, her arms covered in bruises.

Lawless or not, life with Emmett had at least been far more peaceful and far less painful.

"See, Alyce," the gentleman assured the toddler in his arms. "I told you we'd find Owen."

The two siblings greeted one another in a flurry of incomprehensible gibberish. They were a striking pair with their large, cobalt blue eyes and matching blond hair. Twins by the looks of them. The resemblance was even more pronounced by their clothing. Alyce wore a starched blue empire-waist gown cut from the same sky blue fabric as her brother's sailor shirt.

The children must have inherited their mother's looks, because the gentleman's hair was a deep, rich brown, and his eyes were the translucent green of a tender new leaf.

"Ball," Owen offered by way of explanation.

The gentleman flashed a boyish half grin, sending a little flutter through Tessa's stomach.

"The name is McCoy," the man said. "Shane McCoy. Thank you for returning Owen. He's quite the escape artist."

"Tessa Spencer," she replied, extending her hand.

The quick clasp of his fingers sent a stirring of goose-flesh up her arm.

He angled his body toward his companion. "This is the children's aunt, Mrs. Lund."

"Pleasure," Tessa replied, her tone clipped. The woman had her on edge.

As though addressing someone beneath her notice, Mrs. Lund gave only a slight incline of her head. "God rest Abby's soul. She always did have a knack for leaving her troubles on someone else's doorstep."

Tessa absently rubbed her arms. The poor man was a widower. No wonder he was overwhelmed. Especially considering his sister-in-law hadn't offered any additional help. Without a word of explanation, Mrs. Lund had set off in the direction of the ticket office.

"You must excuse her," Mr. McCoy said. "She's still in mourning."

Tessa smothered a snort. *Not hardly.* She'd seen people express more grief over the loss of a wooden nickel.

Unlike his acerbic sister-in-law, the bleak look on the widower's face mirrored her own despair. As much as it shamed her to admit it, she'd gladly assist Emmett with one of his swindles if only to see him once more. She'd taken for granted how much her world had orbited around caring for him. Oh, he was a capable grown man, certainly, but of the two—she'd always been more of the parent. Maybe that was why the haunted look in Mr. McCoy's eyes resonated with her.

At a loss, she gestured toward the heap of bags and coats at his feet. "Is there anything I can do to help?"

"Thank you for the offer," he replied, his light tone not quite ringing true. "But as you can see, I'm beyond help." He nuzzled the top of Alyce's head. "Isn't that right, my dear?"

Alyce bussed his cheek with a delighted squeal, and something inside Tessa melted a little. "I don't believe that for a moment."

Mr. McCoy flashed his boyish grin once more. "Perhaps not."

Certainly it was the early fall sun warming her cheeks. If only her own troubles weren't quite so overwhelming. The little family was obviously in need of a good deed, and good deeds were her new stock-in-trade.

The previous year, she and Emmett had attended a tent revival on a lark. The edifying experience had set her on a path of atonement. While she hadn't been completely sold on the itinerant religion, the preacher's words had given voice to the nagging unease in her heart.

That little voice had turned out to be her conscience. Each day with Emmett, that pesky voice had grown louder until she'd realized there was only one way to silence the clamoring. Since Emmett's moral compass had never been set to true north anyway, he'd taken her desertion badly.

Tessa squared her shoulders. "It was a pleasure to meet you, Mr. McCoy. I wish you all the best on your journey."

She wasn't certain if he was coming or going, and she didn't suppose it mattered.

"Likewise," he said. "What about you? Are you on the first leg of some grand adventure?"

"Actually." She let a small, self-indulgent sigh escape. "I'm not certain where I'm going."

"You're all alone, then?"

His innocent question had her eyes burning once more. If only her last words with Emmett hadn't been harsh. Her change of heart concerning his dubious activities had driven a wedge between them, and she should have tried harder to make him understand. If they'd been on better terms when the Fultons had approached him, she'd have talked him out of consorting with the dangerous gang.

The Fultons.

Her heartbeat picked up rhythm and her gaze darted around the platform. "Being alone isn't such a bad thing."

She'd been standing here like a dolt instead of keeping an eye out for trouble. A dangerous mistake.

Satisfied her lapse hadn't been fatal, she assumed her most serene smile. "I believe I'll go wherever the wind takes me."

She sure hoped the wind picked up soon.

"I miss those days," Mr. McCoy replied a touch wistfully. "Enjoy the freedom."

Alyce snatched his ear and tugged, replacing his melancholy expression with an indulgent chuckle.

Tessa's gaze lingered on his face. My, but he had striking eyes. She gave herself a mental shake. What sort of woman mooned after a widower? Quite a few, judging by the admiring gazes he received from several female passengers strolling past.

Bending to Owen's eye level, she smiled. "Stay out of trouble."

"Ga."

Unable to resist, she ruffled his hair, prolonging the moment. Her gaze locked with Mr. McCoy and they remained frozen, cocooned among the porter's calls and the shouted greetings tossed toward departing passengers. Never in her life had she felt such an immediate connection to someone. Or was her continued solitude simply taking its toll?

"I'm in your debt," Mr. McCoy said, breaking the taut thread of awareness stretching between them.

"Anyone would do the same." She tightened the ribbons on her bonnet and turned away. She mustn't leave her trunk unattended for long. As she knew firsthand, there were thieves lurking everywhere. "Perhaps we'll cross paths again one day."

Tessa tossed the last comment over her shoulder, wondering if he'd felt the same instant kinship. Probably not. Her shoulders sagged a notch before she straightened them. That sort of nonsense wouldn't do at all. She wasn't the sort of person who indulged in fits of melancholy. His obvious affection for his children had stirred up her guilt over Emmett, nothing more.

Mr. McCoy appeared lost and overwhelmed, emotions she understood all too well. Though the encounter felt unresolved, she resumed her seat on her trunk, retrieved her ledger and carefully searched out an offense.

Distracted shop owner while Emmett stole a hat.

In the opposite column she wrote "Returned lost toddler to his father."

Tapping her pencil against her bottom lip, she considered her admiration of the children's father and then discarded the lapse as an offense. He was a fetching gentleman and she'd always been drawn to kindness. No harm in that. Maybe someday, after this was all over... She shook her head. *No.* That was a foolish thought.

Love always came with expectations, and if one fought against those expectations, life was a misery. Her mother had expected a child would domesticate Emmett, but he'd left all the same. Emmett had expected her unwavering loyalty for his rescue, though he conveniently forgot he'd left her with those awful people in the first place.

While there were things about her years with Emmett that she'd genuinely enjoyed, her ledger of offenses was thick and her bank balance thin. She sensed Mr. McCoy was someone who lived by a rigid code of honor. A man who'd expect the same in others.

She closed her book with a snap, blocking out her pages of dishonorable deeds.

After tucking away her ledger, she studied the chalked destinations once more. Her spotty schooling had left her without much knowledge of geography, and she was at a loss. She'd settled in Wichita only because she'd liked the sound of the name.

"If You're up there…" she began, lifting her face to the warming sun. "If You're up there and You have any ideas, I sure could use one now."

A distinctive wooden toy struck the base of her trunk.

"Ball," a familiar small voice declared.

Planting her hands on her hips, Tessa leaned forward. "You are a troublemaker, aren't you?"

Looking inordinately pleased with himself, Owen grinned. "Ga."

Tessa squinted at the sky. "You and I need to work on our communication."

The train whistle blew, startling Alyce, and Shane murmured soothing nonsense. He forced his thoughts away from the lovely Miss Spencer and concentrated on the task at hand. *I am doing the right thing.* Maybe if he kept repeating those words, they'd feel right, they'd feel true.

Unaware of the changes about to upturn her young life, Alyce fiddled with his collar and kicked her feet. *I am doing the right thing.*

Having left Owen with the pinch-faced Mrs. Lund, he arranged for the twins' baggage as well as his own return ticket. Crowds of people surged around them, agitating Alyce and further darkening his mood. This was Abby's dying wish—she wanted her children raised by her family. Only Abby wasn't here anymore, and she didn't see how the children's smiles had faded beneath her sister's dour countenance.

When he returned to where Mrs. Lund was standing, Owen was nowhere to be seen.

"Where is he?" Shane demanded.

Mrs. Lund lifted one shoulder in an unconcerned shrug. "Perhaps if he isn't showered with attention upon his return, the boy will cease running off."

Taller than average, Shane quickly spotted Owen pestering Miss Spencer once more. His rush of relief quickly morphed into anger. There was no way Mrs. Lund had seen Owen from this distance. For all she knew, he'd wandered onto the tracks.

Singularly unrepentant, she crossed her arms over her chest. "Proper discipline is what the boy needs, not coddling. I hope these sorts of antics won't be commonplace with the children."

Her voice grated on Shane's nerves. The woman had all the warmth of a root cellar in winter, but she was also the twin's closest kin.

"They've been cooped up," he replied shortly. "They're bound to wander."

He and Abby had been childhood sweethearts. They'd paired up mostly because their ages matched and they were always seated together in the one-room schoolhouse. At seventeen, Abby had pressured him for an engagement. He'd thought them too young and he was already overwhelmed with his own responsibilities. His father had abandoned the family three years before, and Shane had taken over as the man of the house. Despite his best efforts to soften the blow, urging Abby to wait instead, his refusal had incensed her.

They'd gradually lost touch after her parents had died and she'd moved away. Years later, she'd arrived at his ranch, pregnant and alone. Compelled by honor and loyalty, he'd thought he was doing the right thing by marrying her, hoping their past friendship might grow into something deeper. Except she'd never stopped loving the man who'd betrayed her.

Mrs. Lund harrumphed, and her gaze shifted. "Have you made the arrangements with the bank?"

His jaw worked. "I'll finish up this morning."

That figured. Abby's older sister may have lost sight of Owen, but she hadn't lost sight of the money he'd offered for the twins' care.

How had such a simple arrangement become this complicated? Ten years older than Abby, her sister had been married and gone by the time he and Abby had started school together. After Abby's death, their correspondence had been brief, but Mrs. Lund had been well aware of her sister's wishes and hadn't balked. He'd put off the inevitable for as long as he could, but the time had finally arrived.

As though sensing his tension, Alyce squeezed her small hands around his neck. He absently rubbed her back in soothing circles.

"Everything will be fine," he said, though his blood simmered. He turned toward Mrs. Lund and, with an effort born of sheer will, kept his tone calm. "It's been hard on them, losing Abby. They need patience."

"Fine talk coming from you," she snapped. "A man foisting off his children as though they were so much chattel."

"You know what Abby wanted," he said quietly. "The ranch is isolated. If anything happened over the winter..."

"Or perhaps my sister regretted her choice of a husband."

Her words slashed at his conscience. "We can finish this discussion later."

As though his day couldn't get any worse, he locked gazes with a pair of sparkling blue eyes. A flush crept up his neck. He didn't know how much Miss Spencer had heard, but it was probably too much.

"We meet again, Mr. McCoy." Despite her casual words, Miss Spencer clenched her hands before her stomach, her knuckles white. "I believe this little fellow belongs to you."

Assuming his most stern expression, Shane switched Alyce to his opposite shoulder and reached down. "Owen, that's twice today."

The boy grinned, not at all sorry. Shane raised his eyebrows. Leave it to Owen to find the prettiest girl at the depot. The child was a positive flirt.

Miss Spencer's gaze darted around the platform. "I believe Owen was chasing his ball and became a little lost."

The tight coil he kept around his emotions eased a notch. Owen's champion was smartly dressed in a traveling suit the color of a ripe peach. The cheerful hue brought out the luster in her flaxen hair and the flecks of gold in her sharp blue eyes. Though clearly nervous about something or someone, she exuded an air of confidence and grace.

Her presence felt out of place on the crowded platform. As though she belonged in a private parlor—sipping tea and waiting for her Pullman car. She was the sort of woman Abby had always admired. The rope around his emotions tightened once more. The sort of woman who'd find him boring and suffocating, no doubt, just as Abby had.

"Thank you," he said. "For returning Owen. *Again.*"

"My pleasure."

Her voice had a husky quality that stirred long-dormant yearnings. Though she kept a calm visage, there was something troubled about the way Miss Spencer kept glancing over her shoulder. The more time he spent with her, the more he realized there was an air of mystery surrounding his lovely Good Samaritan. That ambiguity made her all the more alluring, and he fought against his curiosity. Mysteries had a way of ending badly.

While Shane struggled for a suitable reply, Owen tossed the ball toward Mrs. Lund.

She squeaked and dodged sideways, then snatched the boy's shirt and cocked back her arm. "You did that on purpose, you little—"

"No!" Shane shouted helplessly. With Alyce in his arms, he struggled to reach Owen.

Miss Spencer threw herself before the boy and grasped Mrs. Lund's wrist.

Gratitude rushed through him.

Mrs. Lund's face suffused with color. "Get your hands off of me!"

"I will not stand by and watch you hit a child," Miss Spencer declared.

Sensing the trouble he'd caused, Owen whimpered behind her skirts.

"I wasn't going to harm the boy." Mrs. Lund sniffed. "Not that it's any business of yours. A woman, traveling alone. You're no better than you should be."

Shane moved between the two combatants. "I won't have you insulting Miss Spencer."

"And I won't have this…this *person* questioning my intentions."

"What were your intentions?" he challenged.

His sister-in-law gasped. "How dare you question me!"

Now what? It sure looked as if Mrs. Lund was getting ready to haul off and wallop the boy. And if that was the case, then her actions changed everything. No matter how desperate, he wasn't leaving the children with an abusive guardian. They might not be his children by blood, but he loved them all the same, and he was honor bound to ensure they were well cared for, no matter what Abby's wishes.

Mrs. Lund's mouth worked, and after several tense seconds, she gathered herself. "We had an agreement. There's no need to fuss."

Shane rubbed his forehead. *Impossible situations.* He had a singular talent for landing in impossible situations. With winter coming, he'd lose the help he hired from town. The weather isolated the ranch, sometimes for weeks. He'd kept Abby's secret about the babies—everyone assumed he was their father—and he was bound to abide by her request concerning the children's care. Yet he questioned her sister's intentions.

People were always hiding their true motivations. Abby had claimed she still loved him, even though she was pregnant with another man's children. Mrs. Lund had claimed she wanted to raise the twins, when clearly she was more interested in the money. Even he was keeping secrets—Abby's secrets. Of the three of them, only Miss Spencer had no reason for duplicity.

As though only just deciphering the situation, Miss Spencer looked between the two of them. "You're leaving the children with *her*?"

Mrs. Lund tossed her head. "After seeing how he manages them, I can understand Abby's insistence that I raise the children. They are in need of a firm hand."

Shane turned his back on his sister-in-law and faced Miss Spencer. The disappointment in her eyes sent his words spilling forth in a hasty confession. "I live on an isolated ranch. We're cut off from everything during the winter. It's just my men and me."

Miss Spencer swayed forward. "Your ranch is isolated?"

"It's just south of Cimarron Springs. Completely off the map."

"That sounds quite remote." Her voice grew breathless. "And inaccessible."

"Uh." He wasn't certain if there was a question buried in her statement. "Yes."

Shane reached for Owen, who clutched Miss Spencer's skirts all the tighter. His chest constricted. He wasn't leaving them with Mrs. Lund, even if that meant defying Abby's wishes. Though she was the children's closest relative, he'd known her for less than twenty minutes. In that short time he'd seen how truly unsuitable she was for the task.

Twenty minutes.

About the same amount of time he'd known Miss Spencer. His gaze lit on Owen's lovely rescuer. She obviously feared something or someone, though she was doing her best to cover her anxiety. She wasn't as excited about her travels as she'd have them believe. He sensed her independent nature and her stubborn resolve, but he had his own streak of obstinacy as well.

For a moment he imagined the world from her viewpoint, and his thoughts left him unsettled. An unmarried woman without the protection of relatives had few resources. Traveling alone was dangerous, more so farther west. Did she know the trouble she courted? Was she aware of the admiring stares she evoked? A very male sense of protectiveness tightened his jaw.

Mrs. Lund reached for Owen, who cowered away. "Come along," she ordered. "We've wasted enough time."

The boy burst out crying.

"No." Shane spoke more forcibly than he'd intended. His gaze fastened on Miss Spencer. "I'll find another way."

Chapter Two

Searching for a way to gently extract herself from the tense situation, Tessa took a discreet step back. She'd already caused enough trouble for Mr. McCoy, and the more she delayed, the more trouble she caused for herself as well.

Mrs. Lund smoothed the hair from her temple. "I blame Abby for this. She never had a lick of sense. Always running with the wrong sorts of people. Look at what it got her. I suppose I should have known she'd marry someone cut from the same cloth. Blood will out, as they say."

Tessa gazed at the two beautiful children. "Yes, blood will out." If the twins were any indication, Abby had not been cut from the same cloth as her sister. "By way of apology, perhaps I could distract the children while the two of you speak alone."

Shocked by her impulsive suggestion, she froze. Really, this was none of her business, and she was being terribly forward, but the poor widower looked as though he had a few choice words for his sister-in-law that were best exchanged in private.

A muscle ticked in his cheek. "I believe you're right, Miss Spencer. Mrs. Lund and I have a great deal to discuss."

"Call me Tessa."

"Then you must call me Shane."

His sister-in-law made an exaggerated show of straightening her hair and pressing her clothing with flattened palms. Tessa glanced warily between the two. There were fireworks coming, that much was certain. Mrs. Lund had best not underestimate her brother-in-law. Tessa sensed a spine of steel behind that even-tempered exterior.

Clearing her throat, Tessa drew their attention. "There's an ice cream parlor across the street. Why don't I arrange a treat for the children and let you and Mrs. Lund have a moment in private?"

Shane hesitated. "Are you certain?"

"Positive." Despite his assurances, she *did* feel somewhat responsible. When she'd thought Mrs. Lund might strike the boy, she'd seen red, and her instincts had taken over. Though she didn't regret her actions, she *had* set this chain of events into motion. "We'll take a seat by the window. That way, you can see us as well."

He gestured toward a young porter standing vigil near the ticket office. "Can you store the lady's trunk?"

"Right away, sir."

Tessa noted the cut of the freckle-faced porter's clothing and took stock of his shiny new shoes. He was obviously well paid, which meant there was no reason for him to rifle through her belongings for valuables.

"Thank you, Shane," she said. "For your thoughtfulness."

"Enough." Mrs. Lund snorted. "I don't have all day while the two of you chatter about nonsense."

"I believe that's my cue." Tessa knelt and gathered the twins close. Emmett had always discouraged the wasting of one's charm on the charmless. "Your dad says it's all right if I take you for ice cream. Is that all right with you?"

The two exchanged a glance.

Owen nodded. "Ga."

"High praise indeed."

She led them across the street and took a table near the window. Their vantage was doubly useful since Shane could keep sight of his children, and she could keep watch for Dead Eye. She didn't suppose outlaws frequented ice cream parlors. So long as she didn't attract more attention to herself, she was safe. For the moment.

Oblivious to the drama unfolding on their behalf, the twins were instead fascinated with the intricacies of the metal scrollwork chairs. Alyce knelt backward on the seat and traced her finger around the twisted heart pattern. Attempting to climb up as well, Owen pushed her aside. Alyce shoved him back.

"There's no need to fight." Tessa scraped another chair closer. "Wouldn't you like your very own seat, Owen?"

He squinted, then crossed his arms over his chest and stubbornly glared at his sister.

Shrugging, Tessa sat and pivoted her legs beneath the table. "How very nice it is to have a chair all to oneself. Makes one feel very grown up."

From the corner of her eye, she watched as Owen carefully rested his ball on the table and claimed his own seat. Though pleased with her success, she kept her emotions hidden lest Owen catch on.

Only a few tables in the parlor were occupied, showcasing the black-and-white tile floor and the blue-and-white-checkered curtains hanging from the windows. During the height of the summer season, the shop must burst at the seams. With a slight chill in the fall air, business had obviously slowed.

She studied the list of choices. "I believe the special today is chocolate. Chocolate is a fine choice, on any occasion."

After taking their order, the grandmotherly shop owner clasped her hands. "My, but your children are well behaved. And so lovely, too. If you don't mind me saying so, they're the spitting image of you, ma'am."

Without waiting for an answer, the woman circled back around the counter.

Tessa tugged her lower lip between her teeth. Explaining her actual relationship with the children seemed unnecessarily complicated. She'd always adored children, though life with Emmett hadn't afforded much opportunity to be around them. Considering her current predicament, she didn't suppose there'd be much opportunity in the future either. A pall fell over her once more. Always before she'd had hope, but the passing of time had relentlessly drained her optimism.

She rolled the ball across the table and Owen stopped it before it tumbled off. Alyce found the game more entertaining than tracing the metal scrollwork and joined in the fun. The task took a great deal of concentration and giggling.

An elderly couple seated nearby watched their antics with indulgent smiles.

The woman leaned toward Tessa. "You have a lovely family. Makes me think of my own children at that age. Enjoy this time. It passes quickly."

Feeling a fraud, Tessa murmured a few polite words

in response. They were strangers. She'd never see them again. And yet she was no better than Emmett was—playing a game of smoke and mirrors based on assumptions. Worse yet, the game was all too familiar, almost comfortable, like donning one's winter coat after a long summer.

The shop owner returned and handed Tessa two folded flour sacks.

"Their outfits are so pretty," the woman said. "I'd hate to see them mussed."

Grateful for the shopkeeper's thoughtfulness, and still feeling a touch guilty, Tessa knotted the sacks around the squirming children. A tug of longing surprised her once again. There was no reason to be maudlin. Emmett had loved her dearly, she'd never doubted that, but he'd always been slightly befuddled with having a little girl around.

Over the years, ladies from the boardinghouses and saloons where they'd stayed had occasionally taken her under their wing, showing her how to fix her hair and dress properly. Sometimes she felt as though she'd had scores of mothers, and other times she felt as though she'd had none at all. Everyone had different expectations, and she'd spent much of her life puzzling out her role with new people.

One way or another, she'd been searching for something elusive all her life. Just once she wanted affection without expectations. Someone who knew who she really was and loved her all the same. Her fingers tightened around Owen's ball. An impossible hope considering her past.

As the shop owner placed two bowls of ice cream before the children, a grim-faced Mr. McCoy stepped inside. He doffed his hat and took the remaining seat.

Alyce snatched her bowl and lapped at the ice cream.

Laughing, Tessa pulled the bowl away. Now sporting a chocolate beard, the toddler groped for her spoon. Tugging the utensil out of reach, Tessa wiped the sticky mess from Alyce's face.

Shane lifted his spoon and turned toward Owen. The boy worked his mouth like a baby bird.

"They haven't mastered the fork and spoon yet," he said. "Sometimes it's best if we assist."

"Of course." Tessa stole a glance at him from beneath her eyelashes. "Is everything all right?"

"We've decided Mrs. Lund is far too busy to watch the children over the winter."

"Perhaps that's for the best. You're a good father, keeping them with you. You've done the right thing."

He flushed beneath her praise and looked away. "Miss Spencer, thank you for your help. I hadn't met Mrs. Lund before today. I had no idea she was quite so…harsh."

Tessa tilted her head. How odd the widower had never met his sister-in-law before today. Then again, she didn't know much about how regular families worked.

His expression turned severe. "She had other reasons for wanting the children. I can't abide falsehoods."

Instantly chilled, Tessa ducked her head. "Have you considered placing an advertisement? An older woman, perhaps a widow, would not attract gossip."

There was a hopeful gleam in his eyes that had her wary. For a moment the idea of living in the wilds had struck her as the perfect solution. Before she'd realized the impossibility of such a plan. Despite having been raised by an unconventional parent, she understood propriety all too well. While she wasn't particularly vain, she was too young and too unattached for the role of housekeeper. Which made losing her job at the Harvey

House all the more catastrophic. There were few opportunities for single ladies. She'd seen the life of a saloon girl firsthand living with Emmett, and while she understood desperation, she'd do anything to avoid *that* fate.

Shane collapsed back in his chair and raked his hands through his hair. "Abby had certain...wishes." A shadow passed over his face. "I've backed myself into a corner. With winter coming, I'm running out of time. An advertisement could take weeks. I'd have to wait on the post. Then the applicants must be carefully scrutinized. We live in tight quarters on the ranch."

Tessa stared at the spoon clutched between her fingers. "I should never have interfered in something that was none of my concern. I've had a lot on my mind recently."

"You're afraid of someone, aren't you?"

Her head snapped up. "Why would you say that?"

Her acting skills had obviously rusted.

"A few things. Like the way you sat so you could keep an eye on the door. And before, at the train station, you were as jumpy as an outlaw in a room full of deputies. Are you a runaway heiress or something?"

Tessa fiddled with the lace at her collar. "Nothing so romantic, I'm afraid."

Clearing her throat, she glanced away. The outlaw-and-deputies analogy had struck a little too close to home.

"If someone is bothering you," he said, "perhaps I can help."

"We're quite a pair, aren't we?" Though she hadn't expected an instant shower of riches, she'd thought living a moral life might result in a bit more reward and a bit less trouble. Carefully choosing her next words, she said, "I've attracted the attention of a somewhat shady character."

That wasn't too far from the truth. Nor was it a lie. Dead Eye Dan was definitely a shady character.

Shane's eyes widened. "Who is this person?"

"He, uh…he came into the Harvey House where I work. *Worked.* He's been asking about me." Which was also the truth. Maybe not the entire truth, but a good portion of it. "I have reason to believe he's an outlaw."

A really, *really* good reason.

She imagined Dead Eye Dan trolling through town with the daguerreotype picture of her that he'd flashed at the Harvey House. The picture he'd obviously stolen from her father. She'd seen such events play out before with startling predictability. As long as the outlaw concocted a believable tale, each person she'd met this morning would proudly declare her whereabouts. People enjoyed feeling helpful. Meaning the more time she spent with Mr. McCoy, the more she put him and his family in danger as well.

Shane offered Owen another bite and caught her gaze. "Outlaws dine at the Harvey House?"

"Everyone dines at the Harvey House. We have the best prices and our service is impeccable."

"I don't doubt it." He paused. "You don't happen to know this fellow's name?"

Skirting the truth had the unfortunate side effect of leaving too many openings for pointed questions. Tessa considered making a run for the door, then discarded the idea. She'd only attract more attention. And, really, what harm was in a name?

"He's called Dead Eye Dan Fulton."

Shane scoffed, "That is the worst outlaw name I've ever heard."

"Not very clever, I know." Tessa laughed in spite of herself. "He has a meandering eye. It's terribly difficult to carry on a conversation with him because you never can tell which eye is looking at you… I'm rambling again."

"I'm curious." Shane removed the flour sacking from around Owen's neck and wiped his chocolate-covered fingers. "Why don't you simply turn him over to the sheriff?"

"Staying out of his way seemed the best solution. I wouldn't want to anger him."

Or his brothers. She couldn't very well tell Shane about the rest of the Fultons either. Just like she couldn't tell him that if she turned in Dead Eye, the outlaw would guess her involvement in a heartbeat.

The Fultons might not be the smartest men, but they weren't the dumbest either. "As you can probably imagine, one does not rebuke the advances of an outlaw without consequence."

"I see your point." Shane tipped the glass bowl and scooped out another bite. "Then you've decided to abscond like a thief in the night."

Tessa sighed. There it was again, that unfortunate reference to thievery. "Despite what the poets say, absence does not make the heart grow fonder. He'll forget about me soon enough once I'm out of his sight."

She hoped.

The door opened and she leaped halfway out of her chair then sat back down with a thud. The elderly couple who'd admired the children earlier were leaving. No need for panic.

"Sorry," she said. "Thought I saw someone I knew."

To her immense relief, Shane appeared unfazed by her weak excuse. "You've had a rough go of it, haven't you?"

A sharp pain throbbed in her temple. She wasn't lying, though, not exactly. She was withholding certain facts for his protection. Men like Mr. McCoy didn't understand men like Dead Eye.

Despite the bolstering thought, or maybe because of it, she averted her gaze before biting the inside of her cheek.

Emmett had been certain she'd fail on her own, certain she'd come crawling back, begging for his help. He could have at least had the courtesy to be available for the begging-and-crawling portion when the time arrived. "I'm starting on a new adventure. It's very exciting."

Exciting in the sort of way a catastrophic train wreck was exciting, but rousing all the same.

A shadow passed before the window, and she shrank back, dipping her head and covering her face. Everyone simply assumed they were a loving family enjoying the afternoon, and she'd relaxed into the illusion. She'd taken for granted the respectability of traveling with Emmett. Alone, she attracted all sorts of unwanted stares and attention.

Bolstering her courage, she stood. She'd made her choice, and she had no one to blame but herself if the going was difficult. Her heart heavy, she reached out and brushed the backs of her knuckles along the cushion of Alyce's cheek, then ruffled Owen's hair.

The twins had devoured what ice cream hadn't melted and claimed their spoons. They were having great fun sweeping their fingers around the glass bowl, seeking every last drop. The task took a great deal of concentration, which meant Tessa had lost her last excuse for lingering.

The ticking clock above the counter propelled her forward. "It was a pleasure meeting you, Mr. McCoy. You have a beautiful family. Despite your difficulties this morning, I feel certain you will prevail."

She squared her shoulders and focused on the door. The important part was not looking back. Emmett always said that life was not meant to be traveled backward.

Shane caught her hand. "Wait."

She mustn't turn around. All of her instincts screamed that he expected something from her. She knew full well she'd never live up to those expectations.

Certainly she'd never been one to linger over little heartbreaks and trivial disappointments. This morning when she'd realized her time at the Harvey House was at an end, she'd set out with dogged resolve. Though she mourned the loss of her delicate new friendships, she hadn't faltered.

Yet her feet remained rooted in place. She didn't believe in fate, but something had brought them together on that platform. Of all the people passing through the station, Owen had found her. Surely that meant something in the grand scheme of things.

The preacher at the tent revival had said that in helping others one helped oneself. But what did a retired thief have to offer?

Shane released her hand. "Hear me out. Please."

The appeal in his voice scattered the last vestiges of her good sense. "I'm listening."

Chapter Three

Miss Spencer's direct gaze had Shane tied up in knots again, and he immediately forgot what he was about to say. There was a chance they might help each other—if he took care of the problem plaguing her first. Just once he wanted to do the right thing and have something good come of it.

Before Shane could speak, Owen reached for his spoon and slipped. His body fell forward and he splayed his hands, nicking the edge of his bowl. The glassware slid across the table. Tessa lunged. The bowl dodged between her fingers and careened off the edge. Melted chocolate splattered her skirts before the glass shattered.

Owen sobbed and rubbed the spot on his chin where he'd bumped the table. The boy reached for Tessa and she immediately resumed her seat, pulling him onto her lap while carefully avoiding the shattered glass. Owen grasped at her white lace collar with sticky fingers and buried his chocolate-covered face in her neck. Oblivious of the damage marring her pristine outfit, Tessa rubbed his back and murmured soothing words.

Shane swallowed hard once. Then twice. The twins

had sought that affection from Abby, craved her attention. Instead, she'd drifted through their lives like a marionette, going through the motions without any more warmth than a carved wooden block. Everything he'd done to help had only made matters worse.

As Owen's cries turned into hiccups and eventually subsided, Tessa glanced up, her expression troubled. "I have to go. My shift normally starts at dinner. When I don't arrive, Dead Eye will start looking for me."

She was paler by the moment, her movements jerky and frightened. Shane blew out a breath. He'd always had a weakness for the marginalized. All the men he'd hired on the ranch had conquered adversity in one way or another. Finch had lost his right arm and the vision in his left eye during the war. Wheeler was a freed slave Shane had met on a tortuous stagecoach ride through the sweltering Texas heat.

The others…well, the others had seen more than their fair share of hardship. Probably that was why Abby had returned once she'd realized she was in trouble. She knew he'd never turn her away. Yet he suspected a difference in Tessa. As though she'd take any offer of protection as an affront, though clearly she was in need of assistance.

Shane scowled. The outlaw deserved a throttling for terrifying her. Barring that, he'd do the next best thing.

"Let me help," he said quickly. "Please."

Owen fidgeted in her lap and she produced a coin he hadn't noticed before. With a deft flick of her wrist, the coin disappeared. Owen snatched at her fingers and frowned in confusion. She fisted her hands a few times, turning her arm this way and that. With an exaggerated frown of confusion, she brushed Owen's temple.

"Hmm," she said solemnly. "What have we here?"

With a flourish she produced the coin from behind Owen's ear. The boy squealed in delight.

Alyce stood in her chair and leaned over, eagerly joining the game. Without answering him, Tessa absently repeated the trick. Much to the delight of the children, the coin dropped from noses and sprang from beneath dimpled chins with an elegant and imperceptible sleight of hand. Shane was as mesmerized as the children with the rapid disappearance and reappearances of the coin. Only when she dropped the money into her reticule was the spell broken.

She glanced up and he shook his thoughts back to the problem at hand, grasping for a convincing argument.

"The next train doesn't leave for hours." He charged ahead. "I have an idea that may help us both."

Her face softened and his persuasions died on his lips. Abby had an odd habit of staring at a spot over his shoulder, never looking directly at him. The practice had left him feeling invisible. Tessa met his gaze dead-on, her expression open and forthright.

"I'm not sure how you can help." She quirked an eyebrow. "Unless you have a freshly pressed dress handy or a private stage for a hasty exit out of town?"

"No." Her directness was refreshing and disconcerting at the same time. "I'm afraid not, but I can offer you a room at the hotel." At the startled look in her eyes, he quickly added, "To freshen up."

She gave a sad shake of her head. "I wouldn't mind staying out of sight and cleaning up, but I can't displace you."

"As you can see, our plans have changed."

A riot of color suffused her cheeks. "Because of me."

"Never say that. My plans have altered because Mrs.

Lund wasn't a good choice for a guardian. I might not have realized her unsuitability," he added, "if Owen hadn't pestered you into returning him."

Owen grinned at the sound of his name, revealing his two front teeth. "Ball."

"Don't paint me as the hero," Tessa replied, raising her delicately arched eyebrows. "I was a little reluctant to return him. He's a very good listener."

Shane dug through his pockets, producing the metal key. "This is the only key. I have some business in town. If you need to change, I can fetch your trunk as well."

"Not the trunk! I mean to say, that won't be necessary. I'm sure a dab of water will take care of this."

Shane didn't know much about laundry, but he figured it was going to take a lot more than a spot cleaning to erase that damage.

His doubts were forestalled by a flutter of activity. Summoned by the commotion, a woman in an apron bustled over. Together they plucked shards of glass from the floor and wiped up the mess.

Tessa brushed at the stains on her gown. "I can't very well travel like this."

"Definitely not."

Reaching out, she rested her hand over the key. "You said there's only one key."

"Only the one." He'd bought himself some time. With a little effort, his plan would erase the fear in her eyes and make up for the trouble they'd caused her. Then maybe he could convince her they each had something the other needed. "I'll walk you the distance and be on my way."

Owen showed no signs of surrendering his perch, and Tessa absently tucked him closer. The boy rested his head in the crook of her neck and stared at the shiny locket nestled at the base of her throat.

With a last glance over her shoulder, she nodded. "I accept your offer."

Shane blew out a relieved breath. "You'll be on your way in no time."

Keeping vigil for outlaws with wandering eyes, Shane escorted his motley bunch to the hotel and made arrangements with the clerk. Miss Spencer was obviously not well-known in town, as none of the staff showed even a flicker of recognition.

Not that anyone could get a good look at her anyway. She spent much of the time helpfully chasing after Owen and Alyce as they reached for the vase of flowers on the round table in the lobby and crawled between the spindly legs of a settee.

The room he'd procured was at the end of the corridor and he walked her that way, then gathered the twins. Owen yawned.

Tessa hesitated. "How long will your business take?"

"An hour. Maybe two."

"The children appear tired."

"They usually nap around this time."

She reached for Alyce, who eagerly took her hand. "I could…I could watch them. You know, while you accomplished your task."

He hesitated, not wanting to take advantage of her. "If you're certain."

Her offer was ideal. Better than he could have hoped. While he was fully prepared to take the twins on his errand, he moved faster without them.

"Aren't you afraid I'll abscond with your children?" she asked, turning the key in the lock.

Her bright smile stole his breath. Her eyes sparkled and a delightful dimple appeared in her left cheek. He'd been immersed in his own troubles for so long, he'd forgotten the simple pleasure of a moment of joy.

"I'm more afraid they'll send you screaming into the streets," he said at last.

"I'm much stronger than I look."

Her dimple disappeared and he mourned the loss. "I don't doubt it."

Tessa turned the key a few times, but no click of the lock sounded.

She removed the key and studied it closely. "The numbers match but one of the teeth is bent. That must be the problem."

"I'll see if they have another."

"No need."

She reached behind her head and pulled a hairpin from the coil at the nape of her neck, then inserted the slender metal into the space beneath the key. Her brow knit in concentration, she jiggled the hairpin a few times and the door sprang open.

Shane gaped, nonplussed by her odd talent for disappearing coins and difficult locks.

"I—uh," Tessa stuttered. "I once had a temperamental lock on a boardinghouse door. I learned a few tricks."

He supposed there was nothing too odd in that. "You're quite the locksmith."

"It comes in handy at the oddest times."

The twins hugged him around the legs before he left, but seemed content to remain with Miss Spencer. Relieved at Owen and Alyce's easy acceptance of the situation, he made his way toward the train depot with only a twinge of guilt for taking advantage of Tessa's good nature. The twins had been roused earlier than usual this morning and should sleep easily. Tessa appeared as though she could use the rest as well.

Her intervention with Owen, though unplanned and unexpected, had pushed him out of his stupor. While he'd like to believe he'd have seen Mrs. Lund's duplicity eventually, viewing her through Tessa's eyes had forced him into acknowledging her unsuitability.

The telegraph office was devoid of customers, and he accomplished his task in short order. Having a cousin who served as a telegraph operator was convenient. Having a telegraph operator for a cousin who was also married to a lawman was even more helpful.

A flurry of messages were received and dispatched over the following hour, and he took a seat on the bench tucked into a corner of the small office, impatiently tapping his heel. A fine bead of sweat formed on his brow. Miss Spencer must be pacing the floors by now. He checked his watch for the thousandth time. Another forty-five minutes passed before the sheriff appeared. Shane met him at the door in three long strides.

The man was tall and slender and as weathered and thin as a strip of beef jerky.

He presented Shane with a wanted poster. "There's a reward for Dead Eye. Where would you like it sent?"

A reward. His stomach twisted. Glancing at the picture, his eyes widened at the sum listed on the bottom of the page. Tessa could hire her own private Pullman car with that amount. She certainly wouldn't need a housekeeping job. He stuffed his free hand into his pocket and shook his head. At least one good thing had come out of this mess.

"You've got him, then?" Shane prodded. "He's locked up?"

"Picked him up straightaway. Didn't put up too much of a fight. I suppose he didn't figure anyone around these parts would recognize him."

For once, doing the right thing had resulted in something good. Maybe not for him, but that wasn't the point anyway. "Excellent."

The sheriff pushed his hat back on his head with the tip of his index finger. "And how did you come to recognize him, Mr. McCoy?"

Shane scratched his temple and stared at the floor. "Long story."

The question had nagged him as well. How had Tessa known the identity of the outlaw? He shrugged. She probably saw all sorts with people coming and going from the café.

"Understood." The slender man touched the gun strapped against his thigh. "You'd best not stick around, just in case."

"Trust me, there's not a chance he'll connect me with his capture, but I'll be on my way all the same."

"Not so fast. You haven't told me where you'd like the reward sent."

Shane considered and discarded several possibilities. Best not to leave a trail that might lead back to Miss Spencer. "Send the money to Marshal Cain in Cimarron Springs. He'll know what to do."

Once Miss Spencer was settled, he'd make arrangements to have the money transferred. She'd spotted Dead

Eye first, after all, and the money was hers. The sheriff jotted down a few notes and went about his business.

His steps dragging, Shane returned to the hotel. Separating from Tessa was for the best. Being around her stirred up a sting of loneliness. Always before he'd thrown himself into work when the yearnings for companionship had grown too distracting, exhausting himself in body and spirit. The children had forced him to keep a part of his heart open, and he'd be wise to be on his guard in the future. Tessa reminded him of Abby when they were young, full of hope and hungry for adventure. He didn't want to see that optimism fade.

He rapped on the door and Miss Spencer appeared, holding a finger over her lips. A scowl darkened her brow.

"Shh," she ordered. "They've fallen asleep."

Somehow or another she'd draped the stained portion of her skirt like a fall around her waist, cleverly disguising the spots. There were damp portions around her collar where she'd scrubbed at the rest of the marks, and he forced his gaze from the charming sight. His was an honorable mission, and he did her a disservice by thinking of her in any way other than an unexpected acquaintance.

She slipped into the corridor and quietly shut the door behind her. "Where have you been? What took so long?"

"I'm sorry. I can explain." He handed over the wanted poster. "They've picked up Dead Eye Dan. You're safe now."

Her face grew ashen. "What have you done?"

He gripped her shoulders, shocked by her violent trembling. "He's behind bars. He can't bother you anymore."

She vigorously shook her head and backed away. "You don't understand. This is worse. This is much worse."

"There's a reward." His declaration only sent her stumbling farther back, and his hands dropped away. "I had it sent to Marshal Cain in Cimarron Springs. The outlaw will never guess your identity. Contact the marshal and he'll make the arrangements."

Her pale lips pinched together. "I wouldn't touch a dime of that money if my life depended upon it."

"Why not? You spotted him. You've earned that reward."

"Because it's dangerous, that's why. Claiming the reward money will lead the rest of his gang directly to me."

Her fear instantly made sense, but there was an easy enough solution. "Come with us to Cimarron Springs, help me with the children. I'll pay you for your trouble. I'll even claim the money myself and hand it over to you. That way, you're not involved."

She jerked her head in a negative gesture. "You'll put yourself in danger. I won't allow that."

"I'm a grown man."

"You're a father. You should consider your children. Lawmen aren't always honest."

The skeptical edge in her voice stiffened his spine. "I trust the marshal in town. He's married to my cousin. He won't put either of us in danger."

Her shoulders slumped. She opened the door once more and stared into the room. He caught a glimpse of Alyce and Owen asleep on the bed, curled around each other like puppies, a bolster of pillows surrounding them.

"I know you're strong," he said. "I know you don't need my help, but I need yours."

Blood rushed in his ears. He couldn't recall the last time he'd asked someone for help. He'd been independent since the moment his father had walked out on them, and he liked it that way. As long as he didn't count on people, they didn't let him down. Since arriving in Wichita, he'd felt as though he was unraveling bit by bit. If he let this go on any longer, there'd be nothing left of him.

"Never mind," he said, reaching for the key. "It's been a long day. I appreciate everything you've done. I had no right to ask for more."

She yanked her hand out of his reach. "I'll help you."

It was too late to take back his offer, and gratitude and shame warred in his chest. She'd agreed to help him. She'd agreed because she'd seen him weak.

Tessa hesitated. "I'll leave Cimarron Springs as soon as the reward arrives. You know that, right?"

"I know." Earlier, a selfish part of him had hoped she might consider staying on, just until he found a suitable replacement, but she'd obviously anticipated his appeal. "I understand."

Tessa had called him a good father before. She'd said he was doing the right thing by keeping the children with him. The truth was far less charitable. He wasn't a fit parent for the children any more than Mrs. Lund. By refusing to face the impossibility of the situation, he'd been lying to himself rather than doing what was best for the children.

"Four o'clock," he said, replacing his hat. He was done being weak. Once they were all back home, he'd finally make things right, even if it shattered him. He'd put himself back together before; he knew how the pieces fit. "We leave at four."

Now that he'd committed to his decision, a cynical relief surged through his veins. The reward money made everyone's life simpler. Without Tessa, there'd be one less person in town who'd been disappointed by him.

As long as nothing unforeseen happened, they'd never see each other again after the journey's end. She was as good as gone. At least there was nothing left to go wrong.

"The reward money has hit a snag." Marshal Garrett Cain spoke from his seat behind his desk.

"What kind of a snag?" Tessa demanded, covering the panic in her voice. "I was hoping to avoid a delay."

She needed the money quickly. She'd already been in town for three days. That was long enough. Too long, really. She feared she'd run into Shane once more, and the cold shoulder he'd given her upon their arrival had made it abundantly clear that her presence was unwelcome.

"Let's give Shane a few more minutes." The marshal shook his head. "He needs to hear this, too."

Tessa stifled a groan. Perched on the edge of her seat in Marshal Cain's office, she tucked the edges of her skirts around her frozen ankles. Wind whistled beneath the door and frost coated the windowpanes.

She shivered and tugged her coat tighter. "There's no need to bother Mr. McCoy, is there? This really doesn't concern him."

Though Shane's rejection had hurt her more than she cared to admit, his absence was for the best. She was putting them all in danger the longer she stuck around.

"He's on his way already," the marshal said.

Perfect. She offered a tight-lipped smile of acknowledgment. Just what this day needed.

All the little nagging worries she'd harbored piled up around her in a suffocating heap. She'd had no more success in contacting Emmett, which meant her meager savings must stretch indefinitely. Though she'd scoffed at the reward before, a few days of introspection had given her clarity on the matter. Considering her situation, money was a good thing. Someone was going to collect that reward, and it might as well be her. Since she was no longer an outlaw, the code didn't apply anyway.

She glanced across the desk separating them. The marshal held her gaze with a benevolent expression she imagined he normally reserved for relaying the news of untimely deaths.

"I don't suppose your news is good news?" she asked.

"Nope."

On that less-than-cheerful note, he stood, plucked several pieces of wood from the stack near the potbellied stove and stoked the fire. Though clearly not the best conversationalist, he was a fine-looking man with dark hair showing a feathering of gray at the temples. The lawman had a forthright manner and a direct approach that compelled honesty. The kind of man Emmett avoided at all costs.

Her mouth went dry. "You have me worried, Marshal Cain."

And that was saying something.

The door burst open in a flurry of cold air and a young girl scooted inside. Realizing she had a brief reprieve before Mr. McCoy arrived, Tessa forced the tension from her shoulders. The newcomer flipped back her coat hood and stomped the snow from her boots on the rag rug.

The young beauty was in her midteens, showing the first blush of womanhood with her bright blue eyes and curly corn silk hair. "Shane is on his way," the girl said. "He's talking with Mama now."

The marshal assisted her with her coat. "This is my daughter, Cora. Cora, this is Miss Spencer."

The girl held out her hand. "Hello. I've heard so much about you."

Tessa tucked an escaped tendril of hair behind one ear. "Surely not. I only met your father this morning."

"I didn't hear about you from Papa."

Heat crept up Tessa's neck. Shane must have spoken of her—but why? She doubted she'd made much of an impression. Touching her cheeks, she hoped they weren't flaming as hotly as they felt.

The marshal ushered his daughter through a second door at the rear of the office. Tessa caught sight of a jail cell and a flight of stairs through the opening.

"Enough, Cora," the marshal ordered. "You're making our guest uncomfortable. I'm guessing your mother will be along soon. Why don't you run along upstairs and put on some coffee? You know where to find everything."

Yep. Tessa's cheeks were definitely flaming.

A gust of winter bluster indicated another arrival. Her heartbeat thundered and the freshly stoked fire suddenly turned the room blistering hot. Shane stepped inside and turned toward the coat hooks, presenting her with his profile. The corners of his mouth drooped at the edges and his eyes were tired and bloodshot, as though he hadn't slept in a month of Sundays.

He hung his hat on the peg near the door and ducked his head. "Miss Spencer."

"Mr. McCoy," she replied, matching his formal tone.

He didn't appear at all happy to see her. Not that she'd expected cartwheels and a jig, but a friendly smile might have been nice. He'd asked for her help before and she was only here at his request, yet he was treating her as though she'd somehow offended him. Crossing her arms, she looked away.

He didn't even have the courtesy to bring the children. Certainly he knew how much she missed them.

The marshal resumed his seat behind the desk. "Thanks for coming out, Shane. I figured the two of you should hear this at the same time. I just got word from Wichita. Dead Eye Dan Fulton has busted out of jail."

Chapter Four

Tessa gasped and bolted upright. "When?"

"Last night."

Panic rose like bile in her throat. "Who broke him out?"

As though she had to ask.

"His brothers," the marshal replied grimly.

She didn't believe in luck, but she was starting to believe in bad luck. Here she'd been lulled into a false sense of safety, thinking she might actually claim the reward money and sleep a full night through for once.

Tessa turned her fear on Mr. McCoy. "I knew this would happen."

"I was trying to help," he wearily replied.

She splayed her fingers over her eyes. Terror definitely had a way of making her forget herself. While she had perfectly valid reasons for being angry with Shane, the outlaw's escape wasn't one of them. If she'd told him the truth about her connection to Dead Eye in the first place, then they wouldn't be in this mess. She had no one to blame but herself for this particular disaster.

"I'm sorry," she said. "Of course you meant well. I was surprised, that's all."

"What about the reward?" Shane demanded.

"Rescinded." The marshal held up his hands in supplication. "Didn't say I agreed with the decision."

"We caught him." Shane's voice vibrated with suppressed anger. "It's not our fault they couldn't hold him."

Tessa unconsciously touched his hand, instantly realized her mistake and snatched it back. "The money is the least of our worries. What if he follows us here?"

Ten minutes ago all she'd cared about was the reward money. This news had her caring more about saving her own hide. She'd given the Fultons two reasons for tracking her down: she'd serve as bait for Emmett, and they'd have their revenge as well.

Her hands trembled and she balled her fingers into tight fists. She had no desire to experience Fulton revenge.

The marshal kicked back in his seat. "Without the reward, there's no way the Fultons can trace the money back here. You're sheltered in that regard."

"I suppose that's something," Tessa muttered. The men gaped at her. "That's good for us. For both of us," she amended.

Talk about a tangled web. If only her father had been a cook or blacksmith or a farmer. Something simple and ordinary. At least Mr. McCoy and the children were safe. Dead Eye was much more likely to connect the dots between her disappearance and his capture than a handsome widower and his children passing through Wichita.

"I have some contacts," the marshal said. "People I trust. I'll put out the word, see if we can track them."

"I'd appreciate that," Shane replied.

Her slim hope of ever living openly as Tessa Spencer evaporated like the mist. Here she'd been twiddling her thumbs while searching for Emmett, thinking he'd fix his problem and solve hers as well. No more. She had to disappear. Really disappear. Not this skulking about, hoping for the best. She'd go so deep into hiding, not even Emmett could find her. She'd become an entirely new person, with a new name and a new identity, someone no one would suspect.

She'd worry about honesty and good deeds later. Staying alive was a key factor in accomplishing those tasks anyway.

She tipped back her head. "Why are You doing this to me? I'm trying. I'm really, really trying."

You'd think there'd be a little more grace and a little less punishment for those folks who put in the effort. Why did it always seem the dreadful people of the world like Dead Eye always landed on their feet like spry cats, whereas she'd only tried to right a wrong and tumbled right off the ledge and into the abyss? Even Emmett had a talent for squeezing out of difficult situations, and he wasn't exactly a saintly figure.

The marshal frowned. "Who are you talking to?"

"God," Tessa replied with an apologetic wave toward the ceiling.

Railing against God probably wasn't the best solution. Clearly she had more work to do on her spiritual training.

Shane followed her gaze upward. "Does He answer?"

"Yes." Tessa grimaced. "Only His answers are very perplexing."

The lawman didn't appear shocked by her outburst, which was something at least. In his profession, he'd probably seen far more unusual things than a woman talking to the ceiling.

"Do you mind sticking around for a moment?" The marshal straightened. "Shane and I have another matter to clear up as long as he's here."

"Don't give me a second thought," she replied gingerly, ignoring his piercing stare.

He was making excuses to hold her here, no doubt, waiting her out in case she collapsed into hysteria. Which she had no plans on doing. She was made of sterner stuff. Emmett hadn't raised a wilting flower. She might have drooped a touch, but she definitely wasn't wilting.

Hugging her arms over her chest, she stood, crossed the short distance and stared out the window. Towns had personalities, the same as people. This one screamed *respectability*! The boardwalks had been swept clean of snow, lethal icicles had been chipped from the eaves and black smoke pumped merrily from the chimneys. Emmett had never lingered in towns like this. Respectability made him nervous. Perhaps that was why Shane had been so cold once they'd reached town. Maybe he sensed she didn't belong.

Which begged the question—where *did* she belong?

Since arriving on the train, she'd known there was no way of watching the children without attracting unwanted attention. Her previous hunch had been correct; she was too young and too, well, too unattached. She'd spent twenty minutes escaping an interrogation from Mrs. Stuart in the mercantile yesterday. Even arriving on the same train with Shane had piqued the woman's curiosity.

The marshal focused his attention on Shane. "How's that mare? The one that ran into the barbed wire?"

Letting the conversation ebb and flow behind her, Tessa formulated a new plan. First, she'd take on an assumed name. While the subterfuge went against everything she'd fought for, in order to live an honest life, she had to remain alive. Even God had to understand that. Next, she needed an income. She'd checked the board outside the church the day of her arrival, but the only listings were for cattle hands and train workers. Neither of which was suitable. She wasn't returning to Wichita with Dead Eye on the loose, and the next larger city was even farther away. She was counting her pennies already.

"Shane, you're wound up tighter than an eight-day watch," the marshal said. He indicated the fresh blanket of snow outside his window. "You'll end up frozen in a snowdrift if you insist on traveling in this weather."

"It's not so bad," Shane said.

"Jo is worried."

"About the children?" Shane scooted forward. "What's wrong?"

Tessa's attention perked.

"They're fine," the marshal said. "It's you she's worried about."

Rubbing his forehead with the heel of his hand, Shane slumped back. "Jo's got no cause for worry."

"Don't do this to yourself," the marshal continued. "The kids miss you. Of course they do. They'll get used to the change. You might as well let them adjust now. When the weather turns ugly, you won't be able to make the trip anyway. We all know that. Things will all work out. You'll see."

The space between them thrummed with emotion. Tessa held her tongue for a full minute before blurting, "What do you mean the kids miss you?"

The two men blinked.

Shane spoke first. "The marshal and his wife, my cousin, are watching the twins over the winter."

"You didn't keep them with you?"

"You said I was a good father." He stared at his clasped hands. "I'm trying to be. They're better off this way, with people who can give them attention. This is my solution. It's for the best. Better than Mrs. Lund, that's for certain." His startling admission ignited a flurry of self-recriminations. All this time she'd thought she'd done something wrong, that he was annoyed with her or, worse yet, embarrassed by her. Even with his face averted, she sensed his guilt.

A tumble of comforting words balanced on the tip of her tongue and she held them there, hugging herself tighter. He didn't want or need her pity. Having faced tough times herself, she knew the frustration of trite phrases and meaningless assurances.

Why hadn't she listened closer before? What had the marshal said? Something about the weather. And Shane *did* look exhausted.

Tessa's thoughts raced. Instead of running again, what if she stayed put? The town was far and gone from all the Fultons' usual haunts. Dead Eye would stand out like a sore thumb around here.

"Mrs. Lund was not a good choice," Tessa agreed. Perhaps Agnes would consider letting her stay on at the boardinghouse full-time. There'd be no changing her name, the cat was already out of the bag, but she'd worry about that minor detail later. "Anyone can see you only want to do the right thing."

"It's a big change." He heaved a sigh. "We're all doing our best."

Her stomach rumbled, and she pressed one hand over the noise. The boardinghouse provided a nice breakfast and lunch, but she'd been hoarding the bread and cheese for the next leg of her journey. Though she'd counted on the reward money, she'd also been prepared for a hasty exit. Another one of Emmett's rules: hope for the best, and plan for the worst. If she ever saw him again, she'd thank him for all the excellent advice.

Right after she read him the riot act.

She recalled the reason she was in the marshal's office in the first place and her optimism faded. She couldn't put these kind people in danger.

The door Cora had disappeared into earlier opened once more and Owen and Alyce raced through. They caught sight of Tessa and charged. A wave of pure longing sprang forth. With a shriek she knelt and gathered them into her arms.

Cora followed close behind. "I tried to stop them, but when they found out Tessa was here, they were determined."

"It's all right," Shane said. "I planned on fetching them after the marshal said his piece."

"I've missed you," Tessa squealed in delight. "Have you been keeping busy?"

Owen held out his hand. "My ball."

"Yes, your ball." Tessa beamed at Shane. "That's two words together."

His grin was tinged with pride. "He started that just yesterday."

Alyce patted the ribbon at Tessa's neck. "Pretty."

Tessa's eyes burned. She'd been away from them for only a few days, and already they'd changed. They'd changed but they remembered her. She couldn't recall a time when someone had greeted her with such unabashed joy.

She scooped them close and laughed, then glanced at Shane and her smile faded. She'd never seen a man more crushed, more defeated. Being separated from his children was obviously tearing him apart, and her heart went out to him.

Though they were little more than strangers, she'd give anything to take away that pain, even for a moment. He reminded her of Emmett, making all the wrong choices for all the right reasons. Trying his best in a bewildering situation. While she assumed the marshal and his wife were good people, clearly the twins belonged with their father.

Cora planted her hands on her hips. "Shane, what you need is a wife. Why don't you send away for one of them mail-order brides like the blacksmith did a few years ago? I've never seen that man smile so much since he got hitched."

Marriage.

Tessa smothered a gasp. How had she overlooked such an obvious solution? She'd been so wrapped up in the details that she hadn't seen the broader picture. The most obvious solution had been sitting right in front of her all along. Like it or not, the only guarantee of respectability was marriage.

The edge of her ledger protruded from her satchel. The project was a lifetime of work. Instead of piecemeal efforts, what if one grand good deed erased all the other entries?

The idea took hold and gained shape. She'd have everything she ever wanted: security, safety and, best of all, anonymity. Well, everything but authenticity. Her past must be left in the past.

Owen touched the locket at her throat, fascinated by the shiny metal. The twins seemed genuinely fond of her. They adored her in the way only children could, without artifice of expectations. She envisioned their future in light of their current arrangement, shuttled from family to family, always searching for a place where they belonged. Memories of her own childhood returned with an unsettling jolt. They deserved better.

Although this was hardly a perfect solution for all of them, it was the best one she could think of. What other choices did any of them have? She glanced at Shane and a curious sensation passed through her, a gentle warmth, like the heat of the sun shining through a glass windowpane.

She'd learned his wife had passed away almost six months before. How much did he miss her? What would he think of such a suggestion? She sensed an unyielding resolution about him. Most folks took the easy way of things, drifting along like flotsam. Not Shane. He hadn't given up his children because that was the easy way out; he'd given them up because he felt it was the right thing to do.

What of her own situation? This was a clean slate. A new start. They were strangers with no preconceived notions about each other. He was a kind man, and she was a good person at heart. She'd simply never had the opportunity for demonstrating her better qualities.

There was only one little snag in her plan. Unlike the children, Shane definitely didn't adore her. She wasn't certain if he even liked her. Then again, he was a widower, and no one expected him to fall at her feet. They only needed to get along. She'd seen too much of the darker side of human nature to harbor any hope of a fairy-tale ending anyway.

"Find yourself a wife, Shane," Cora declared. "I'm brilliant. A mail-order bride solves all your problems."

Cora was brilliant, all right. The idea was as inspired as it was obvious.

All Tessa had to do was convince a virtual stranger to spend the rest of his life with her.

Brilliant indeed.

Alyce tugged on Shane's pant leg, and he hoisted her into his arms.

The marshal shook his head. "Leave Shane alone, Cora. He doesn't want to marry a stranger."

"You did."

Garrett's ears flamed. "I knew your mother. She wasn't a stranger. She was from town."

Shane had never seen the marshal shaken, but Garrett sure looked shaken now. Wondering if Tessa was enjoying the exchange as well, Shane grinned at her, but her expression was distant and shuttered, as though she was puzzling out some great difficulty.

"Yes, Mama was from town." Cora rolled her eyes. "But you weren't. You'd only been here a few months. You barely knew her."

"I knew her well enough," Garrett muttered, his scarlet ears turning even redder. "You've been listening to rumors again, haven't you?"

"Mrs. Stuart does ramble on," Cora continued. "But that doesn't mean getting married isn't the perfect solution. Shane is quite a catch. Any lady would be privileged to have him. Let's put his picture on the church bulletin boards in Wichita."

"No." Instantly panicked, Shane broke into the conversation. He figured his ears matched the marshal's right about now. "No one is putting my picture anywhere. Ever."

Agitated by his raised voice, Alyce hugged his neck. Shane tickled her stomach until she grinned. Taking good-natured enjoyment from the marshal's discomfort was one thing; hearing Cora talk about him as "a catch" was a whole different matter.

Garrett scrubbed his hand down his face. "Your mother and I didn't know each other very well, I'll admit that. But not everyone can be as fortunate."

Shane's amusement faded, and their friendly quarrel disappeared into the background. Alyce was staring at him with her wise, solemn eyes, and his whole chest ached. Freezing in a snowdrift didn't seem so bad if it meant seeing the children. Even if he saw them only once a week. Even if he didn't get a full night's rest until they were full-grown. He was used to hardship.

Cora's voice grew exasperated. "Maybe if Shane left the ranch once in a while, he might have more options. Except for that trip to Wichita, he doesn't go anywhere. How's he supposed to meet anyone around here? Miss Spencer is the only new single female we've had in town in months."

A strangled noise sounded from Tessa's direction, and Shane kept his attention averted. Cora was three for three—she'd mortified all the adults in the room.

The marshal ushered his daughter toward the back of his office once more. "This conversation is over. We'd best check on that coffee and find your mother. Can't leave the stove unattended." He motioned for Shane. "Bring the kids by the house when you're ready." He touched his forehead. "Miss Spencer, it was a pleasure meeting you. Let me know if I can be of any further assistance during your stay."

The door closed resolutely behind them.

While grateful the awkward conversation was at an end, Shane didn't relish being alone with Tessa after that mortifying exchange.

She craned her neck, following their hasty retreat. "What is behind that door, anyway?"

"A jail cell and stairs to an apartment on the second level. The marshal keeps the space closed off unless there's a prisoner. The deputy lives upstairs when there's an inmate overnight."

Cora's words rang in his ears. Tessa was definitely the only single female they'd had in town in a while. He almost laughed out loud before catching himself. Even if she didn't have one foot out the door, she'd never settle for someone like him. She was too smart and too pretty for a lonely widower who lived on an isolated ranch with nothing but a bunch of uncouth men for company.

All the same reasons she couldn't watch the children. Mrs. Stuart at the mercantile had practically tackled him when he'd stepped off the train with Tessa by his side. No doubt the old busybody had been watching them like a hawk, searching for any sign of impropriety.

At least Tessa didn't appear shocked by the Cains' ribbing. Their candor could be disconcerting. He shook his head. The idea was crazy. Out of the question. He'd already got married once for the sake of the children. What kind of fool made the same mistake twice? Clearly he wasn't marriage material. As for sending away for a bride, who in their right mind would come all this way to marry a man sight unseen? The idea was ludicrous.

Tessa perched on a chair and lifted Owen into her lap. "I was starting to think that door had mysterious properties."

Shane chuckled. "JoBeth, the marshal's wife, comes in through the back as well. It's a shortcut from the telegraph office where she works. She must be around here someplace. The kids didn't make that walk alone. She's probably upstairs."

Voices and footsteps rumbled overhead, and a welter of emotions swirled around him. He envied the Cains' easy camaraderie and close-knit family. After his father left, he'd quit school and supported his mother by working as a cattle hand. A man's job that hadn't left him much time for anything but eating and sleeping.

Following his mother's death, he'd worked even harder, saving up money for his own place. That was all he'd ever known—work and responsibilities. The kids were the best thing that had ever happened to him. They deserved a childhood. Although he supposed most folks didn't think about such frivolous things, having surrendered his own youth, he wanted more for them.

A burst of laughter from overhead filtered through the vents. The Cains liked each other and enjoyed spending time together. Sometimes they tried to pull him into their antics, like this afternoon, but he always kept a distance. Even when his family had been together, they'd never shared that sort of lighthearted connection, and he wasn't certain how to fit in.

He caught sight of Owen and grimaced.

The boy had turned away, making an exaggerated point of ignoring Shane. Of the two children, Owen had taken the change the hardest. He'd been sullen and withdrawn since the move. While understandable, his rejection still hurt.

Owen glared. "Want Scout."

The demand had Shane shuffling his feet. "He's at home. I'll bring him for a visit next time."

Tessa glanced between the two. "Who is Scout?"

"A horse." Visiting Scout each morning had been part of their daily routine since before Owen could walk. He'd even had his own currycomb and took great pride in brushing the feathered hair above the animal's hooves. Over seventeen hands high, the enormous draft horse had taken a shine to Owen as well and always remained docile beneath his ministration. "Owen wasn't happy about leaving him behind."

That was an understatement. Shane briefly closed his eyes against the memory of the boy's pitiful sobs.

Tessa pressed a hand against her stomach, and Shane recalled the rumblings he'd heard earlier.

He'd been almost rude with her before. The decision to leave Alyce and Owen with the Cains had weighed heavily on him, and he hadn't been very good company on the train ride back or even today, for that matter.

In an effort to atone for his previous behavior, he asked, "Have you eaten yet?"

She glanced up. "Not yet."

He studied Tessa's upturned face and his gut knotted. Lines of tension framed her mouth and dark circles showed beneath her eyes. He recalled the trunk he'd seen in the haberdashery window and realized why the familiar-looking luggage had caught his eye. She must be pawning her belongings. Most telling of all, she'd been frantic about the reward this morning when she'd been hesitant about the money before. Those hints might have clued him in earlier if he hadn't been wrapped up in his own concerns.

Tessa was obviously short on funds.

She'd been adamant about leaving town as soon as the reward arrived. What was she going to do now? What were her plans for the future? Forcing his questions aside, he reached for his coat.

Curiosity was holding up what needed to be done. "Join me for lunch at the hotel. I could use a bite." Actually, he'd eaten an hour ago. "I insist. You can fill me in on the gossip from town."

Owen had practically attached himself to Tessa. Most likely she'd be gone soon, another disappointment for the boy, yet he couldn't deny them their visit. At least the twins were smiling for once. All three of them had been more somber than usual lately. The finality of their situation had left Shane troubled and distracted. Assisting someone else was the perfect way to take his mind off his worries.

"Um," Tessa began. "There is one small matter I'd like to discuss over lunch."

Chapter Five

Alyce and Owen were bundled into their coats and Shane assisted Tessa with hers. After a quick scurry down the boardwalk, their heads bent against the wind, the hotel dining room was warm and inviting with the mouthwatering aroma of fried chicken filling the air. Chairs were quickly arranged and orders placed.

Tessa rested her hands on either side of her plate and straightened her silverware. "The marshal and his wife, are they happy?"

Rolling his eyes, Shane said, "Sickeningly so."

He laughed and Tessa's mood lightened. She'd tread carefully. This was an extremely delicate situation and she must present her solution with the utmost care. If she structured the conversation correctly, he might even make the suggestion himself. Another one of Emmett's handy tricks.

Shane removed his hat and threaded his fingers through his hair. "JoBeth's courtship was the talk of the town some years back. Garrett and JoBeth married after the marshal accepted guardianship of his niece, Cora. She calls them Mom and Dad now, which seems fitting enough. It's a tough job, being the only parent. Around these parts, marriages are arranged for practical reasons as often as not."

Excellent. His story fit her plan perfectly. Already he must be thinking about the two of them together. Cora had set the wheels in motion by mentioning mail-order brides and the fact that Tessa was the only single woman available. Soon he'd put the pieces together and catch the drift of her thoughts.

"People get married for all sorts of reasons, you say." She nodded slowly, her eyes locked with his. "Like caring for children?"

He rubbed his chest as though something pained him. "Yep."

Well, that wasn't a good sign. He didn't appear to comprehend her meaning at all. He looked as if he had indigestion. "You must miss the children terribly. Not being able to see them every day. If only there was another way."

Surely that was obvious enough. She was dropping all the hints she could think of. Giving him every opportunity to realize she was open to his offer.

"Owen and Alyce love the Cains," he said quietly. "And certainly Jo and Garrett are excellent guardians, but nothing replaces seeing them every day."

Tessa drummed her fingers. Perhaps if she approached this from another direction. "And you can't possibly hire anyone because folks will gossip."

"Exactly."

"I thought before…" She inhaled deeply. "On the trip back from Wichita, the children and I did well together."

Maybe if she backed up the conversation and reminded him of the time they'd spent together already, he'd catch the drift of her thoughts. Once he recalled the past, maybe he'd look to the future.

He fumbled for the coffee mug the server had set before him. "You did real fine with them."

Though she'd never been around small children before, they'd got along well. There'd been the usual tantrums and spills. She'd even scolded Owen and he hadn't appeared to hold it against her. Children didn't seem to hold grudges.

Owen teetered and Tessa instinctively steadied him. Yep. She was definitely developing her instincts with the children.

She folded her hands before her. "And we got along well, too, didn't we?"

"You know I'd hire you in an instant," he blurted. "After meeting Mrs. Stuart, you can understand the difficulties. I won't let you endure that sort of gossip. That doesn't mean you can't see them as often as you want."

"Don't misunderstand me," she added quickly. "I realize now how impossible it would be for you to hire me as a housekeeper."

"Exactly," he declared. "I couldn't put you in that situation. There'd be talk. There's always talk. You're a fine-looking woman."

A jolt of pure feminine pleasure surprised her.

She'd never much thought about her looks one way or the other before. Discreetly rubbing her damp palms against her skirts, she caught sight of Owen and Alyce peacefully rearranging their table settings. Those two never got along for this long.

Shane jolted upright. "You need money, don't you? I should have realized that sooner. What with losing out on the reward and all. You just have to ask. I'm happy to help."

Tessa nearly pounded her fists on the table. He'd picked

up on the clues, all right. The wrong clues. "I don't want to borrow money from you. I want to help out with the children. But not as your housekeeper."

He frowned. "I can talk to JoBeth. I'm sure she'd appreciate the help."

Nope. He was not catching the drift of her meaning at all. Not even close. Worse yet, they were drifting further off point with every word.

"All three of you get along real well." He rushed ahead before she could say anything else. "Both Owen and Alyce adore you. If you settle here, the Cains will let you visit as often as you like."

"I'd like that." Her knuckles whitened around her own coffee mug. "Sometimes we have to change our plans. Sometimes things don't work out as easily as we think they should."

"No. They don't."

Shane cleared his throat. "I think I know what you're hinting at."

"Excellent." She resisted adding a *hallelujah*. "I was beginning to think we'd be here all day."

"You think I should consider Cora's suggestion."

"Yes!" *Finally.* At last they were on the right track.

"I can't send for a mail-order bride," he declared forcefully. "Even for the children. I know you're all trying to help. I appreciate it. Truly, I do. But it's out of the question." Owen tipped a cup and he lunged before the liquid spilled. "I'm not really the mail-order bride kind of fellow."

Tessa covered her face with her hands. What did a woman have to do to get a marriage proposal around here? She lowered her hands and sucked in a restorative breath. If he wasn't catching the hints, she'd have to do this herself.

"Why don't we get married?" she declared just as forcefully. They'd be here all afternoon if she waited on Shane to decipher her hints. "We already know each other. Sort of. And you said it yourself before. We each have something the other needs." Before he could speak, she rushed ahead. "No one could take the place of your first wife, I'm sure."

Something flashed across his face, an emotion she couldn't read. "I wouldn't expect anyone to."

"It's what you said before," Tessa went on, relieved they were at least finally speaking on the same topic. "Things are different out West. Marriages are arranged for practical reasons. We're simply being practical."

"I just want to get this straight," he said, not appearing at all eager. "You're saying we ought to get married? You and me?"

Her enthusiasm deflated, and she pressed two fingers against her temple. This had seemed much more logical back in the marshal's office. Sitting here before Shane, trying to think of a good way to convince him that she was the perfect choice for a bride, nothing seemed clear. What qualifications did she have? She could pick a pocket and spot a cardsharp from across the room. Not necessarily what most men were looking for in a bride.

Now that the words were out, her courage fled. Covering her unease, she snapped, "Of course you and me!"

"You caught me off guard." Shane forced the pent-up air from his lungs, remembering to breathe. "Just making sure. You see, um, you said you had a small matter you'd like to discuss."

"Yes. Marriage."

"I think I see the problem," he replied, still feeling a bit dazed. "Maybe next time you should say that you have something important to discuss rather than something small. That way I'm prepared."

For a moment she appeared annoyed, but her expression quickly shifted to one of uncertainty. The sudden change left him even more confused.

Tessa sighed and studied the tines on her fork as though they were the most fascinating things on earth. "When Cora spoke of mail-order brides before, I couldn't help but think about the children."

"The children?" He was still catching up with the conversation. And who could blame him? Usually when someone wanted to discuss a small matter, they meant a broken heel on a shoe or an overdue bill at the boarding-house.

Something small.

A marriage proposal was not a small matter.

"Clearly they're better off with their father," Tessa said. "They're better off with the person who loves them most." Her eyes took on a misty appeal. "This all must be very confusing for them. Losing their mother, moving from the only home they've ever known."

Her reasoning put him at ease. She liked the children. Maybe it was because they were twins that they had that effect on people. But was affection for Alyce and Owen enough for a lifetime together? He'd been down this road before with disastrous results.

Her too-pale lips pinched together. "I realize we haven't known each other very long, and this is an enormous decision, but I really think we could make this work."

While he was busy reeling from the unexpected announcement, she'd obviously thought through the details already. Any man would jump at the offer, himself included. Except he didn't want her making a lifelong decision because she was backed into a corner. He didn't want her to do something she'd regret later.

His collar had grown alarmingly tight, and he tugged on his string tie. Adding the minutes together, they'd known each other only a matter of hours, and yet he'd known Abby for most of his childhood and still managed to marry a stranger.

"We could make a list—" her voice quivered "—of all the reasons for and against the marriage."

She had the look of a wide-eyed doe, softly innocent, ready to flee at the least disturbance. She'd been strong and brave since the moment he'd met her, and he'd never considered how much energy that courage cost her. For a woman on her own, harassment from men like Dead Eye must be all too familiar. He felt her desperation as though her plea had taken on a physical presence. If he refused, if he turned her away, where would she go next? Because of his interference with the outlaw, she appeared more frightened than ever.

"Like I said before, you caught me off guard." A fierce need to shelter her from harm welled up inside him, and he stalled for time. "It's not a bad idea. Unexpected, sure. But not crazy."

These past few days without the children had been miserable. Being together again was right and good, the way things were supposed to be. He desperately wanted that feeling back. He wanted the same peace he'd felt the first time he'd held Alyce and Owen in his arms nearly two years ago. There was only one problem. He didn't want that peace at the price of someone else's misery.

Snared in his memories, the quiet stretched out.

Tessa held out her locket for Owen's fascinated inspection, and Shane marveled at the silky lashes sweeping against her cheeks, the delicate translucency of her eyelids and the brilliance of her hair catching a shaft of afternoon sun.

She broke the silence, jarring him from his musing.

"What?" he asked. "I didn't catch that."

"I should go," she said. "I've kept you too long."

"We don't need a list." Her hesitant uncertainty spurred him into action. "After thinking things through, getting married is the best solution."

He wasn't exactly a silver-tongued charmer. Tessa deserved a proper courting, but that wasn't in the cards. He didn't have the time or the skills. Best not to give her false hope anyway. He'd begin this relationship as he meant to go on. He was a practical man and this was a practical decision.

"Are you certain?" Tessa asked softly, a heartbreaking note of doubt in her voice.

"I'd ask you the same. It's a hard life. Be sure you know the bargain you're making. They'll catch those outlaws sooner or later. You'll see."

No regrets. If they agreed to this marriage, he wanted no regrets for either of them.

He didn't doubt her abilities or her resolve. She wasn't weak, not by a long shot. He'd eaten in Harvey House restaurants plenty of times during his travels. He'd seen waitresses lift trays that would bend a grown man. Though she was little more than a slip of a thing, she'd taken care of herself well enough up until now. It wasn't her fault she'd attracted the notice of Dead Eye.

Owen wrapped his arms around Tessa's neck and snuggled close.

She had an effortless, nurturing quality about her that left him curious about her past. "Do you have brothers and sisters? Family?"

Why wasn't someone looking out for her? He'd settled in Cimarron Springs because of his family. His aunt was the closest thing he had to a mother with his own gone. His uncle, guilty about his brother abandoning the family, had taken it upon himself to fill in the empty space. Though their attention was occasionally stifling, he appreciated their concern.

"No brothers or sisters, I'm afraid." Tessa's smile was strained. "I'm an only child. My mother died when I was eight. My father raised me after that. He's not around anymore." Her gaze skittered away. "That's all there is to know about me."

Shane very much doubted that. Her face had got that shuttered look once more, and he didn't press her any further. There'd be time enough for them to get to know one another later. A lifetime.

The thread between them was fragile, and he feared one wrong word might snap the delicate connection. "You can change your mind, you know."

"I know." She rested her cheek on Owen's head and sighed. "This is about something different."

In the first months of his marriage, he'd wondered about the man who'd abandoned Abby. The man who'd made her so miserable, she'd wasted away from the heartbreak. He didn't think about it anymore, because thinking didn't change anything and only made the hurting worse. He didn't care beyond a lingering sadness for what might have been.

Something weighty and ragged settled in his chest. "I don't want you making a mistake you can't take back."

"You're not a mistake, Mr. McCoy."

"Shane," he said, his throat working. "Call me Shane."

The last time he'd plunged into a marriage, he'd been confident that friendship would turn into love. Never again. He'd go about things differently this time. With this marriage, he'd keep his distance, treat the relationship as a partnership in the business. He'd give her space instead of stifling her.

He wouldn't give either of them a reason for regrets.

Her eyes grew unfocused and looked beyond him. "My father raised me after my mother died. Just him alone. I know the challenge. I'm well aware of the sacrifice."

The distant look in her eyes returned. Already she was shutting him out. He bent his head. At least this time there were no surprises.

"Cimarron Springs is a nice town, but it's small," he said. His initial impression of her came rushing back. In another life, she might have been the tea-sipping heiress. Fate had left her in a far different situation. She hadn't given up yet, and he admired her pluck. "There's not much excitement around these parts."

"I've had all the excitement I can stand in one lifetime." Her gaze turned intense. "I've lived everywhere, Shane. Just once I'd like to live *somewhere*. I want to feel safe."

Owen slapped his hands on the table, rattling the dishes. "Ga."

Tessa smiled. "Even Owen agrees."

She was more than he deserved. How could he explain that his hesitation had sprung from his own unsuitability, not hers? At least they'd have the twins between them. Her affection for the children had obviously instigated her precipitous suggestion. Though he lauded her compassion, someday Owen and Alyce would be grown and gone, and there'd be only the two of them. What then? Would they have enough in common after the years to survive the loss of what had brought them together in the first place?

"You're certain?" he asked.

Her chin came up a notch. "There's one thing you should know about me. Once I make up my mind, I don't change it. I'll feel the same in a day, a week, a month and a year. There's no reason to wait."

The twins, normally full of energy and chatter, were oddly, blissfully quiet. Their silence gave him the opportunity for reflection. Too much opportunity. Just once he wished for a little noise. A tantrum or another spill.

For this union to work, he required Tessa's unfailing loyalty, which meant giving his in return. "This isn't just about finding a caretaker for the children. I want this to be a partnership. My ranch is doing well, growing. I need someone I can build a life with."

Growing bashful, she smoothed Owen's hair. "I don't know much about running a household."

"We'll take things slow. Real slow." He might have been married before, but he'd wager he knew even less about being a husband than Tessa knew about being a wife. This time, though, neither of them would have any false expectations. "We'll figure out the relationship together. There's no need for love or any of that nonsense gumming up the works."

There. He'd said it. There'd be no awkward scenes like the one with Abby. Her last words to him rang in his ears. *I tried to love you—really, I did.* He wondered if his father had thought the same thing. Had he tried to love his only child, but simply couldn't?

"No need at all," Tessa scoffed. "Love. Really? I shudder at the thought."

He ignored his unexpected shock of disappointment. "Absolutely. We'll have something that's better—mutual respect."

This was going well. He'd set the expectations. There were no secrets, no false hopes. Only an agreement between two people brought together by fate. He'd finally be in control of his own destiny, not pushed along by forces outside his control. He should have felt powerful. Instead, he felt hollow. Empty.

"Yes," she agreed with a faint, polite inclination of her head. "Respect. That's far, far better."

"We should shake on it."

"Shake?"

He stuck out his hand. "Yeah. We'll shake on it. Like a true business deal."

She clasped his fingers and his resolve immediately disintegrated. Everything about her was soft, gentle and unintentionally inviting. From the touch of her hand to the curve of her cheek, she embodied all that was feminine. A good mother for the children, she was everything they needed, everything they'd been lacking in their short lives. She was loyal, he sensed that, and he owed her loyalty in return. He'd made her a promise and he'd keep that promise. They could be business partners, all right, as long as they never touched.

Two people, living in close quarters in the middle of nowhere, never touching. That shouldn't be too difficult, right?

He lifted his gaze to the window and groaned. He'd been so focused on Tessa, he'd missed the fat snowflakes sheeting before the window. The ominous haze that had been hanging in the air had finally broken loose in a squall. If this weather continued, they'd be snowed in before long. He'd run out of time already. It wasn't unusual for a foot or more of snow to fall in a day. He'd find out soon enough if Tessa had spoken truthfully about her resolve.

She followed his gaze and gasped. "Oh my. When did that start?"

"I'm sorry—truly, I am," he said. "That weather changes everything. I can't afford to be stranded in town. I have to stay ahead of that weather. I'll come back with the next thaw. If you're…if you're still here. If you haven't changed your mind."

They'd been granted an unexpected reprieve. Why, then, was this irrational panic welling in his chest?

"Today." She spoke with gritty determination. "There's no reason for waiting. I'll leave with you today."

Shane's heartbeat thundered in his ears. Now which one of them had lost their nerve? "There'll be no going back."

She leaned forward, her earnest gaze pinning him in place. "I'm ready to start over. Now. Today. There's no reason to wait any longer. I'll be a good wife to you, I promise. I've taken care of my father for years. I'll be a good mother to the children. You wanted a partnership, and that's what I'm offering you. We both know what we expect from each other."

Doubts clung to his resolve like cobwebs. He didn't want her regrets.turning into resentment. "And what is it you expect of me?"

Her eyes glittered and he unconsciously took her hand once more. She squeezed his fingers. "I don't want to be afraid anymore. We barely know one another, but you make me feel safe. I haven't felt that way in a very, very long time."

As though the confession had cost her, all the fight drained out of her.

His determination crystallized. He tucked two fingers beneath her chin and gently forced her to meet his steady gaze. "I'll keep you safe, I promise."

Her lovely, expressive eyes wreaked havoc with his senses. She should have been nestled safely away in a warm house, with someone looking out for her. He could do that much for her at least.

The weather outside gave him an idea. From now until Christmas he'd give her plenty of space. That way, if she eventually decided they didn't suit and she wanted to leave him, she wouldn't feel beholden.

He doubted she expected anything different. She'd wanted only safety.

Safety...the one thing he could offer her. He only hoped that would be enough for a lifetime, because that was all he had to give.

Chapter Six

"You look like a tea person. Am I right?" JoBeth McCoy, the marshal's wife, squinted at Tessa.

Tessa waved away the tin. "Tea is far too extravagant."

Everything was moving at a wonderfully brisk pace—the preparations, the wedding, even Jo's rapid-fire speech. Tessa hadn't gathered a breath since she'd agreed on marrying Shane within the hour. Things were definitely different out West, as she was quickly learning. Without batting an eye, Shane's family had sprung into action. They hadn't seemed shocked by the announcement at all.

Cora had even winked. *Winked.* She'd deliberately dropped those hints about marriage. Although someone should tell the poor girl that Shane was oblivious to hints. Tessa sighed inwardly. The whole town had clearly been trying to marry off the widower, and Tessa was, as Cora had so bluntly stated, the only new single woman in town in ages. They'd obviously exhausted all the other possibilities.

Ignoring her refusal of the tea, Jo stuffed the tin into the crate before the counter. "Never underestimate the edifying powers of small luxuries."

A twinge of guilt nagged Tessa. She should have waited out the weather, given Shane more time. Except whenever he was near, the heavy weight on her chest eased. For the first time since she'd parted ways from Emmett, she felt as though she could take a full breath. The sensation was heady, intoxicating.

She'd give their relationship until Christmas to take hold. If Shane was still indifferent to her by then, she'd reassess the situation. Although she didn't plan on giving him any reason to be indifferent.

She'd be a good wife, a good mother. She was a quick learner, and she'd figure things out along the way. "Never mind the tea. Tea is a waste of money."

"You'll thank me later." The dark-haired woman gestured out the window. "We don't have much time. The boys are meeting us at the church in twenty minutes. I'm guessing you won't be back in town for another few weeks. Maybe a month. Better be quick about your purchases."

"I don't even know where to begin." The boxes and cans blurred together in one overwhelming mass.

While she'd taken care of all the purchases with Emmett, she'd never taken care of little ones before. "I'm not certain what I'll need. What the children will need."

"That's why I'm here," Jo said brusquely. "Why don't you pick out a nice shawl? Something special for the wedding since there isn't time to change."

She steered Tessa toward an out-of-the-way display of fabrics and continued shopping. Tessa grimaced. Clearly Jo didn't want or need her help. Probably for the best—she was only slowing down the process. Though she hadn't lied about her resolve before, she was still adjusting to the abrupt change. The inclement weather had sent everyone into a flurry of activity that left her little time to think.

The preacher had been fetched, Shane had ordered the horses hitched and the marshal had returned home for the twins' belongings. The bustle hadn't given her any chance for second thoughts or regrets. She only hoped Shane felt the same. The intense look on his face had worried her.

A book caught her attention and she touched the faded cover. *Bartleby's Encyclopedia of Household Management.* On impulse, she snatched the heavy volume and added it to her purchases. If Bartleby had written that tome, he must know a whole lot more about household management than she did. Caring for her and Emmett was one thing, but she had two children counting on her as well.

A gust of snowflakes and a blast of frigid air signaled the arrival of another customer. Marshal Cain appeared, his hat dusted with snow.

He shook off the flakes and grinned. "The wagon is hitched, the kids are packed and Shane is waiting at the church. How are you two doing?"

"Almost ready," Jo said brusquely. "Walk Tessa over and I'll join you in a tick."

Her nerves drew taut and Tessa hesitated. "I should stay and help."

Jo marched over, carrying a heap of crocheted items crafted in a cheerful emerald green. "You'll need these as well. Mrs. Edwards makes the warmest hats and mittens. That piece of felt you're wearing won't offer much protection in this weather."

Touching the brim of her sad little bonnet, Tessa acknowledged the thin material. "It was the warmest hat I own."

Her winter wardrobe had been designed for a brisk walk from a train station to a hotel or a quick scamper across a crowded street. She'd never had to choose clothing for anything more rigorous than a short dash.

"Don't worry." Jo filled her arms with the woolens. "You'll be fine. I'll take care of everything."

"Are you certain?" Tessa asked, hoping they hadn't caught the wobble in her voice.

The marshal drew his wife into his arms and kissed her forehead, then turned toward Tessa. "Leave the supplies to Jo. She knows what you'll need better than anyone."

At their affectionate display, Tessa stifled a sigh. How she missed the warmth of companionship. She'd always considered herself independent. These past few months had taught her the difference between independence and solitude.

With a resolute nod, Tessa wrapped the emerald green scarf around her throat and replaced her felt bonnet with her new cap.

A young boy hovering over the penny candy caught her attention. Tessa snapped her fingers and the boy cast a guilty look over his shoulder. The temptation of the penny candy was no match for the sight of the marshal's tall figure by her side. The boy stuffed his hands in his pockets and scurried away.

The marshal frowned down at her. "What was that all about?"

"Saving him from himself, that's all. Everyone needs a reminder about right and wrong now and again." Although some people clearly never got the message. "It's best to turn them young, before they can get into any real trouble."

Before they became caught up in the thrill of danger and lost sight of good and bad altogether.

"Ah, sticky fingers." The marshal nodded sagely. "I'll keep my eye on him."

She'd recognized the boy's look well enough. She'd seen the slightly glazed longing on Emmett's face plenty of times. Over the years she'd gradually realized he loved the game more than the prize. Why he couldn't receive that same thrill from an honest day's work, she'd never know. Life would have been so much simpler for everyone.

As she reached for the door, Jo called out. Tessa whirled around.

"Take this." Jo thrust a cinnamon-colored silk scarf into her outstretched hands. "Something new. We'll figure out the old, borrowed and blue later."

Tessa touched the collar of her dress. "This will serve as something old. And if the temperature drops any lower, my lips will serve as the blue."

"You look lovely." Jo squeezed Tessa's shoulders. "Stop worrying."

"I'm not worried." That was mostly the truth. She wasn't worried, more like uncertain. While she didn't regret her decision, she feared the unknown. "Thank you. For everything."

Her chin trembled and she clenched her jaw. The only opinions Emmett had ever trusted were those of babies and animals. He always said that children and beasts saw the true heart of people and not what was falsely presented on the outside. She'd seen Shane with his children; she'd seen how they adored him. He was an honorable man. Except she wasn't drawn to him only because he was a good man. Her decision was based on far more than his fatherly abilities.

There was a spark between them. She ticked off her self-imposed time frame in her head. She had until Christmas to fan that spark into something beyond companionship. Surely by then the Fulton brothers would have given up on her as well.

The more time they spent together, the more her past would recede. She'd watch it fade into the distance like a departing train. Would Shane do the same? His affection for his first wife obviously ran deep. Could he ever feel that same affection for her?

Jo flipped the dark hair from her forehead. "A few jitters are normal. If this is something more, only say the word. We'll put a stop to this whole event at once."

Though she'd known Jo only a short time, Tessa didn't doubt her words. "No, no. It's not that."

"You'll do well together." Jo placed a reassuring hand on her shoulder. "Take good care of him."

"What if I can't?" she asked in a ragged whisper.

Tessa was grateful when the marshal moved away and studied a display of tinned milk, giving them a moment of privacy.

"You can." Bending her head, Jo spoke quietly. "Be patient with Shane. He's had a rough time these past few years. It's not my place to say, but I don't think life with Abby was easy."

Tessa grasped for an appropriate response, but the marshal interrupted her reply. She had so many questions and yet she feared the answers.

"We'd better go," the marshal said. "This weather isn't letting up, and Shane will be waiting."

With a last glance at the heap of purchases piling up on the counter, Tessa followed him into the frigid afternoon. She sure hoped Shane wasn't angry about all the money she'd spent. She hated starting off their marriage on a bad note. Up until this point, saving money had consisted of what she'd managed to squirrel away beneath her mattress. The only budgeting she'd done had been hiding the surplus from Emmett—his taste ran to the expensive. Life with her father had been a series of ups and downs. He spent money freely when they were flush, and Tessa economized when they weren't.

After stepping outside, the marshal held out his hand. "It's slippery. Be careful."

Clutching his arm, she ducked her head against the howling wind. Snowflakes blurred her vision and she blindly followed his lead. The cold whipped at her legs and a sharp, stinging gust brought tears to her eyes. By the time the marshal escorted her into the warmth of the church, her toes had gone numb. They shuffled into a small vestibule brightened with twin glass lanterns.

The marshal gestured toward his right. "There's a room over there where you can hang up your coat."

The cramped office space was overflowing with books. They were stacked and stuffed on every available space. Considering the variety of subjects, she wondered if the collection served as a sort of library for the town. Cautiously navigating the clutter, she removed her coat and cap and smoothed her hair. Standing on her tiptoes, she checked her reflection in an oval mirror perched on a shelf. At least the wind had whipped some color into her cheeks. She brushed at her skirts before abandoning the effort. The scarf Jo had chosen added a bit of elegance to her outfit.

A soft knock sounded at the door, and Tessa greeted a kindly gray-haired man with pale blue eyes.

"I'm Reverend Miller," he introduced himself with an outstretched hand.

She clasped his fingers in greeting. "Tessa Spencer."

"Are you settling in all right? Is there anything I can get you?"

"I'm fine. Thank you for asking. I appreciate your help on such, um, on such short notice."

He offered a gentle smile. "You have to be ready for anything in this neck of the woods."

"I'm learning that."

He studied her face and she resisted the desire to squirm beneath his piercing scrutiny. After a moment he nodded, as though coming to a decision.

He reached for the door and hesitated. "Shane is a good man."

How many people had said the same? She hoped she was worthy of him. "I know."

He expelled his breath in an audible rush. "I'll see you inside, then. Welcome to Cimarron Springs, Miss Spencer."

Feeling as though she'd passed some sort of test, Tessa followed him out the door. The marshal was patiently waiting for her. He'd removed his hat and heavy coat and his hair had obviously been finger combed into place. While she appreciated his solicitous behavior, she hadn't had a moment alone since they'd set the wedding into motion. She felt as though she was under scrutiny, and any moment they'd discover a flaw.

"Shane is inside with Cora and the children," Marshal Garrett said. "Jo will be here any minute. We'll start the ceremony then."

"All right." She tucked a lock of hair behind one ear. "Thank you for helping to arrange everything."

He nodded. "Life can be tough out here. If you need anything, Jo and I are close."

Feeling a fraud, she stared at the plank wood floor. "You're all being so kind."

They were all loyal to Shane, and she didn't know if she deserved their kindness. When she'd imagined the marriage, she'd pictured the isolated ranch. She hadn't given much thought to Shane's friends and family. What did they think of her? Were they worried?

The marshal circled the brim of his hat with his fingers. "Shane is a grown man. He knows what he's doing."

While his words didn't exactly put her at ease, she appreciated his honesty.

"Since your father isn't here," the marshal continued, "I was wondering if I could have the honor of walking you down the aisle."

Tessa touched her locket and swallowed around the lump in her throat. "Thank you. I'd like that."

The familiar ache took hold once more. Emmett would have enjoyed playing the father of the bride. He had a way of attracting a party even when there was nothing to celebrate. He'd have enjoyed her wedding if only for a new audience to regale with his stories.

Though wary of the lawman, she appreciated his thoughtfulness. She'd listened as the other girls at the Harvey House had waxed poetic about their future wedding days, but she'd never joined in the game. She'd never been one for daydreaming.

The marshal checked his watch and rocked back on his heels. "I did a lot of traveling before I settled in Cimarron Springs. Met a lot of people in that time."

"I imagine your job was very exciting," Tessa offered.

While she preferred the silence, she supposed he thought small talk might pass the time. She glanced over her shoulder. What was taking Jo so long?

The marshal shrugged. "Sometimes it was exciting. Sometimes not. The thing about traveling is that you meet all kinds of folks. I met a fellow named Spencer once. I think his first name was Earl or Edgar or something."

He knew. Tessa jerked her head up and sucked in a sharp, frightened breath. Why else would he mention the name? She searched his face for any sign of condemnation and found none. Pressing her hand against her racing heart, she masked her expression. Perhaps it was a coincidence. There was no reason to assume he knew about her father. Or her.

"Spencer is a common name." She kept her reply deliberately vague and her voice dispassionate.

"I'll never forget him." The marshal rubbed his chin and gazed at the door. "Craziest thing I ever saw. There was a poker game in the saloon and old Frank was in deep to this stranger named Spencer. Frank was a known drinker and a known gambler, but he also had three children and a wife at home, so the regulars had a gentleman's agreement. They steered clear of Frank when he got wound up that way. Only Spencer wasn't exactly obliged to honor that agreement."

"I suppose not."

Her legs grew wobbly and she locked her knees. The story sounded all too familiar. He was almost certainly speaking of Emmett.

Voices sounded from deep in the church and she started. Had the marshal orchestrated a delay to expose her? Why was he toying with her? If he planned on revealing her past before Shane, she wished he'd speed up the story. Or was he simply baiting her? While she hadn't pegged the marshal as a blackmailer, she didn't know him well enough to decipher his motivation.

The marshal gave a slow shake of his head. "By the time I got to the saloon, poor Frank had gambled away all his money. Frank was desperate. The very next deal of the cards, he bet the deed to his farm. Now, I might have been the law in that town, but a game is a game and I had no right to interfere. Near broke my heart when Frank lost his home to Spencer. I've never seen a man look like that before, like he'd lost his spirit."

Tessa took a cautious step toward the door. She wasn't certain where this story was leading, and she had a bad feeling about the ending. Either way, she was hedging her own bets this time. "Gambling is a wicked addiction."

"Most of the regulars lit out real quick. No one likes to see a man like that, trounced. I stayed behind, worried about Frank's state of mind. Spencer stayed behind as well." The marshal scratched his temple. "Spencer waited until it was just us three, then handed Frank back the note for the deed and all but twenty dollars of his winnings. Old Frank was blubbering and crying like a baby. Spencer said, *Some lessons you gotta learn the hard way.* Those words, they stuck with me."

She glanced behind her, searching for any sign of a deputy waiting with wrist shackles. "This Mr. Spencer sounds like a wise man."

There was a three o'clock train. If she scraped together all her pennies, she just might make the fare. Her shoulders sagged. There probably wasn't a place west of the Mississippi that wasn't plagued by Emmett's past capers. She was well and truly trapped.

"Don't get me wrong." Marshal Cain chuckled. "I'm certain Spencer was cheating, though I never could prove it. But Frank never gambled again. He'd learned his lesson, all right, and cheaper than he might have with a less compassionate cardsharp. That's the trouble with being a lawman sometimes. Figuring out what to do with people like that Spencer fellow. I couldn't decide if I should put him in jail or give him a medal."

"What did you do?" Tessa pressed her quaking hands together. "You said you couldn't prove he was cheating."

Emmett might not have been out-and-out cheating, but he was most certainly double-dealing. He had a whole bag of tricks. Often his strategy was as simple as counting the cards or ensuring the other man drank too much. He was adept at noticing the little ticks people assumed when they were dealt a winning or a losing hand. Nothing with Emmett was ever as entirely straightforward or as simple as cheating.

"You know what I did?" The marshal studied her intently. "I tipped my hat to him. Then I suggested he move on to another town. I'll tell you this—I wouldn't mind meeting up with that fellow again someday."

She narrowed her gaze, wary of the trap in his words. "You're a very tolerant lawman."

"Experienced, more like. After a while in this job, you stop seeing everything as black-and-white and you notice a whole lot of gray."

As Tessa cautiously eyed the marshal, JoBeth arrived in a breathless rush.

She skidded into the vestibule and pecked her husband on the cheek. "Sorry I'm late."

After giving Tessa a brief hug, she rushed inside.

Tessa stole a peek through the narrow opening in the double doors, hoping for a glimpse of Shane.

Marshal Cain stuck out his elbow. "Ready?"

She looped her hand through the bend in his arm and nodded.

He gave her hand a quick squeeze. "As long as you're honest with each other, the rest will take care of itself."

An uncomfortable sensation settled in the pit of her stomach. *Honesty.* His random tale hadn't been so random after all. Did he know for certain, or did he simply suspect she and Emmett were related? Either way, according to the marshal, the one thing she needed for a successful marriage was the one thing she couldn't give.

The doors from the vestibule opened and Shane stood, tugging on his coat sleeves, then lifted his gaze and flinched. Her face pale, Tessa clung to Garrett like a prisoner being led to the gallows. Shane sighed quietly. Just once he'd like a bride who didn't appear as though she was ready to bolt for the nearest exit at any moment. Tessa greeted him at the altar with a tremulous smile and he offered what he hoped was a reassuring smile in return.

The rest of the ceremony passed in a blur. Reverend Miller was well aware of the time press and moved the ceremony along at a clipped pace. This wasn't the first hasty marriage the reverend had overseen, and it wouldn't be his last. Tessa didn't hesitate over the promise to "love," but he doubted she even knew what she was saying. Her gasping responses sounded slightly dazed. Owen lost his ball during Shane's portion of the vows, briefly halting the ceremony, which meant no one noticed his garbled replies.

Since there'd been no time for procuring rings, Reverend Miller simply skipped over that part of the ceremony.

Shane cast a sidelong glance at Tessa, wondering if she'd noticed the oversight, but she appeared unperturbed.

When the preacher pronounced them man and wife, Shane cupped her cheeks and leaned down, directing his kiss toward her forehead. She tipped back her head and their lips collided. Her hands fluttered gently to his shoulders, then drifted upward, entwining in the hair brushing the nape of his neck. Time slowed and everything drifted away, leaving only the two of them. A tender flood of emotion shuddered through him.

A movement caught his attention and he wrestled hold of his senses, pulling back. Her eyes glassy, Tessa swayed forward. Shane steadied her before scooting away.

Garrett reached between them and clasped his hand, covering the awkward moment. Following a few hasty goodbyes and promises of future meetings, the children were bundled onto a makeshift bed in the back of the covered wagon. Snow sheeted around him, catching on his collar and trickling wetly down his back. He pulled his woolen muffler tighter.

Tessa lifted her foot onto a spoke of the wagon wheel and reached for the buckboard. He caught a glimpse of her trim ankles encased in wholly impractical half boots. He adjusted his leather gloves, hoping JoBeth had followed his instructions and outfitted his new wife with some sensible winter clothing. Judging by the stack of boxes in the back of the wagon, his cousin had taken him at his word.

Tessa kicked off and raised herself only halfway up before collapsing back onto the snow-packed street. Tipping back her head, she glared at the high seat. Without giving her time for protest, Shane gathered her around the waist and easily lifted her onto the bench. She squeaked and quickly scooted toward the opposite side. As he pulled himself up, the wagon tipped, and Tessa slid across the seat, bumping against his shoulder. She lurched away with a muffled apology.

"You warm enough?" he asked.

Her head jerked in a nod. "I'm fine."

The sudden change in her demeanor had him on edge. She'd seemed fine before the ceremony. During, even. Had the reality of her situation finally set in? Was she afraid of him? The thought was like a punch in the gut. What had he done to frighten her?

He cast her a cautious glance. "The trip takes an hour on a good day. Probably two hours in this weather."

"All right."

His new wife wore matching bright green woolen mittens, a hat and a muffler in a familiar pattern he recognized as the work of Mrs. Edwards. She'd wrapped the muffler completely around her face, leaving only her eyes visible. Crystal snowflakes clung to her eyelashes like cottony powder. He reached beneath the seat and produced a red plaid blanket, offering her the warmth without quite meeting her eyes. She dutifully tucked the material around her legs.

Flipping back the domed canvas cover, he made certain the twins were warmly bundled as well. Tessa followed his gaze and frowned.

"They'll be fine." He answered her unspoken question. "The canvas covering and the blankets trap the warmth. They'll be a lot more comfortable than you and me. Don't worry. You tell me if you need another blanket."

She tugged down her emerald woolen scarf, revealing her pert nose and full, pink lips. "I will." Then she quickly replaced the covering.

Gazing at the sky, he considered putting off the trip and quickly realized the futility of such a plan. If he hadn't been able to talk her out of a wedding, he doubted she'd be content with staying in town another night.

He didn't feel the cold like other folks. The kids were fine, so he didn't worry about them. Even if the wagon became stuck in the snow, they had plenty of supplies and his ranch hands would fetch them soon enough. He was worried about Tessa and her impractical boots of the thinnest kid leather. The horses jerked their heads, jangling their harnesses, and he reached for the brake. He'd worry about her shoes later. It wasn't as though she was walking the distance.

He'd know by Christmas whether or not she regretted her decision. All he could do until then was wait and keep his distance. He'd come this far—there was no use turning back now.

Chapter Seven

As Shane made to flick the reins, Garrett shouted from the stairs of the church. The marshal loped the distance and lifted a bundle toward Shane.

"JoBeth thought you might need this," Garrett said.

He touched the brim of his hat in Tessa's direction and dashed for cover once more.

The wrapped bundle warmed Shane's hands and he flipped back the covering, revealing a heated brick. He leaned toward Tessa and she recoiled.

"It's a warm brick," he said tersely. "For your feet."

She hadn't jolted away from him in the church. She'd actually leaned toward him. If they hadn't been standing before other people, he'd have been sorely tempted to take the moment further. She hadn't been protesting then. What had changed?

As the wagon lurched into motion, she braced her mittened fingers against the buckboard, her hand appearing impossibly small and almost childlike. He must have at least a foot of height on her as well as a hundred pounds. Some people were intimidated by his size. Next time he was in town, he'd ask JoBeth for advice. He'd see if she had any insight on how to put Tessa at ease. His cousin sure wasn't scared of him. Then again, Jo-Beth wasn't scared of anything. Maybe she wasn't the best person to ask.

For now, he'd keep his distance. It was what he'd planned on doing anyway. With that settled, Shane slapped the reins against the horses' backs and the horses picked up speed. Glancing over her shoulder, Tessa sketched a wave at the Cains.

They smiled and waved in return. Before long, the swirling white curtain of snow obscured everything but the faintest outlines of the buildings in town. The children fussed for the first half an hour or so, and Tessa spent most of that time with her back turned, quieting Owen and Alyce and keeping them warm and occupied. By the second half hour, the movement of the wagon had lulled them, and they curled around one another and dozed.

A sound caught his attention and his head swiveled. Tessa sat tall and straight, her hands clasped in her lap. Without turning his head, he kept an eye on her.

When he thought he caught her shivering, he whipped around. "I can rearrange the boxes, make some room with the children. It's warmer."

"I don't think there's any room even if you rearranged things." Worry clouded her face. "Jo near bought out the whole store."

"You're probably right. I hope cattle prices are good this spring to pay off the tab," he said, hoping to lighten the moment.

"You don't mind, do you?" She asked with tentative uncertainty. "About all the things Jo bought? I'm not even certain what she purchased. I'm sure we can return some things if it's too much. Or not."

Her continued hesitancy troubled him. They were too new to each other. They didn't know each other's moods yet. They hadn't developed the shorthand of shared experiences and private jokes. "I don't mind. Jo knows what she's doing." He glanced at the supplies heaped in the back of the wagon. "I told you before. This is a partnership. Don't feel like you're beholden to me."

She didn't appear convinced, and he caught a glimpse of her knotted hands once more.

"Looks like the weather might let up," he offered hopefully.

"Don't worry about me. I'm fine. And I promise you, I'll keep a good budget. I'm good at saving money."

"You won't beggar me anytime soon," he said easily. "You can help me tend the books. That way, you'll know how much you can spend."

He understood pinching pennies. The first year after his father left had been miserable. There'd been no money. His mother hadn't known the first thing about their financial situation. He'd ensure Tessa had a better grasp of their capital.

"I'm not good with numbers." Weariness showed in her eyes. "I know my letters. I can read," she continued with a hint of challenge in her voice. "I can keep a budget—truly, I can. Just as long as the numbers aren't complicated."

"Keeping the books isn't difficult. I'll teach you."

"You will?"

"Sure."

He caught the gratitude in her wide blue eyes and faced forward once more, remorse settling in his gut. After her bold proposal, he hadn't expected the emergence of this shy, uncertain creature. He much preferred the cheeky Tessa he'd first met in Wichita. He racked his brain for ideas, but couldn't think of a single thing that might put her at ease.

"Are you certain you're warm enough?" he asked lamely.

"Quite comfortable," she replied primly.

He lifted his shoulder in a slight shrug. She must be all right. Why lie about something as simple as whether or not she was cold? That didn't make any sense.

She tipped her head to look at him. "I know it must not seem like I'm very capable, but I can manage quite well, even in the leanest of times. Emmett always spent just a bit more than whatever we had. I grew quite adept at economizing when necessary."

"Some folks are like that." The snippets she dropped about her past made him curious for more information. "How did your father make a living?"

"A little of everything. Emmett was easily distracted. We moved around quite a bit."

"Hmm," he replied noncommittally.

At least they had that much in common. His own father had been a drifter. The similarity explained why Tessa was eager for the permanence of ranch life, and he prayed she didn't regret her decision. Sometimes wanting something and getting that something were two different things.

Snowflakes melted against his cheeks and dampened his collar. Tessa tugged her knit hat lower over her ears. He thought he caught her shivering again from the corner of his eye, but when he turned, she was stock-still.

The wagon wheels cut a path in the snow and he followed the hazy tree line, stark, leafless branches the only things visible against the white. Dense sheets of snow churned in a mesmerizing dance on the wind. With visibility down to a few yards at best, the sight was hypnotic, isolating them in the winter storm.

Tessa brushed the flakes from her lap, her head swiveling to and fro. "How can you tell where you're going? Everything looks the same to me."

"I've done this enough, I can see the landmarks." Without thinking, he gave her hand a quick squeeze. "I know the way. I won't get lost."

"I trust you."

His chest swelled with both pride and trepidation. She trusted him. She must—she'd married him, after all. In the coming months she'd realize any lingering doubts she might have about his intentions were unfounded. She'd find out soon enough she had nothing to fear from him.

He studied her face, searching for a clue to her thoughts. What had she said before? *You're not a mistake, Shane.*

He sure hoped she felt that way once she'd settled into ranch life.

"Don't worry," he said, his anticipation building the nearer he got to home. The past week had been full of change. Once they were at the ranch, they'd develop their own routine. Things would go back to normal. A different sort of normal, maybe, but they'd work out the details later. "We're almost home."

The worst of the trip was behind them.

Home.

This trip was interminable. Tessa clamped her teeth against their chattering and nodded rather than answering outright. Something had happened back there in the church. She couldn't explain it. One minute she was mumbling her vows; the next minute the touch of his lips had sent her nerves sizzling. When the pitch of the wagon had thrown her against him, the result was electrifying. He'd pulled back just as quickly, and she'd been keeping a space between them ever since.

Clenching her jaw, she repressed a shiver. She was freezing. Doing her best to hide her misery, she wrapped her arms around her body and concentrated on taking deep, even breaths. By her calculations, they had less than a half hour before they arrived at his ranch. She'd prove herself worthy of the task she'd undertaken even though her lungs had practically crystallized with the cold. At that moment, she feared the blizzard just might do her in before she'd passed a single day as Mrs. McCoy.

This was her first test, and she'd endure. Shane had warned her against the harsh conditions, and she'd assured him of her fortitude. She wasn't showing weakness now. Pride held her tongue. She wasn't giving voice to her misery. Not after he'd offered her every chance of staying in a nice, warm hotel, and she'd insisted on traveling instead. Her own discomforts were of little significance anyway. As long as the children were cozy and safe, nothing else mattered.

Aching from holding herself still, she groaned into her muffler. There might be a few things other than the children's comfort that mattered. The sensation in her toes probably mattered. She'd lost all feeling in her feet sometime during the past mile or so. Probably that wasn't a good thing. The tantalizing heat of Shane's body beckoned, but she kept her distance. Being close to him did something odd to her stomach.

A shudder racked her body and his head spun toward her. "I can stop, you know. Clear out a space in the back and you can sit with the children."

"I'm fine," she replied, her lips stiff with the cold. Pride was a powerful motivation. She'd practically railroaded him into marrying her; she wasn't giving him a reason to doubt her now. "Don't worry on my account."

"Suit yourself," he said, his voice clipped.

Another uncontrollable shudder caught her unaware. She rubbed her upper arms and peered at her new husband. He didn't seem the least bit chilled or uncomfortable. As all the little discomforts piled together, the realization left her unaccountably annoyed. Emmett had never taken to the cold weather. He tended to drift south during the winter and north during the summer. At the thought of him, a curious mixture of grief and anger gripped her.

She was exhausted and spent from worrying about him. He should have at least sent a telegraph. Didn't he care about her? Even a little? Perhaps something dire had happened that prevented him from reaching out. She'd know if he was dead, wouldn't she? Surely she'd feel his loss in her soul. What if he was injured? *No.* That didn't make any sense either. Emmett had never been much of a brave patient when ill. If he needed assistance, he'd have no qualms about contacting her. He wasn't a prideful man when it came to his own discomfort.

More than anything she sensed his absence was typical of Emmett's abiding negligence. Since he clearly wasn't worried about her, it probably never occurred to him that she might be worried about *his* safety. He'd reach out when he was good and ready, no matter how much his silence frightened her. Not because he was a cruel man, only thoughtless.

Blurry figures appeared in the distance, a line of horse and riders remaining ominously still, and she clutched

Shane's arm. "Who are they? What do you think they want?"

There was no good reason for anyone to be out in this miserable weather, which left the alternative.

He switched the enormous tangle of reins to one hand and brushed a spot of snow from the tip of her nose. Her stomach did that odd flip once more.

"Those are my men." A tinge of pride crept into his voice. "They must have been keeping watch. I'm later than usual. With the weather, they'd have been keeping a lookout."

She scooted farther away lest he feel her chilled trembling. "Will they mind? About m-me, I mean?"

Shane frowned. "Why should they mind about you?"

"Well, um, won't our marriage be a s-surprise?"

He shrugged. "I suppose. They'll get over it."

Not for the first time she found his economy of words frustrating. Emmett had always managed to fit three sentences into a place where one would do. While the quirk had sometimes been annoying, at least she'd never had to guess what he was thinking. Other worries crowded out thoughts of Emmett. Despite her best efforts, the shaking began anew. It seemed her body had a will of its own.

She considered asking Shane how long until they arrived, then abandoned the idea. If she appeared impatient, he might catch on to her misery. Instead she concentrated on the approaching riders, squinting through the snow as they took shape.

One man separated from the other three and took the lead. Something covered part of his face, and as he approached, she realized he wore a patch over his left eye.

The man's good eye widened at the sight of her while the other three riders openly gaped.

The man with the patch turned toward Shane, his right arm tucked at an awkward angle against his side. "You're late, boss."

By his tone, the words were a statement rather than an accusation.

Shane shrugged. "I'm surprised you spotted me."

"Parker saw the movement. He's got eyes like an eagle." Though clearly curious about Tessa, the man was obviously waiting for an explanation from Shane. "We were saddled and ready. Thought you might have trouble in the whiteout."

"No trouble. The kids are in the back. This is my wife."

The man's good eye nearly bugged out of his head. "Pleasure to meet you, Mrs. McCoy."

Tessa started. No one had spoken her new name before now, and the sound of it brought home the permanence of her situation. This was her new life, her new home. She'd best get used to the change. Though aching from the bitter cold, she assumed her most polite expression.

She leaned around Shane, seeking a better view of the men he employed. "Call me Tessa. I didn't catch your name."

Shane had gone oddly silent. He hadn't even attempted an introduction. She wondered if he was embarrassed or uncertain.

The first ranch hand touched the brim of his hat with one hand, his other still bent against his side. "Call me Finch. This here is Red, Milt and Wheeler."

Tessa's violent trembling hadn't yet abated and she gritted her teeth against the chattering once more. "It's a pleasure to meet y-you all."

Even bundled in their winter gear, the men were distinctive. There was Finch with his patched eye, Milt with his ragged gray beard and Red with a shock of ginger hair peeking out from beneath his hat. Wheeler was the most striking of all, a tall black man with an amused expression in his dark eyes. He kept looking between her and Shane, a smile twitching at the corner of his mouth.

When he caught her staring at him, his grin widened as though someone had told a joke and he was the only one who understood the humor. "Nice to make your acquaintance, Mrs. McCoy."

The men's mounts seemed oversized for horses. Even sitting in the wagon, they towered above her. Their breath puffed white and they pawed at the ground.

"We can finish the introductions later," Shane said. "Finch, drive the wagon the rest of the way. I'll ride your horse back with Tessa. Red can stay behind and make sure you don't get stuck. Wheeler, why don't you head on up to the house and get the fire started, maybe put on a pot of coffee."

Wheeler glanced between Tessa and Shane once more, his dark eyes glistening with suppressed laughter, then nodded. "Sure thing, boss."

She touched her head and caught sight of her mittened hand, recalling her matching woolen muffler with a grimace. He was probably wondering what was beneath all that knitting. No doubt she appeared two stones heavier as well. They were probably curious as to what had possessed their boss to marry such an odd creature.

Shane and Finch quickly swapped places and Shane urged his behemoth mount around to Tessa's side of the wagon. The animal was as dark as midnight with flecks of snow catching in its hide and melting just as quickly. She kept her gaze focused ahead, blinking her watering eyes against the flakes pelting her face.

Shane motioned with one hand. "You'll ride with me."

She gazed up at him, light-headed at his superior height atop the enormous horse. There were limits to one's endurance, and she'd just discovered hers. "I'll stay with the children."

Finch stiffened beside her and she considered offering him an apology. Continuing back to the house with a woman swathed in green knitting was probably not to his liking, but she'd reached her boundary for new adventures as well. She absolutely wasn't giving up the safety of the wagon for that enormous beast, no matter how chilled.

"Finch can handle things," Shane said. "They'll only be twenty minutes behind us."

"*We'll* only be twenty minutes behind," she corrected him. Even if she was frozen solid by the time they arrived, she wasn't budging. "Right, Finch?"

Finch blanched and looked away.

Shane leaned down and pitched his voice low. "Riding is quicker. And it's a whole lot warmer back at the house."

"I doubt I'll ever be warm again," she grumbled, having exhausted her good nature as well as the limits of her resilience. The frigid cold had seeped into her very marrow and she figured it'd stay that way until the spring thaw. "I'll be fine."

His jaw tightened and he extended his arm. "You're making Finch nervous. Now give me your hand."

"I'm not making Finch nervous. He's perfectly fine."

Finch shrugged.

Shane's fingers waggled encouragement and his face reflected command. There was compassion and understanding there, too, but the command remained. If he'd ordered her, she could have resisted easily. Instead he'd gentled his voice into a soft appeal.

"Please."

She huffed. "All right."

With obvious hesitation, she gathered her skirts and rose unsteadily. Before she reconsidered, he grasped her around the waist and tossed her onto the horse before him.

She yelped and clutched the arm he'd wrapped around her waist, then glanced down at the nauseating expanse between her new perch and the ground. "Why are all your horses so tall?"

"I raise draft horses. They're bigger than average. I train the runts for saddle. No sense in wasting good horseflesh."

Tessa gaped. "This horse is considered a runt?"

His chuckle rumbled against her back. "Yes. This horse is small by dray standards."

Her fingers dug into his arm and he eased her closer. "Hook your right knee around the saddle horn and brace your left foot on my boot. You'll have more balance and feel more secure that way."

She didn't exactly feel insecure. Though she was alarmed by the height, the arm holding her steady was strong and sure. Settling into position with her frozen and stiff limbs was awkward at best, painful at worst. After elbowing Shane in the stomach and butting the back of her head against his chin, she stilled.

He grunted and she muttered an apology before saying, "I'm ready."

Finch had taken on an amused expression remarkably similar to the one Wheeler had assumed earlier. Tessa sighed. If nothing else, at least she'd been a source of entertainment for the men.

As Shane expertly spun the horse around she stifled a squeak.

"Meet you back at the house," Shane called.

Tessa peered around. "Will you be all right, Finch?" She gazed up at Shane, her thoughts veering into panic. "What if the children wake up? Won't they be scared?"

"They'll be fine. They know Finch. Since Abby died, the men have taken turns helping with Alyce and Owen."

His eyes were inches away, and she noticed the flecks of amber surrounding his irises and the way the green darkened around the edges. Her breath hitched. Already the heat of his body had seeped through his jacket, promising the first hint of a thaw. The tantalizing warmth relaxed her and eased the ache in her bones.

He kicked his horse into step and Tessa yelped once more. "A little warning, if you please."

He tightened the arm holding her. "I won't let you fall."

"I know."

"Relax, Tessa." He pried her grasping fingers from the folds of his shirt. "You're cutting off my circulation."

She tried to loosen her grasp—really, she did. But her fingers wouldn't mind. Self-preservation had taken over her muscles, and they refused to loosen. In order to keep her seat, she remained staunchly upright. Never the best of riders, she hadn't been on a horse in years. Usually Emmett borrowed some horribly expensive animal from a friend of a friend if he needed a mount. Those horses were always delicately boned and much, much closer to the ground.

The jerky gait sent her bumping against Shane. Taut and sore from the cold, she collapsed deeper into abject misery with every step. Feeling wretchedly sorry for herself, she cataloged her discomforts. Beginning with her frozen ears and ending with her frozen toes, she mentally counted her list of aches and pains.

"Relax," Shane soothed. "Don't fight the horse's gait. Sink into the movement."

She'd much rather be sinking into a hot bath with lavender-scented oil. "I've never ridden double before," she offered by way of excuse.

Of all the things she'd worried about, neither freezing to death nor breaking her neck in a tumble from an oversized horse had been on the list. She hadn't considered whether riding would be part of her new life. Considering Shane lived on a ranch, she probably should have thought that one through. What other surprises did her future hold?

She'd face whatever came next with courage and grit. Well, with grit at least. The courage might come later.

"Don't worry," Shane said. "If you like, I'll buy you a nice, docile mare. Something small and meek. Perhaps a Shetland?"

"Absolutely not! A poor little pony amongst all these dray horses? They'll trample the wee thing underfoot."

"You might be right. Something a little larger, then."

"Yes, but not too large."

The conversation had temporarily distracted her from her dangerous perch, and she gradually relaxed back into the gait. After a few strides, she caught the rhythm of the animal and swayed in unison. Nothing could distract her from the miserable weather. Snowflakes pelted her face, stinging her cheeks. She turned her face into Shane's jacket, clutching his lapel. Raising his arm, he adjusted the fluttering edge of her muffler, tucking the loose end between their bodies. The gesture was absurdly comforting and protective, banishing some of her earlier fears.

Fatigue crept up on her once more, and her eyes grew drowsy. She was exhausted, but the cold wouldn't let her rest. Though she fought against them, violent tremors racked her body, and there was no hiding her suffering from Shane. Though he said nothing, she felt him urge the horse into a faster pace.

"Just a little bit longer," he said near her ear, his warm breath puffing against her temple, "and we'll be out of this weather."

"I'll be f-fine once we're inside."

The past few weeks caught up with her in a rush, sapping her strength. She'd set out from Emmett with all sorts of lofty aspirations and high hopes, and she'd failed on all accounts. Truth be told, she'd left with more than her fair share of arrogance as well. Like an errant child, she'd harbored a bit of an "I'll show you" attitude toward Emmett. She'd come to believe that she'd done most of the work in keeping them afloat, and maybe she had. But Emmett had always solved their most pressing problems. Perhaps not in the most conventional way, or even the most legal way, but he'd always kept them one step ahead of disaster.

What a fool she'd been. She'd apologize to him for her foolish overconfidence if they ever met up again. He'd treated her as a child and she'd behaved like one. Emmett had preferred her as a little girl, staring up at him with wide-eyed devotion. He preferred being adored to being chastised. Didn't everyone?

Slackening his hold, Shane tucked her arms between them and adjusted the lapels of his coat, cocooning her against his body. "You'll be warmer this way."

His masculine scent teased her nostrils and a tremor that had nothing to do with the cold shook her. The familiarity was foreign and disturbing, but exhaustion prevented her from resisting his comfort. Sagging into the solid wall of his chest, she slipped her arms inside his coat and anchored them around his waist. The heat of his body sparked life back into her icy fingers.

She'd never been this close to a man before. That same foolish longing for unconditional love pierced her heart like a spear, overwhelming any vestige of good sense or restraint. Husbands and wives were allowed a greater degree of affection, and she'd only just realized how much she craved the touch of another human being. She felt as though she'd been given her first sip of water and discovered a desperate, unquenchable thirst.

The rough wool of Shane's coat scratched against the chilled patch of skin exposed between her forehead and her muffler, the discomfort barely registering against the rest of her complaints. "R-really, I'm f-fine. Just a little ch-chilly."

"Sure."

"I don't want you to think that I'm ill-suited for the w-weather."

His chuckle rumbled beneath her ear. "Out here, everyone is ill-suited for the weather."

"You don't s-seem to mind the cold."

"I mind. Not as much as other folks, but I mind."

She angled her head and caught sight of a modest ranch house, the chimney already billowing dark smoke into the sky. Relief flooded through her. The building was a neat structure, one story with a porch that stretched across the entire front. The house was dwarfed by enormous buildings set farther back and a third, smaller structure off to the left.

Shane leaned away and slipped two fingers against her chin, lifting her head a notch.

"Look, we're nearly there."

Wind whistled between their bodies, robbing what little warmth she'd captured.

Home.

She was damp, cold, miserable and homesick for something she couldn't even name. She craved a sense of familiarity, of recognition. Her life had changed in the blink of an eye this morning. No one could blame her if it was all too much to absorb. This wasn't her home. Not yet. None of this felt any more memorable than the copious number of hotels and boardinghouses she'd stayed in over the years.

She glanced at the silent man she'd married. Could she make this her home? How did someone who'd never had a home make a home for someone else?

Chapter Eight

Tessa's violent trembling reminded Shane that she was huddled against him only for his shared warmth. He should have left her in town, though a part of him knew she'd have refused. His new wife definitely had a stubborn streak.

He watched her reaction to his homestead, unable to read her response. He'd never much considered how his place looked to other folks. The ranch had been arranged with the house facing the road, two enormous barns sitting back and to the east, the bunkhouse between them. He'd built every structure on this land alongside his men. He'd planted all the trees a decade before. Fast-growing elms and poplars, along with slower-growing evergreens that were already making a fine windbreak. Though sturdily built and neatly arranged, the ranch house was woefully inadequate. He hadn't been thinking of a family when he'd laid out his plans.

After Abby had arrived, the small space had quickly filled with supplies for the babies. His aunt Edith, the local midwife, had taken one look at Abby and warned them of the possibility of twins. Abby had been miserable in those last months, and his presence had only aggravated her. Eventually, he'd moved to the bunkhouse. Even after the children were born, he'd stayed away. The ladies from town had clustered around, taking turns and helping out. His presence had seemed unnecessary.

Tessa blinked, her eyes welling with tears in the sharp wind. "This all belongs to you?" she asked, her voice filled with wonder.

"To us," he replied. "You're my partner now, remember? This all belongs to us."

Something had been missing from his life for a long time. Too long. He sensed a kinship with Tessa and a renewed sense of purpose. The past couple of years had been difficult, harder than he'd even admitted to himself. He hadn't realized how glum he'd been until the first ember of hope had illuminated his discontent.

Between the twins' birth and Abby's illness, there'd been no time to plan for the future. All the change and tragedies had narrowed his focus. Like moving through this blizzard, he'd only been able to take the steps immediately before him. For the first time in a long time he caught a glimpse of a fresh start, and he felt the faint stirrings of enthusiasm once more.

He'd planned on adding a second story to the house after the twins were born, but the addition had no longer seemed necessary after Abby's death. He'd dig out the plans this winter and get Tessa's opinion.

She shook her head, her encompassing gaze full of wonder. "How many acres do you own?"

"A thousand." At her gasp he added, "Only about one-third of that is fenced for pasture. The rest is prairie. I'll fence more as needed."

"Was this your parents' farm?"

"Nope," he replied, his pride evident. "I saved and bought a couple hundred acres, then bought a couple hundred more. Everything added up over time."

She pressed back into his chest, her head ducked against the wind. Though he'd insisted they ride as a matter of expediency, he hadn't counted on the way she'd melt against him. Her trust in him was part of the reason he'd agreed to the hasty marriage, after all. She put on a fine air of sophistication, but it hadn't taken long to realize she was little more than a babe in the woods. She was far too innocent for her own good. How had she got this far without someone taking advantage of her?

"You didn't tell me you were a land baron," she said, her voice muffled against his jacket. "I guess there's a lot of things we don't know about each other."

"I know. I rushed things."

She stiffened and he immediately regretted his words.

"Don't worry," he said. "We've got plenty of time to find out about each other."

"A-ages," she replied, her words nearly incomprehensible over her chattering teeth.

Everything had seemed more urgent in town. Here, the wind biting like a thousand teeth, her suffering apparent, he questioned his choice. He should have given her more time, no matter the weather. His men were plenty able to look out for the ranch while he was gone. He wasn't so all-fired important they couldn't last a few days without him. Part of keeping her safe was keeping her warm and dry.

Except he didn't like being away. When he was gone, even for a short time, he felt the pull of home.

The arms wrapped around his middle tightened and Tessa nestled her head beneath his chin. "I know you think we should have waited, but I'm glad Owen found me that day at the train station. I'm glad we met."

"Me, too," he said, truly meaning his words. "Me, too."

She murmured something unintelligible, her words garbled by her shivering, and his worry over her comfort increased. Illness was always a risk. Abby had suffered from a vague malaise even before the children were born, but the fever that had taken her life had been swift and unexpected. A sense of urgency tightened his knees against the horse's flanks, urging the animal into a faster step. The sooner Tessa was inside, the better.

She was still trembling when they reached the house. He looped the reins around one of the posts anchoring the porch, knowing Wheeler was near and would care for the animal. The snow had lightened but the cold hadn't let up yet. The wind alone was brutal.

He swung down first and reached for Tessa. He grasped her waist and she braced her hands on his shoulders. She stared at him with her wide blue eyes revealed between the silly green muffler and knit cap.

"I look ridiculous, don't I?" she asked.

"You look charming. Mrs. Edwards does enjoy bright colors. I recognize her work. Or her color choice at least."

He set Tessa on her feet and her legs collapsed beneath her.

Catching her against his chest, he scooped her into his arms. She was solidly built, but not heavy.

"Oh my," she gasped and circled her arms around his neck. "I guess I'm not used to riding. I'm far too heavy for you to carry."

"Do you doubt my strength?"

"Not your strength—your endurance."

Wheeler had unlatched the door and Shane nudged it open with his foot. A burst of warm air ruffled his hair.

She tugged down her muffler and grinned. "You've carried me over the threshold like a proper bride."

His chest constricted. The gesture was more personal than he'd imagined, more intimate. The stove had been lit and a pot of coffee percolated on the burner. Books and papers lay scattered over the kitchen table. A pile of clothing was visible through the open door of his bedroom. He grimaced at the mess. After leaving the children with JoBeth and Garrett, he hadn't felt like doing much of anything, and his lack of enthusiasm showed. Dishes were piled in the dry sink and he caught sight of the muddy prints his boots had tracked.

He set Tessa on her feet and she teetered a bit before catching her balance. "I'm getting my sea legs again."

Hovering near as she took a seat beside the potbellied stove, he stepped away only once she'd been safely seated. She scraped her chair nearer the fire and whipped off her gloves, warming her fingers.

"Be careful," he said. "Don't warm them too quickly."

Her face screwed up and she groaned, folding her hands against her stomach. "It feels like pins and needles."

He knelt before her and forced open her fingers, chafing them between his own. "They're like ice. Why didn't you say something earlier?"

"It's not bad."

Her violent trembling intensified and he realized this wasn't the time for lectures. He slipped her damp coat off her shoulders and draped a blanket around her. Kneeling before her again, he reached for the laces of her boots.

She brushed his fingers aside but her own were too

stiff and clumsy for the sodden laces. He pulled them off and realized her socks were damp as well. "You're fortunate you didn't get frostbite."

Her small toe peeked out from a hole in her sock, and she curled her feet, covering the hole with her opposite foot. The gesture was guileless and endearing.

She offered a weak smile. "At least I can feel them. My feet."

He carefully wrapped her chilled toes in a woolen blanket and pulled over a footstool, resting her heels on the surface with her feet toward the fire. "No closer," he admonished.

He crossed to his room and dug out a pair of clean wool socks from his drawer, then draped them over the warmer atop the stove.

A knock sounded on the door and he discovered Parker on the threshold holding a steaming covered dish. "Thought you might like some leftover stew." Parker lifted the pot. "Wheeler said, uh… He said you had a guest."

Parker was the second man Shane had hired after Wheeler. The old cook was stout and solid, his beard as gray as his squinted eyes. He peered around Shane with unabashed curiosity. Word of their unexpected visitor traveled fast.

"This is my wife, Tessa. Tessa, this is Parker. He does most of the cooking around the ranch."

The grizzled cook advanced farther into the house. "Pleasure to meet you, miss."

"Mine as well," she said. "You'll excuse me if I don't get up. I'm afraid the ride from town has left me a little worse for wear."

Parker grunted and cast a reproving glare at Shane.

"It's not fit for man nor beast out there. Not sure why anyone would want to travel in this weather."

"I—" Shane began.

"I'm afraid that's my fault," Tessa interrupted smoothly. "I forced the matter. I was anxious to see my new home."

Parker flushed beneath her warm smile. "You let me know if you need anything settling in. I'm just across the way."

"Did Wheeler take care of Scout?" Shane asked. He couldn't have anything happening to Owen's favorite horse.

"The animals are tucked away in the barn already."

"Excellent."

Clearly they'd exhausted their pleasantries, yet Parker lingered in the cozy heat of the house. "I can see the wagon just over the rise. They'll be here soon. Wheeler says you brought the children. The place isn't the same without them younglings running underfoot."

"My thoughts exactly."

Parker remained just inside the door, appearing as though his feet had sprouted roots and anchored him to the floor. "Do you need anything else?"

"We'll be fine." Shane steered him toward the door. "I'll explain everything to the boys later." He spoke low enough that only Parker could hear.

The man grinned. "I can't decide whether we should send you into town more or less often."

"Some discretion is in order."

"All right, all right. Don't get your back up. You better take care of your missus, there. She looks a mite chilled."

"As soon as you finally leave, I'll see to Tessa. Except you don't seem to be able to leave, do you? Did someone nail your feet to the floor when neither of us was looking?" Shane muttered, growing more exasperated by the minute.

"Right, boss."

After firmly shutting the door behind Parker, Shane crossed back over to Tessa. She'd wrapped her arms around her body and was rocking back and forth in an effort to chafe some heat into her arms. He took the socks from the warmer on the stove and knelt before her.

As he pulled back the wool blanket, she gasped in protest. He slipped the warmed wool socks over her feet and her expression instantly transformed. She went from ragged annoyance into pure bliss in the space of a heartbeat.

"Oh my," she breathed out in a sigh. "That is absolutely the most wonderful thing I've ever felt. I had no idea I could be that miserable and cold."

Shane ducked his head. Not even three hours married and he'd nearly frozen his wife. Things were not starting off well at all.

Things were not starting off well at all. Tessa woke before the children the following morning and soon realized Shane was gone.

Not just gone. Most of his belongings were gone as well and all the drawers in the bureau were empty. The previous evening, she'd fallen asleep in the enormous bed while reading Alyce and Owen a bedtime story. This morning they were safely tucked in their cribs in the adjoining room, the covers neatly tucked over their shoulders.

An ignominious start to any marriage. Shane had promised her space while they got to know each other, and while she hadn't been entirely certain of the living and sleeping arrangements, she hadn't expected completely separate dwellings. Near as she could figure, he must be staying in the bunkhouse with the men. Where else would he be?

She padded into the kitchen and took stock of her dwellings. This was a new chance for a first impression, and she was making the most of the opportunity.

The house wasn't terribly large, featuring a long main room with a kitchen on one end and a living area at the other with a table and chairs for eating in the middle. Having a kitchen open to the rest of the house left her feeling oddly exposed, but she wasn't exactly in a position to complain. Off the main living area, two bedrooms flanked the west side of the space with a washroom in the middle.

The pantry was well stocked, and the crates filled with JoBeth's purchases were stacked along the wall. Her trunk was there as well, and a blush crept up her neck. Shane must have seen it in the window of the haberdashery. Though embarrassed, she appreciated the gesture.

Like a child on Christmas morning, she carefully unwrapped each item and marveled at the selection. Jo had even thrown in two calico dresses, a sturdy pair of boots and several pairs of wool socks. Tessa savored the memory of her warmed socks from the previous evening. Stove-warmed socks were her new favorite thing.

After everything was unpacked and neatly arranged, she opened *Bartleby's Book of Household Management* and discovered a recipe for biscuits. She'd seen the cooks at the Harvey House rolling out the dough plenty of times, and with only a few wrong turns, she soon had a fine batch of biscuits prepared.

Her cooking skills were adequate and she relished the

time for improving them. She'd always found baking an enjoyable activity. Since the cooks at Harvey's were always complaining that stoves could be temperamental, she carefully monitored the progress of her first batch until they'd achieved a perfect golden brown. By the time Owen and Alyce called from their room, she had six dozen biscuits cooling on every available surface.

Frowning at the surplus, she penciled a note into the margin of the book. *Recipe makes 72 biscuits. Considering cutting recipe by ½ or ¼.*

In the following hours, she had Alyce and Owen fed and dressed, the coffee percolated and the kitchen back in order. In all that time, Shane had yet to make an appearance. While she accepted full responsibility for falling asleep before they'd spoken of their plans for the day, she'd expected he'd at least check in on her and the children.

Planting her hands on her hips, Tessa pivoted. "How about we go exploring?"

Owen clapped his hands. "Ga. Scout."

"Would you like to see Scout?"

"Ga."

"Excellent."

Soon she had the two children bundled into coats, gloves, hats and scarves. Sweating, Tessa sat back on her heels and swiped the moisture from her forehead. She'd never considered the difficulties of pressing tiny feet into tiny boots and tying wool hats beneath dimpled chins.

The moment she had them both prepared, Owen tore off his hat. "Hot."

"No, no," Tessa admonished. "I'll be ready in an instant."

By the time she'd donned her own hat, gloves and coat, the twins had shed theirs. With tears of frustration burning behind her eyes, she quickly accomplished the task once more. Owen wailed and tugged at the knot she'd tied in his hat strings, and she quickly opened the door.

"There." She pointed. "Why don't you wait on the porch?"

Owen's tears instantly dried and he toddled outside, Alyce close on his heels. Sweat trickled down Tessa's back from her exertions, and her skin itched. She scrounged a burlap sack and had it filled with biscuits in record time, the door open and the cabin filling with cold air. Her attention darted back and forth between the children as she clumsily finished her task.

Once she'd stepped outside and closed the door behind her, the sheen of moisture covering her instantly chilled.

"Really," she said in Owen's direction. "There simply must be a better or more efficient way of doing things."

Owen only pointed toward the red barn. "Ga. Scout."

Hoisting her bag into the air, she gestured in the opposite direction. "First we're delivering these to the bunkhouse, and then we'll visit Scout."

Stubbornly shaking his head, Owen pointed. "Scout."

"Bunkhouse."

Owen shook his head.

Tessa shrugged. "Then I guess we can't visit Scout after all. Back inside, everyone."

This time Alyce burst into tears. Tessa scrubbed one hand down her face, smothering a sound of frustration. Children were proving much more difficult than she'd expected.

She felt a tug on her sleeve and glanced down. Owen stared up at her. He pointed toward the bunkhouse. "There. Ga there."

The battle of wills had been struck. Alyce hiccuped and ceased her tears. Tessa warily eyed Owen. She might have won this skirmish, but she anticipated resistance at every turn. It appeared Owen enjoyed testing his limits with her. She'd keep a close eye on that one.

"That's better," she said brightly. "Off we go."

Feeling both excited and apprehensive, she set off down the shallow stairs. The ranch featured the main house, a bunkhouse that was quite a bit larger, an enormous red barn and another barn that had been painted an indistinguishable shade of mud brown. Trees dotted the area and a lengthy line of enormous evergreens had been planted as a windbreak. In the distance, fenced pastureland stretched as far as the eye could see. She spotted horses, cattle and even what looked to be a sheep.

The men had already cleared paths leading to all the buildings. Fascinated by the fresh blanket of snow, the twins dutifully trailed behind her, occasionally sticking their mittened fingers into a drift and licking off the snow.

"Remember, only clean snow," she admonished, brushing a patch of grayed flakes from Owen's mitten.

Once she reached the bunkhouse door, she rapped sharply. A moment later Finch appeared.

"Mrs. McCoy," he said, blinking his good eye rapidly. "Shane isn't here. He's in the barn."

A noisy burst of activity sounded from inside and several figures darted past. A distinct mixture of scents wafted through the door. She recognized tobacco, bacon and coffee, all blended together into something that undeniably declared the bunkhouse a male-only domain.

She lifted her burlap sack. "I'm actually here to see you."

Finch silently opened and closed his mouth a few times, then said, "Well, uh, come in. Don't stand out there in the cold."

Tessa and the twins shuffled inside. One of the men stood at attention as though waiting for an inspection. Wheeler straightened his collar while Red hopped on one stockinged foot, clumsily tugging his boot onto the opposite limb.

Finch cleared his throat. "You met the boys last evening. You remember Red, Wheeler and Parker."

Only Parker appeared at ease. He sat before an enormous tin washtub filled with a pile of peeled potatoes, his shirtsleeves rolled up while he scraped the peel from yet another. As she nodded a greeting, she caught Finch shoving playing cards beneath his pillow out of the corner of her eye.

Alyce plucked something from the floor and lifted it to her mouth.

Wheeler lunged and pried the object from her fingers. "You don't want to eat anything off this floor, little missy." He stuffed the offending object into his pocket. "You be careful, Mrs. McCoy. They'll give you a run for your money at that age."

"Everything to the mouth." Red planted his hands on his hips. "That's what my mother always used to say about my little brothers. Everything to the mouth."

"I'm learning that," Tessa said with a roll of her eyes. "I can't thank you enough for taking care of the children and unloading the wagon."

Owen reached for Parker's sidearm and the man scooted away. "No, no, little partner. Remember, we talked about that."

Alyce approached Wheeler and reached out her chubby

arms. He held up his hands and took a step back, casting a wary glance in Tessa's direction. The move had her wondering about his past. Had his family been touched by slavery? Considering his age, older than Shane, but younger than Parker, the idea wasn't that unlikely. Clearly the man was uncertain of her welcome, and Tessa's heart ached for the past. Over twenty years since the war, and he was still guarded around newcomers. Not that she blamed him.

She lifted Alyce into her arms and crowded the man. "You'd best accept the inevitable, Wheeler, and hold her. She's quite persistent."

Clearly wary, he accepted the child. Alyce grasped his cheeks with both hands and gurgled. Wheeler's broad grin revealed his white teeth against his dark skin.

Tessa turned toward Finch. "I made far too many biscuits this morning. I was hoping you gentlemen could assist."

She held out the bag and he reached for it with his left hand. Only then did she notice his right sleeve was pinned back. He'd lost his arm beneath the elbow. She'd thought he'd held the limb at an odd angle the previous evening, but she'd been too immersed in her own misery for closer inspection. Anchoring the bag against his side with what remained of his upper arm, he retrieved one of the biscuits.

She fidgeted beneath his close scrutiny. This was her first real effort, after all, and there was no need for such a meticulous critique, was there?

After turning the biscuit this way and that, he took a bite and nodded. "This is good."

Tessa expelled a breath she hadn't even known she was holding. "Thank you."

"Where did you learn to cook like this?"

"I cooked for my father some. I bought a book from the mercantile in town. I simply followed the recipe. The first batch didn't turn out as well. The stove was too hot, I think."

"That stove runs hot. Let me know if you need any help."

"I will."

He glanced at the biscuit and back at her. "You just followed the recipe?"

She wasn't quite certain what he found odd about her explanation. "Yes. The instructions were quite clear. There are more recipes in the book I'd like to try. I'm short of ingredients, though."

"There's a meat shed around back and root cellar near the house." He jerked one thumb over his shoulder, indicating the general direction. "I'm sure Shane will show you around today. Do you need anything else?"

She had to give them credit. If the men were surprised Shane had brought a wife home from town as well as the supplies, they kept their curiosity well hidden.

"That was all. It was nice meeting you." She reached for Alyce. "You said Shane was in the barn?"

"Yep."

After that brief reply, the silence stretched out uncomfortably. Okay, maybe their curiosity wasn't that well hidden. The four men stared at her as though some exotic creature had wandered into their midst. As she stepped outside once more, the cold hit her like a blast and she held Alyce closer. At least the wind wasn't blowing and the snow wasn't falling. With the bright morning sun sparkling off the snow, she might have lingered over the enchanting sight.

The barn was only a few degrees warmer than the

outdoors, but even the slight change was welcome. A man she recognized from the previous evening, Milt, sat on a low stool surrounded by heaps of corn he patiently shucked, tossing the cobs into the center.

Shane stepped from one of the stalls and halted. "What are you doing here?"

Tessa hesitated. It was more than a little disconcerting how surprised he was to see her. The easy companionship they'd shared the previous evening had vanished, leaving a wary edge to Shane.

What had she done to make him watchful of her? They barely knew one another. What about her, then, made him brace for a showdown each time she appeared?

Chapter Nine

Taken aback by his demand, she halted. "Well, uh, look-ing for you."

Owen dashed toward the open stall door. "Scout!"

She caught him beneath one arm midstride and hoisted him onto her opposite hip. "Let's hear what Papa has to say first."

Her arms strained against the increased weight of carrying both children. Though Alyce remained still, Owen squirmed against her hold. The men were clearly working, and she didn't want to disturb them more than necessary.

Milt stood and brushed the corn dust from his hands. "I can take the little fellow around for a visit."

Alyce cantilevered her body toward the man and Tessa set her down.

The little girl tugged on his pant leg. "Scout."

Milt grinned. "Yes. You can come, too."

Tessa set Owen down as well, rolling her shoulder in relief. "Are you certain?"

She turned her head toward Shane, and he gave a slight nod.

Tessa followed their progress. "He'll keep a close eye on them, won't he?"

"You can trust Milt."

She nibbled on the inside of her cheek. Left alone with her husband, Tessa's unease increased. There were no road maps for this new relationship, no past experiences on which to build. She wasn't certain how wives were supposed to act, but judging from the odd look on Shane's face, she wasn't hitting the mark.

She stared at her clasped hands. "I thought I'd see you at breakfast."

"I ate with the boys."

"I figured as much. I made biscuits."

Well, that was certainly a good start. *I made biscuits.* She'd have him swooning at her feet in no time with those honeyed words.

"I'll probably eat with the boys most meals," he said, his gaze not quite meeting hers. "You don't have to cook for me."

By her self-imposed timeline, she had until Christmas to convince him they suited. How was she supposed to do that if they never saw each other?

"How about dinner?" She scuffed at the ground. "Will you at least have dinner with us? For the children," she added quickly. "You can spend time with the children that way. We can develop a proper routine. From what I read in Bartleby's book, routine is very important for a successful family life."

Then again, Bartleby had also stressed the importance of accurate references when acquiring new servants and the proper etiquette for receiving morning callers, neither of which applied here. As she'd discovered after reading the first few pages, Bartleby must have been

English, and the English obviously had far more rigid procedures and customs.

The chapter on entertaining sprang to mind. If she ever threw a formal ball, she knew the lady of the house should perform the first quadrille. Whatever that was. Yet the basic advice throughout the book had seemed sound, and stressing the importance of having a routine felt a whole lot more acceptable than begging for a scrap of companionship like an eager chicken pecking for feed.

"Good idea." Shane rubbed his chin. "The ladies from town were big on routine as well."

"They sound like very wise ladies."

"Dinner is a good idea, then, too. What time?"

Wow. She'd had two whole good ideas in a row. She was on a roll. "Six o'clock."

The concession rang of victory, though she felt anything but victorious. Too bad Bartleby hadn't included a chapter on wooing widowers. She craved something more than this stilted awkwardness. She'd find a way for them to work comfortably together as friends, with or without his cooperation.

She sucked in a breath and started over. "Finch said you'd show me the root cellar and the meat shed."

He tilted his head. "When did you see Finch?"

"Just now." She motioned in the vague direction of the outbuilding. "I stopped at the bunkhouse before I found you."

"You went to the bunkhouse?"

Tessa narrowed her gaze. His tone did not sound encouraging. "Yes."

His grim expression had her taking another cautious step back. "Was that wrong?"

His eyes softened and he speared his hands through

his dark hair. "Not wrong, exactly, but steer clear of there in the future."

His impervious tone raised her hackles. She wasn't one of the children and he'd best remember that.

"How come?" She sounded like a recalcitrant child, but since that summed up how she felt, she didn't care. "Why can't I visit the bunkhouse?"

"Because they're doing stuff."

"What kind of stuff?"

"I don't know. Man stuff." He threw up his hands. "They need their privacy. They shouldn't have to worry if you're going to barge in."

He might have a valid point, she conceded. They had seemed rather shocked by her presence. There'd been all that hasty tucking away of shirttails and secreting away of playing cards.

Despite the allowance, she wasn't ready to let him off the hook. "I didn't barge in. I knocked." She huffed. "What if I need you for something? Can I knock then?"

It wasn't as though they were sharing the same quarters. Concessions must be made. He made it seem as though she was a great inconvenience, and she didn't relish being thought of as an imposition.

"Yes," he replied, clearly exasperated by the run of questions. "You can knock if you need anything. Just try not to need anything too often."

Tessa crossed her arms over her chest. "I'll try and keep my knocking at a minimum. I wouldn't want to interrupt all your *man* stuff."

Their conversation smacked of the ridiculous, and the whole arrangement struck her as a bit irregular. Didn't Shane realize that he might be the person she needed? She might not know much about being a wife, but she didn't suppose this was the usual way men and women went about things. Shane had been married before. Surely he knew… She blew out an inward sigh. She mustn't forget about his previous relationship. She'd practice her patience. As long as he didn't take too long to come around.

Battling a surge of remorse for her curt attitude, she searched for a change of subject.

Alyce and Owen had emerged from the stall and discovered the corn. Owen plucked a cob from the dirt floor and stuffed it in his mouth.

"No!" Tessa called.

Owen grimaced and spit out the dried kernels. "Blech. Bad."

"Yes, bad." She took the cob and wiped the drool from his chin. "You needn't taste everything, you know."

Milt gave a slight shrug of one shoulder. "A little dirt never hurt none. My ma always said dirt had healing powers. Why don't you leave the young'uns with me and take a look around the spread. That sun won't stay up forever."

Rather than debate the healing powers of dirt, Tessa hooked Alyce beneath her arms and set her on one of the low stools. "Would you mind helping Mr. Milt while Papa and I take a walk?"

Alyce opened and closed her fists with a nod. "Me help. Me help."

Crouching, Owen lifted another ear from the floor and tossed the whole thing into the center, husk and all. Milt retrieved the corn.

Tessa lifted her eyes heavenward. "Don't help the man too much." She turned toward Milt. "You're sure you'll be all right for fifteen minutes or so?"

"Right as rain."

Shane heaved open the barn door enough for them to pass, then called over his shoulder, "Holler if you need anything."

Once outside, he glanced at her feet and paused. "Those are better boots than the ones you had on yesterday."

"JoBeth picked them out for me."

He halted in his tracks. "Then why didn't you wear them yesterday? They'd have kept your feet a whole lot warmer. You nearly froze."

"Because they're ugly work boots," she grumbled. "I wanted to look nice on my wedding day."

And there hadn't been time to change since he'd been all fired up about the weather. She glanced around the serene setting and the light dusting of fresh snow. Clearly his fears had been unfounded, but she wasn't pointing out *his* mistakes.

He pinched the bridge of his nose. "Never mind. I'm sorry. Let's get on with the tour. We only have a short time before the twins tire of their current activity." He paused before a building not much bigger than an outhouse. "This is the meat shed."

He swung open the door and Tessa gasped. An enormous carcass hung from a hook in the center. She gagged and spun around, holding one hand to her mouth.

Shane heaved a sigh.

Oh no, she wasn't giving him any more fodder. She didn't know why he'd woken up on the surly side of the bed this morning, but she wasn't letting him ruin her day. If Mr. Shane High-and-Mighty McCoy thought she was too much of a tenderfoot for the ranch, she'd prove him wrong.

Him and his big, gusty disappointed sighs.

"How long…?" She swallowed hard. "How long does it hang there?"

"Weather like this, when it stays below freezing, it'll keep for a bit. The meat is cooked or dried or salted. I keep two thousand head of cattle and three hundred horses. The cattle business keeps me afloat when the horses aren't selling. Horses are an unpredictable business, but the cattle is steady. Everybody has to eat."

The carcass wasn't quite as shocking anymore. She'd been surprised, that was all. She'd noted a drawing of prime cuts in *Mr. Bartleby's Book of Household Management*. Although the penciled drawing of that animal had been much less detailed and colorful than the real thing. No matter. With each experience she gained a thicker skin. Later, she'd ask Finch how to carve up the parts. If she caught him outside the bunkhouse, that was. Who knew if butchering was considered important enough for *knocking* and interrupting *man stuff*?

Tessa snorted, her warmed breath puffing vapor into the air. She'd have to skulk around and pounce the instant he walked past. Man stuff indeed.

Shane turned. "Did you say something?"

"I was wondering about the root cellar," she answered blandly.

He led her across the grounds following a well-worn path scraped clear of snow toward a lean-to cut into the side of the hill. He crouched and flipped open the door set at an angle. "Be careful when you go down the steps. When there's a melt, sometimes the water leaks inside and freezes."

She peered over his shoulder.

He motioned with one hand. "Ladies first."

Stooping, she squinted into the darkness. "Are there spiders?"

"In the summer, yes. Now they're mostly dormant."

"What about snakes?"

He heaved another one of his annoying sighs. "The snakes are hibernating as well," he said with exaggerated patience. "As long as you wear your ankle boots, they can't bite you anyway."

Ankle boots were quickly becoming the bane of her existence.

She recalled her morning routine with frustrating clarity. She'd practically torn Owen's boots asunder trying to jam them on his feet. She'd had such enthusiasm this morning.

Six dozen biscuits, three sinks full of dishes and two pairs of boots later, her cheery mood had waned. Suddenly it was all too much. The cold, the spiders, the snakes, the side of beef swinging from a jagged hook and how abominably difficult it was for a grown and capable woman to place tiny shoes on tiny, squirming feet.

Shane wasn't the only one who was a touch cranky this morning. She stared at the jagged edge of the fingernail she'd torn while dressing Owen. A burn on her thumb from the stove throbbed as well. Her new husband's unexpected dour mood didn't do anything to lighten her own thoughts either. The sooner this was finished, the sooner she could sit down with a cup of tea and nurse all her bumps and bruises, the mental ones as well as the physical ones.

She pressed a stiff arm against Shane's chest. "Never mind. Ladies first, remember?"

He staggered back a step. Her torn nail caught on

his wool coat and she winced, then glared at the spot of blood.

"I'll rip out their tongues tomorrow," she grumbled.

Shane blanched. "Whose tongues?"

"The shoes. The boots. Those tiny little boots with a bend where a foot doesn't bend."

"Oh yes. It's quite a chore, isn't it?"

His weary resignation softened her anger. They were in this together, the two of them, by design, by agreement and by the vows they'd declared before a man of God. This was no time for turning on each other.

"Yes," she returned shortly. "It's quite a chore."

Already this morning she'd changed their diapers twice. Bartleby needed a chapter on child rearing. That thought brought her up short. How did one transition a toddler out of diapers, anyway? She made a mental note to ask Jo the next time they saw one another.

Yes, Bartleby definitely needed a chapter on child rearing. Instructions on dealing with tantrums seemed far more useful than knowing where to sit a baroness at the dinner table.

With Shane staring expectantly at her, she took a cautious step into the abyss, then another. She'd never been overly fond of the dark. Emmett had conducted most of his more nefarious business after nightfall. He'd slip out after he assumed she was asleep, padding across the floor and slipping out the door. She'd listen for the thud, thud of his shoes as he replaced them in the corridor followed by the raspy turn of the key in the lock.

The moment his shadow disappeared from beneath the door, she'd roll over and light the wick on the oil lamp. After that, she'd wait. The waiting was the loneliest part. She'd imagine all manner of catastrophes the longer the evening wore on. One question had always worried her most. What would she do if he never came home?

At least now she knew. She'd succumb to a keening sense of loneliness within months and marry a handsome stranger with two adorable children. Ah well. She gave a mental sigh. There were worse fates out there.

She wasn't dancing with a smelly cowboy in a saloon for a nickel a song with bells jangling around her ankles. That was something. She wasn't in a shallow, unmarked grave with one of Dead Eye's bullets in her chest. That was another something. All in all, things might have turned out worse.

The stairs had been cut into the dirt and topped with embedded wood slats. Three steps down her false courage ran out and she whirled. "Perhaps we should get a lamp."

"There's plenty of light," Shane assured her. "We're not here to read the newspaper."

"Right. Of course."

She faced the darkness once more and traversed the last three steps. The space was no bigger than the washroom in the ranch house, the ceiling low enough that Shane had to stoop. The air smelled dank and loamy and a fine sheen of dirt covered every surface. Wooden shelves holding jars of neatly arranged preserves lined the walls. There were pickles, peaches, even tomatoes.

"Who did all this work?" she asked, covering her unease.

Shane stood before the door, blocking both the exit and what little light penetrated the inky blackness.

"Finch and Parker, mostly," Shane said. "Finch grows a garden out behind the barn in the summer."

"Even with his…" Her voice trailed off and she made a vague motion with her arm.

"The loss of his hand has never slowed him down, near as I can tell." He cleared his throat. "Abby liked to keep the household supplies separate from the rest. This set of shelves is for the main house. Everything else is for the men."

"How come?"

"How come what?"

"Why did Abby want the supplies separated?"

"I don't know," Shane replied, a touch of sorrow in his voice. "She liked things a certain way."

Tessa frowned at his halting explanation. Something brushed her arm and she yelped. Leaping aside, she collided with Shane.

He stumbled back and crashed into a shelf, rattling the jars.

She scooted away and brushed at her arms. "Something touched me."

"Probably cobwebs."

Shivering, she backed toward the stairs. "You said there were no spiders."

"The cobwebs are left over from summer. It's winter. Like I said, they're mostly dormant. Spring is when you have to watch out."

The more she thought about spiders, the more she felt the cobwebs everywhere. In her hair, grazing her legs, touching her cheek. She discreetly brushed at her arms, concealing her unease from Shane. If he knew she was terrified of this tiny, cramped space filled with who-knew-what kind of creepy crawlies scurrying about, he'd sigh and take up what little oxygen remained in the heavy air.

"As long as we're down here," he said, then snatched

a jar from a shelf and extended his arm. "Apple jelly. It's excellent on flapjacks."

"Bartleby has a recipe for French pancakes."

"Are those like flapjacks?"

"I think so."

At least he was matching her for witty conversation. What a pair they made. If this was an example of the scintillating conversation they'd have over the next twenty years, they were both in trouble. Once they'd exhausted the fruits and vegetables in the pantry, they'd be well out of topics unless they planted something more exotic next spring.

"That reminds me." Shane tilted his head. "Who is Bartleby?"

"Something I found at the mercantile. *Bartleby's Book of Household Management.* It's quite useful. Well, mostly useful. For example, in England, lobsters are best purchased during July and August. I don't suppose I'll ever use that little tidbit."

Shane chuckled. "Cimarron Springs is a long way from the coast."

A rare burst of insight had her clutching the jar against her chest. They were no good with each other alone; they needed the children between them. Each encounter they'd had up until this point had been with the children. As time wore on, would they become better or worse at dealing with each other when the children weren't present? She didn't want to contemplate the answer.

The walls closed in around her and her future pressed against her with suffocating and endless finality. She had to escape. Scurrying past him, she bolted up the stairs. The brush of cobwebs swept against her face and she batted them aside.

Her annoyance sprang from her insecurity. What if he never developed an affection for her?

In the sunlight once more, she brushed her face and arms. A shudder swept through her from head to toe.

Shane followed close behind her and the silence stretched out between them.

Tessa set her jaw. She'd always thought she was a strong woman, but this relationship was testing her courage more than the spiders had. She'd rather face the dark cellar than his disappointment. When she'd given herself the arbitrary deadline of Christmas, she'd been certain she'd prevail. No more.

Even as she worried for the future, the idea of never seeing him sent an ache through her soul. They'd figure things out eventually. They had to.

"Since this is all new to me," Tessa began, "I thought it best we keep things out in the open. What exactly do you expect of me?"

Shane blanched. "Expect? How do you mean?"

She didn't know whether to laugh or cry at his panicked expression, but at least they were having a conversation about something more than preserves.

"You know, we need to talk."

She mustn't panic. This was only their first day together. There were bound to be a few bumps in the road. Things would get better. They had to. Except Shane didn't seem to want her around the men, and the children weren't the same as having the company of another adult.

Surely he'd want to spend more time with her eventually. Because if they didn't find some common ground between them, she feared she'd drown in her own loneliness.

Chapter Ten

Since this was only their first full day together as man and wife, Shane wasn't prepared for the questions. All his previous experience had taught him that women mostly wanted to be left alone. That didn't seem to be the case with Tessa, and he wasn't ready for such personal questions.

She turned her head aside and glanced at him askance. "What do you mean what do I mean? You know, what do you expect of me in regard to the chores and such."

"Oh yeah. Chores. Sure." He scratched his chin. "Whatever needs to be done. The men take care of themselves. Wheeler does the washing and the mending. Parker does the cooking. Everyone chips in."

"I'll need to speak with Wheeler."

"About what?"

"About the washing and the mending, of course." The slightest hint of a glare appeared on her face. "As long as my questions don't interrupt his *man stuff*."

She seemed awfully stuck on that one particular phrase. "I mentioned before, we live in close quarters around here. It's best everyone respect each other's space."

"Can I speak with Wheeler or not?" she demanded, her voice sharp.

"Yes."

"Excellent."

This was all new territory. Abby had rarely left the house, let alone approached the men. He'd never addressed the problem before because he'd never had a problem before. Tessa was not Abby, a fact he was reminded of more and more often.

"Any other questions?"

"Not that I can think of right now."

As they crossed the distance, Milt emerged from the barn, Owen and Alyce trailing behind him.

The older man nudged Owen forward with a gentle hand on the boy's shoulder. "I think this little fellow needs some attention."

Tessa held her hand before her nose. "If our conversation is finished…"

"Yes." He hesitated, then moved closer. "Are your feet and toes all right? No lingering damage from the cold after last night?"

"Not at all." She lifted her chin a notch. "Dinner at six? You promised."

The censure in her voice raised his hackles. At least give him a chance to do something wrong first. He'd already agreed. Why was she hounding the point? Why did he feel as though he'd already been tested and failed? "I'll come by in the evenings."

"Excellent."

She pivoted on her heel and marched back to the house, Owen and Alyce in tow. Shane blew out a breath.

Beside him, Milt grinned. "Sure is a nice day today."

More than nice, the day was positively gorgeous. The

sun was shining, the wind was calm—not a cloud marred the sky. A perfect day for being outside. "Yep."

"Good day for a ride from town."

"Something you want to get off your chest, Milt?" He'd taken the children and Tessa into a dangerous storm, when clearly there'd been no need. For all its bluster, the storm had left only a few inches of snow, making the trip appear all the more absurd. "It might have gotten worse."

"But it didn't."

"Is there a point to all this?"

"You seem a little cranky this morning. Everything all right?"

"Remind me why I hired you."

Milt chuckled. "Because I don't let you get away with anything."

"Fair enough."

It wasn't Milt's fault that Shane had made a poor decision, but he sure didn't need the point driven home. "The weather might have turned. This time of year, you never can tell."

"You never can." Milt slapped him on the back. "How long will you be living in the bunkhouse? The boys are a mite confused. Especially if the new wife will be stopping in to see you during all hours of the day."

"We're figuring things out." Shane pressed a thumb and forefinger against his eyes until he saw stars. "I told her the bunkhouse was off-limits except for an emergency."

"Ah, she's all right. The boys were surprised, that's all. They'll get used to her being around by and by. We all grew accustomed to things being a certain way. Abby rarely came outside."

"Things are going to be different, that's for certain."

Shane watched as Tessa bundled the children into the house. There was something about her, something vibrant and alive. She breathed excitement into every space she occupied. When she entered a room, it was as though she expected something to happen—as though she planned on making something happen if it didn't.

He wasn't really all that comfortable with excitement. "Things are going to be very different."

"Be good to shake things up. We're all too set in our ways."

"I don't know if everyone else will agree." Shane had known these men a long time. Long before he and Abby had married. He couldn't have built the ranch without their help. Even though they were hired hands, he owed them. None of them had to stay; they were free to leave anytime the mood struck. "You don't mind if things change?"

"Owen and Alyce seem comfortable with Tessa. She's good with them."

"She is."

"What about you? Are you happy?"

Shane stopped in his tracks. "What kind of question is that?"

"It's a fair question. A man should have at least one thing in his life that makes him happy."

"I didn't realize we were sharing our feelings this afternoon. What makes you happy, Milt?"

The older man tugged on his ragged gray beard. "I like being a part of something. I like waking each morning knowing that I'll put in a good day's work. I like going to bed bone weary, knowing I did my share."

Shane hooked his thumbs into his belt loops. Leave it to Milt to actually answer the question and turn the tables on him. "What does happiness matter? Happiness doesn't pay the taxes or put food on the table."

Why, then, did he feel such a steadfast pull toward Tessa? He was terrified of examining his reasons too closely. There was a part of him that was missing, something Tessa would never understand. He'd lost that youthful optimism the day his father had left them. Life was precarious, lived on a razor's edge. He'd learned to make his way cautiously, never investing too much hope or too much sorrow in any one event. He didn't want to know what made him happy, because he didn't want to lose out once again. Thinking about happiness only drove it away.

With no place for his anger, he glared into the distance. "I don't know what makes me happy. I never stopped long enough to think about it. I like having the kids around. I don't like when they're gone. I hated the idea of them living in Wichita. I didn't even like the idea of them living down the road. The house feels like home when they're here and empty when they're gone."

Milt hoisted his bushy gray eyebrows. "For a man who's never thought about something, you sure have a lot to say on the subject."

"You asked me a question," he nearly shouted. "I'm answering."

"All I'm saying is that maybe you should think about these things before you go traipsing into town and bringing home a wife."

Milt was an old friend, but even Shane had his limits. "I don't traipse."

"You did bring home a wife. Maybe you should think about what makes you happy and unhappy the next time you make a lifelong decision."

"Why does it matter?"

"It matters because you're shouting at me and all I did was ask a simple question. I could ask Wheeler, Red, Parker or Finch, and I bet they wouldn't be hollering at me. All the years I've known you, and I ain't never heard you raise your voice. Why does thinking about what makes you happy send your blood boiling? Seems like that means something."

What made Tessa happy? Shane was afraid to ask. Afraid to find out. What if he couldn't provide her with what she needed? The questions rattled around in his brain and gave him a throbbing headache. "Everything seemed so simple in town. I'm trying, Milt. I'm really trying. What if I can't make her like me?"

"Is that what you want? You want her to like you?"

"It seems like a good place to start, yes. She seemed really annoyed with me this morning. Do I sigh a lot? What's wrong with men doing man stuff? She seemed really annoyed by that as well."

"Yep." Milt cackled. "There's a great place to start. Maybe next time you should hold off getting married until you decide whether she likes you or not."

"That's the thing." Shane whipped off his hat and slapped his leg with the brim. "I don't pick them. They pick me. She asked me to marry her. What's a guy supposed to say when a beautiful woman wants to marry him? What would you say?"

Sure, there were other men who'd probably make better husbands, but he couldn't imagine Tessa with someone else.

His frustrated admission only sent Milt laughing harder. "I can't help you there. I never once heard of a fellow with that sort of problem. I don't know what you're doing, but I think I'll follow you into town next time. See if I can get me a wife, too. Especially one with pretty blue eyes like Mrs. McCoy."

"They are pretty," Shane conceded. There was no harm in admitting the truth. He may not have married her for her looks, but there was no point in denying her beauty. Even when she was annoyed at him, he caught a glimpse of sardonic merriment, as though she was laughing at a joke only she understood. "She's beautiful," he added, almost to himself.

The next few weeks were bound to be difficult for both of them. Despite their shared concern for the children, they were strangers. How did a pair of strangers go about feeling married? At least he and Abby had had common memories, common friends. He and Tessa had nothing but an awkward meeting on a train platform and a love for a precocious pair of toddlers.

"You and Tessa will do fine by and by," Milt said. "She reminds me of my own missus."

Shane gaped. "You were married? You?"

"Don't act so all-fired surprised," Milt grumbled. "I was a handsome man in my youth. Had my pick of the girls."

Shane chucked him on the shoulder. "I don't doubt it."

Milt's expression grew sorrowful. "I was eighteen when I married Sarah. She was as pretty as a new penny. We only had six months together. It was the typhus. Things were different back then. It was the war, and I was gone. There were no doctors. She never had a chance."

Almost a decade Shane had known the man, and he'd never once realized Milt had been married. "I never suspected."

"I never told you. You did right by Abby, and I'm proud of you for that."

"I never truly loved her. Not like she wanted me to," Shane said, the admission ripping through him. "I sure never made her happy."

They'd reached the corral and Milt braced his arms on the top railing. "People can make their mind up about being happy or unhappy. Abby was like that. She made up her mind to be unhappy. That wasn't your fault."

"Abby and I were kids together, climbing trees and fishing in the stream. We were friends. How could I have been so wrong about everything? We were married a year and I never really knew her." What a fool he'd been then. What a fool he was now. "I was the wrong man for her."

He'd lied before. He wanted things to be different with Tessa. He craved something more. He wanted to be the right man this time. That was his curse. No matter what happened, he'd never let on. He'd never let her know. She'd agreed on the basis of a partnership, and he was sticking by his bargain.

If she seemed content by Christmas, maybe he'd try to move their relationship forward a bit. Until then, he was hanging back and giving her space.

He took a step away and Milt blocked his path. "Six months was all I had with Sarah, and we fought almost every minute. People die and it's easy to forget all the little things that annoyed you about 'em. Sarah was a real pain sometimes. Opinionated. Stubborn. Dying didn't change that, didn't make her a saint."

"But you loved her."

"We loved each other, sure." Milt braced his arms on the corral fence once more. "Abby is gone now and nothing can change that, but you and I both know she didn't come here for love. She came here because she knew you wouldn't turn her away. I don't know who she got mixed up with after she left town, but I know when a person is ate up by regret. Felt that way myself a time or two. Some people get hooked on suffering the same as people get hooked on drinking and gambling." He fisted his hand. "That's your weakness—you think everything can be fixed. Except you were never going to fix Abby because she didn't want to be fixed. She came here because she wanted a good home to raise those children, and you gave her that."

Shane's chest squeezed with pent-up frustration. "Then why did she insist on sending the children to her sister? Why didn't she want me to keep them?"

"The same reason you went traipsing off to town and got yourself a wife. She didn't expect to die. A man can't raise children alone around these parts. You tried. Everyone knows you did. No one blames you."

"For the last time, I do not traipse. You make it sound like I was skipping down Main Street with a basket of daisies." Turning the topic helped Shane catch his breath. He'd never had a conversation longer than a sentence or two with Milt, and here they were, dissecting his life like a gaggle of women at a quilting bee. "You've been reading Wheeler's penny dreadfuls again, haven't you? Those books will rot your brain."

"Those are good books. Exciting. And don't change the subject. I might not know what you were thinking bringing home another wife, but I do know this—Tessa is different. You can't go expecting she'll be like Abby, because she's not. Things are going to change around here. I can smell it as surely as I can smell a change in the weather."

"That's what I'm afraid of."

Milt guffawed. "You know what your problem is? You think change is a bad thing."

"I thought my problem was trying to fix everything," Shane began, then stopped himself. There was no use arguing. "Never mind. We'll move the smaller herd to the south pasture today. If this thaw keeps up, we'll be knee-deep in mud soon enough. Let's keep the cattle closer to the ranch. I want to keep an eye on things."

He'd leave her alone. Give her space for the next few weeks. Let her settle in and learn the routine. Things would change, certainly, but not that much.

"Sure thing, boss."

Milt took the abrupt change of conversation in stride, though his words haunted Shane in the following weeks.

Tessa was going crazy.

She was going absolutely, stark raving mad. There was absolutely no reason this should be happening. Everything was going wonderfully. Swimmingly. Perfectly. She and Shane had developed a perfectly wonderful, easy routine. He'd done exactly what she'd asked of him.

And yet she wanted to strangle him.

Everything he did annoyed her. She couldn't explain it. She had nothing to complain about—nothing.

She punched down the bread dough, then stuck out her lower lip, blowing a breath and ruffling the hair plastered against her forehead. She wasn't feeling generous toward Shane *or* Bartleby at that moment. She flipped the bread dough and sent up a cloud of flour. Coughing, she waved her hand before her face. Neither man understood what it was like being a woman. Bartleby clearly thought menial labor was for servants. Which was all well and good if one actually had servants.

Shane breezed in each evening and played with the children. Never mind if there were dishes in the sink or laundry hanging from the eaves. Why should he be concerned? He'd clearly had a hard day of work. He clearly needed a relaxing evening.

She punched the dough again. What about her? Did it ever occur to Shane that she might have had a difficult day? That *she* might need some time alone? Oh no. Never. Shane rolled around on the floor like her third child, whooping it up with the twins.

Flipping the dough aside, she nicked the edge of the flour tin and sent the whole thing tumbling off the counter. A plume of flour rose from the floor like a white explosion.

"Drat."

Owen toddled over. "Drat."

"Don't say that word, dear. That's a grown-up word."

"Drat," he repeated.

Tessa wiped the damp hair from her forehead with the back of her hand and reached for the broom. Already she was a day behind in her chores. Alyce had torn down the clothesline the previous day and she'd had to begin the washing all over again.

As she swept up the mess, Owen toddled over. With her hands full, she lifted her foot and carefully nudged him back with a toe against his shoulder. "No, no. Let Tessa clean up the mess."

He appeared mutinous before turning away. With a huff she reached for the dustpan, sweeping up the flour as best she could. It seeped into the floorboards and mixed with the water she'd spilled from the dishes earlier, turning into a thick paste.

"Of all the stupid messes," she muttered. "Never mind. I will finish this later."

She rounded the tall kitchen worktable and gaped. Owen and Alyce had snatched her rising bread from the counter and were tugging it apart.

"No!"

Her teeth gritted, Tessa engaged in a brief tug-of-war, managing to wrest more than half of the dough away. She set the mounds onto the worktable once more and inspected the damage. Bits of dirt and dust adhered to the sticky surface.

"Ruined!" she exclaimed. "It's all ruined."

"Drat," Owen declared.

Her heart pounded against her chest and she had an inexplicable urge to scream. She was going batty and she had no one with whom she could share her frustrations. She'd assured Shane she was fit for ranch life.

He'd explained everything clearly. He'd told her all about the isolation and the hard work. He'd been perfectly honest about the trials she'd be facing. She'd been confident that she was prepared.

She'd been wrong. Horribly, horribly wrong.

She was lonely. She was bored. No, that wasn't right. She had plenty to do. She wasn't so much bored as stagnant. She was heartily sick of doing the laundry on Thursday and baking the bread on Friday. Or was it the other way around? She didn't even know which day it was anymore. She was used to being surrounded by scores of people. She was used to being around Emmett. Emmett was a person who liked to talk. Emmett actually carried on a conversation.

She wasn't used to being in the same house day after day after day conversing with two tiny little people who had only a twenty-five word vocabulary between them. Not that she didn't love the children. She absolutely loved them. Feeling lonely around them felt like a betrayal, which only made her feel worse.

Closing her eyes, she sucked in a few breaths, letting her chest rise and fall. She thought about the brilliant sunset they'd had the previous evening and the time her mother had taken her to see Lake Michigan and she'd thought it was the ocean.

Yes. That was better.

She opened her eyes and formed a plan. "Let's build a fort!"

While the children watched, she arranged the chairs in a square and gathered several blankets from the bedroom, then draped them over the backs.

"There," she declared. "Isn't that lovely? Now you can play in the fort."

A crash sounded.

She whipped around. Alyce had tipped over the pan of beans she'd been soaking for supper. They'd landed on the floor in a splatter, the water mixing with the flour and the bread dough the children had smeared around earlier.

The pressure in her head throbbed. She couldn't do this. She was a failure. Twice in her life she'd set out to do something difficult, and twice in her life she'd fallen flat on her face.

With a sob, she turned and crawled beneath the blanketed fort.

Chapter Eleven

Shane sensed something was not quite right as soon as he neared the house. No enticing aroma of dinner wafted from the kitchen; no little people toddled outside to greet him. He cautiously pushed open the door and discovered Owen without his trousers sitting in a mess of water and beans, while Alyce wore Owen's pants and perched on a mound of flour.

Anxiety danced along his spine.

"Tessa," he called softly.

Upon seeing him, Alyce and Owen greeted him with their usual unabashed delight, then quickly returned to their mess. The children reveled in the unsupervised disorder, drawing pictures in the dust and arranging the beans into piles. The kitchen chairs were arranged in a square and draped with a blanket.

"Tessa," he called again. "Are you here?"

He heard it then. A quiet noise. A soft sniffle sounded from beneath the makeshift fort.

Anticipating trouble, he brought Alyce and Owen a cup of milk as added insurance against a few more minutes of peace.

Shane crouched and peered beneath the blanket. Tessa was sitting with her legs crossed, her fist against her mouth while tears glistened on her eyelashes.

He cleared his throat. "How was your day?"

"Fine." She sniffled. "How was yours?"

He scooted into the fort she'd arranged and let the blanket fall back into place, plunging them into darkness.

"You sure you're fine?" he asked.

"No." Tessa's voice broke in a sob. "Owen won't wear pants, and Alyce will only wear Owen's pants. They knocked over the beans and the flour, and then they started playing in the mess. Oh, and they ruined the bread dough. It's all covered in dirt. Don't worry. They're not eating the beans. They both tasted one, though, and spit them out. They didn't take a nap this afternoon, which meant I didn't get the washing done, and Bartleby says the washing should be done on Tuesday. I shouldn't have even been doing the wash except Alyce tore down the clothesline yesterday."

"Can you switch the days around?"

"No. Wednesday is the day I make bread. There's the kneading and the rising and then the baking. It's exhausting. Have you ever made bread?"

"Can't say that I have. Biscuits sometimes."

"Bread is much more difficult than biscuits." He felt rather than saw her scowl. "You don't understand."

"We could have biscuits next week instead of bread," he prompted.

"Why would we do that?"

"Because biscuits are easier and you said all the bread dough got ruined."

Her hiccup turned into another sob. "You're not helping. You don't understand."

"Then help me understand."

His eyes had adjusted to the dark, and he made out her disheveled appearance.

She swiped at her nose with the back of her sleeve. Reaching into his back pocket, he retrieved his handkerchief and handed it over.

With a hiccup, she fisted her hand over the square. "I lied to you. I can't do this. It's too much."

Why hadn't he seen the signs sooner? Everyone had their breaking point. Tessa had gone through a lot. She'd come to a strange place and married someone she hardly knew, assuming the care of two rambunctious children. She'd tried to make everything perfect. Too perfect. She'd set an impossible standard for herself.

He should have noticed that she was growing overwhelmed sooner. "Sure you can. This is one bad day. Everyone has bad days. You've had lots of good ones, too, haven't you?"

"Yes." She took a few uneven breaths. "I hate Bartleby."

"Then I'll burn his book. I'll have the boys start a bonfire right now."

"No." She hiccuped. "I like his recipe for potted chicken."

Clearly she didn't want her problems solved, which was too bad, because he excelled at fixing things. Instead, he tried another tack. "How about this? First, I'll clean up the kitchen. Then I'll take Owen and Alyce to visit Scout. You can have some time alone to catch up on things. If you're feeling better later, we can all go sledding together."

"That is the worst idea I've ever heard." She huffed. "That's the whole problem. Don't you see?"

He frowned. "I don't."

"Except for the cleanup part. That part wasn't a bad

idea. You can clean up all you want. Whenever you want. The sledding is a terrible idea."

"Why?" He pinched the bridge of his nose. "I can't help you unless you talk to me."

"If you must know, I don't want to go sledding." She crossed her arms rebelliously over her chest. "I'll have to bundle the children and that will take hours because Owen will undress while I'm putting on Alyce's coat and Alyce will undress while I'm putting on my coat and nothing will ever get done."

"We'll bundle them as a team. That way, no one can undress."

"All right." A loud sniffle. "Only if you help clean up and bundle the children."

He would have offered more help earlier, except she'd never asked and everything had seemed fine. If she'd let him know sooner she was growing overwhelmed, things might not have spiraled out of control.

She brushed the tangled hair from her forehead. This didn't seem to be the time to point that out.

The agreement was struck and he emerged from beneath the blanket. He spent the next hour and a half cleaning the house, though he left Tessa and the fort undisturbed. He bundled the children, which took just as long as Tessa had complained about, and led them outside. They visited Scout, feeding the horse a winter dried carrot, then dug the sled out of the loft.

After an hour alone Tessa joined them outside, as cheerful as ever. Her eyes were dried and she looked as bright as the morning sun. He didn't even mention the blob of bread dough in her hair, figuring she'd discover it soon enough.

Following that memorable evening, he'd made a point

of ensuring Tessa had time alone each day. Sometimes she'd finish her tasks and join them in sledding or building a snowman or a snow fort; sometimes she simply stayed in the cabin and brewed a cup of tea. While his daily intervention didn't solve all the problems that cropped up, it seemed to provide Tessa with the endurance to handle whatever the children threw her way.

They were friends of a sort. He'd asked for companionship, and he'd got companionship. Except he feared with Tessa, he wanted something more. Only he'd made a promise, and he was honor bound to keep that promise. Since those first hesitant days together, she'd given no hint that she wanted anything more from him. Nothing. Not even the slightest indication.

Whatever tender feelings she may have harbored in the beginning, those feelings obviously hadn't survived time and proximity. Tessa had kept her end of the bargain. She was a good mother to the children. She'd kept her promise to him, too. She was a good wife in all the tasks he'd set before her. He didn't have the heart, or the courage, to ask for more.

Only one problem nagged him. She was holding something back, and until she trusted him with her secret, a wall remained between them. If he pushed her to trust him, he'd only push her away. He'd been through this with Abby and lost, and he feared he was losing again.

For the second time in his life, he was the wrong man.

Shane was holding something back, and yet Tessa couldn't quite put her finger on the problem. Following her slight hiccup with the beans and the flour and the all-around mess, they'd fallen into a much easier routine. Some of the ice had thawed between them. They didn't exactly share the easy camaraderie of old friends, but at least they'd developed a level of comfort around one another.

Despite this newfound partnership, there was still something missing. She told herself he was mourning his first wife, that he was exhausted, that he just needed more time. No matter what she told herself, she'd begun to suspect the problem wasn't with Shane. She'd started to wonder if she simply wasn't the sort of person who inspired affection in others.

Despite her misgiving, one evening after the children had gone to bed, she blocked his exit. There was no time like the present.

"Shane," she began haltingly. "I was wondering if you'd help me with something."

"Sure. What?"

She reached for *Bartleby's Book of Household Management*. Also following her slight mishap with the beans and the flour and the all-around mess, she and Bartleby had come to an agreement as well. She stuck to the recipes and mostly ignored his other advice. She'd do the washing when she was good and ready, and not adhere to an arbitrary schedule created by some crazy Englishman for the torture of frontier wives.

She set the book on the table with a thump. "Do you know fractions?"

"Sure." He scratched his temple. "Some. Nothing real complicated."

"Hopefully this won't be too complicated." She indicated a list of ingredients. "Some of the recipes make too much, and some of them make too little, but I don't know how to calculate the adjustments."

He grinned and her eyes were drawn to his mouth.

Memories of the way his lips felt against hers flooded her senses. Too bad she didn't inspire affection in others, because she sure experienced it herself.

"That's easy," he said. "I can show you how to do that."

She felt a little breathless. "Right now?"

"Absolutely." He glanced right and left. "I thought we had a slate board around here. That's probably the easiest way to start."

After retrieving the twins' slate board and chalk, she indicated the recipe again. "This made seventy-two biscuits, which is too many. I'd like to cut the recipe in half."

"Let's see here. Knowing how to do something and explaining how to do something are two entirely different things."

Shane prowled around the kitchen. He gathered the measuring cups along with the tin of flour and set them on the table.

She gazed at his eyes, recalling how she'd thought they were the green of a tender new leaf. They reminded her of spring, when everything was fresh and new again. She liked the way he moved. There was an unconscious grace about him, an economy of motion.

As he arranged the flour and measuring cups, her apprehension grew. "I don't need to actually make the biscuits. I just need to know how to change the recipe."

"We're not making anything. I'm showing you how this works in practice."

She lowered herself onto a chair and planted her chin in her cupped hands. "I can't wait to see what you have up your sleeve."

And she definitely liked looking at his arms. His rippling muscles were undeniably masculine and unconsciously enticing.

"I suppose we should start out with something easy. Like a cup."

She studied his shaggy hair, the way it curled over his ears. He really needed a haircut. She'd clipped Emmett's hair before. Maybe he'd let her give him a trim. "That one is easy, silly. Half of a cup is a half a cup."

"Fair enough. Then let's take this next measurement."

Scooping the flour, he filled two measuring cups, then reached for a third. She liked his hands. The dusting of dark hair across the knuckles, the scars from the nicks and cuts he'd suffered over the years, the callouses on his fingers. Most of the men she'd encountered growing up had worked in saloons or storefronts. They'd had soft hands with neatly clipped nails. Shane's were jagged. His thumbnail even had a dip in the center, as though he'd crushed it once and it had never healed. She'd never considered someone's hands in detail before, but she found Shane's fascinating.

"Are you listening?" His voice interrupted her inspection.

"I missed that last part."

The next hour passed in a blink. After seeing him with the children, she shouldn't have been surprised at how incredibly patient he was with teaching her. Nothing quite made sense at first. He wrote the problems on the slate board and solved them, then showed her the solution using the measuring cups.

She scooted closer and followed his directions on the slate board. Their shoulders touched and he didn't move away. Fearful of spooking him, she didn't press nearer. He erased the problem and wrote another. After a few false starts, she completed the task with a frown. "That doesn't look right."

"There's one way to check it."

She scooped equal amounts of flour into a smaller cup and measured them both into a larger cup, eyeing the results. "That's right! That worked."

"Of course it worked. It's math."

Tessa grinned. Reaching above her, she brushed a dusting of flour from his forehead. "You'll need a wash after this."

He caught her hand against his temple. With infinite care, he turned his head and her knuckles scraped along the shadow of his beard. Dragging out the moment, she placed her other hand against his chest, noticing the strength there, the gentle beat of his heart against her fingertips. A soul-deep yearning filled her.

As though it was the most natural thing in the world, he tipped his head and kissed her, his mouth wooing hers. She threaded her hands through his hair, marveling at the sleek texture.

As she sank into the sensation, a call sounded from the children's bedroom and they broke apart.

Her gaze skittered away.

Shane stuffed his hands in his pockets. "Sounds like Owen."

The call sounded again.

"He wants water," Tessa said. "He always wants one last drink of water."

"He doesn't like being left alone."

"This will just take a moment."

While Tessa saw to Owen, the sounds of Shane cleaning up the kitchen drifted through the door. The noise of dishes clinking together was comforting. Such a small thing she'd taken for granted before. Right now the simple task filled her with longing. The familiar sounds of another person bustling in the kitchen were music to her soul.

By the time she'd settled both Alyce and Owen, he was gone. Tears of frustration sprang in her eyes. She longed to turn back the clock and play out the moment once more. She sat in the kitchen for a long time after that, trying to figure out what she'd done wrong.

He wasn't indifferent to her, and yet whenever she approached him, he turned away. Which had her wondering once again if he found some problem with her, if he found something lacking in her. She pressed two fingers against her lips and recalled their earlier kiss.

Her chest ached. Owen wasn't the only one in this house who didn't like to be left alone.

Chapter Twelve

The temperate weather melted all but a few patches of snow, making Shane's life easier while he worked outside. The change also meant Tessa and the children were enjoying the subtle shift in temperature. They weren't underfoot exactly, she took great pains avoiding him during the working portion of the day, but she left an indelible mark wherever she went.

The ranch hands adored her. Each evening in the bunkhouse he lay with his hands threaded behind his head as they spoke of her in glowing terms. She and Parker exchanged recipes. Wheeler, whose mother had been a seamstress, was teaching her how to sew. The other men treated her with kid gloves, watching her from a fascinated distance.

A gradual shift took place in the general mood of the ranch, a change in the rhythm of everyone's routine. Though a perpetual winter haze hung low over the horizon, a quiet sense of anticipation took hold. Usually about this time the men grew surly with the shortened days and he was hard-pressed to keep them in line. Petty fights erupted. Tiny irritations exploded into fisticuffs. Not this year.

Everyone was happy with the changes. Which didn't explain why everything annoyed Shane. He knew his frustrations were unfounded, and that annoyed him all the more. His reactions were irrational and out of proportion. There was no reason or explanation for his surly mood. He'd got exactly what he'd envisioned. If anything, the marriage was turning out even better than he'd hoped for at the start.

The four of them had sunk into a comfortable routine. The exact sort of comfortable routine he'd always desired. Each evening they ate dinner together. Then he played with the children for an hour or two while Tessa worked on one of her numerous projects. She never sat still for long. Either she was knitting a lumpy scarf, mending some stray piece of clothing or experimenting with a new recipe. Like a metronome, she kept up a steady beat of activity.

He had no cause for complaint and yet something bugged him, something he couldn't quite put a finger on. She respected his time with the children, even encouraged their interaction. The house was neat and tidy. Everyone was happy.

Everyone but him. Lord help him if Milt ever found out. The man would never let him live it down.

She'd kissed him, and yet he still felt her hesitancy, as though she withheld a part of herself. She didn't show that same hesitancy around the other men, and that troubled him. Why was she holding back with him and not the others? Why did she prefer their company to his?

The next morning, enmeshed in his troubled thoughts,

he rounded the corner and collided with the source of his agitation. Tessa stumbled back with a warm smile.

"I didn't think you'd be around today," she said. "Last night you mentioned checking the cattle pastures."

Glancing over his shoulder, he gauged her trajectory. "Is that why you're on the way to the bunkhouse? Because you knew I wouldn't be there? Where are Alyce and Owen?"

Her cheeks flamed. "The children are napping and I need Wheeler's help."

"Can it wait? He has other work." They were behind on chores already. He'd let the men know already that today was all about catching up. He didn't want the weather trapping them unaware, and he had a bad feeling there was another storm on the horizon. "Why don't you check back with him tomorrow?"

A flicker of apprehension crossed her face. "Are you angry with me? Have I done something wrong?"

"It's not that." He was torn between wanting to draw her closer and needing to keep her at arm's distance. "The next few days will be busy. The men have other work to do."

She drew back her shoulders. "I always ask if they have time."

Shane heaved a breath. "They're not going to refuse you. You're the boss's wife. Or had you forgotten that?"

"Stop it." She jabbed a finger into his chest. "Stop sucking in your breath whenever you speak with me. I'm sick of it."

"Easy there." Her sudden fury startled him. "What's gotten into you?"

"What's gotten into me? Your stupid heaving sighs.

That's what's gotten into me. Have I done one thing over the past weeks to disappoint you?"

He held up his hands in a placating gesture. "No."

Not once since he'd known her had he seen this side of Tessa. She was quaking with anger, her lips trembling, her face mottled red.

"Then why are you always glaring at me? Why are you always sighing and muttering as though I'm some problem that can't be fixed? I don't know what you want from me. I'm trying. Truly, I am. I don't know what else you expect of me."

Trapped by his regrets, he shook his head. "I'm sorry. I didn't mean to upset you." That wasn't entirely truthful. He'd been itching to lash out at someone for days. He'd felt his control slipping away and he desperately wanted it back. "We both knew this wasn't going to be easy."

"It doesn't have to be this difficult either. You're not helping."

"Me?" Her tirade set him back on his heels. "I've done everything *you've* asked of me as well. I come for dinner each evening and I promptly leave as soon as you usher me out the door."

"I don't ask you to leave." Her stance faltered. "Once the children are asleep, there's nothing left to say, is there?"

Shane rubbed the back of his neck. He was reliving his first marriage all over again. Abby had accused him of being too withdrawn on more than one occasion.

Instead of telling Tessa that it didn't matter how hard he tried, he'd still be a rancher, he paced back and forth before her. He knew cattle and horses and hard work. He'd always be a disappointment because he had nothing else to offer. There was no use trying.

He was making her unhappy. Christmas was around the corner, and though they'd fallen into a comfortable routine, Tessa remained elusively distant. He'd given her space, and she'd drifted further away.

"We did our best," he began, his voice thick with an apology. "Maybe this was a mistake."

He didn't know women. He didn't know Tessa. They had nothing in common but the children. He was making her miserable. That alone was reason enough for ending things.

Her face paled. "This isn't a mistake. We can make this work but you must meet me halfway."

He'd thought she'd leap at the chance of an escape. Instead she was staring at him as though he'd betrayed her, treating him as though he'd gone and done her some great wrong. "I won't keep you from the children, if that's what you're worried about."

"I love them. You know I do. I need you as well."

She didn't need him and they both knew it. That was the whole problem.

"Don't you see? This is all I am." He swept his arms in an encompassing gesture. "This is all I have to give you."

Her eyes wide and pleading, she looked up into his face. "I don't believe that."

All at once he felt vulnerable and exposed. Raw emotion knifed through his chest, sending his heart hammering. He didn't have the words. She wasn't the enemy, this wasn't an attack, and yet he was threatened in a way he couldn't explain.

His mood was precarious, balancing between panic and fear. He needed space between them because his thoughts became muddled when she was near. Away from her, his path was clear and unfettered. Knowing she was near and didn't return his affection would drown him. He needed a firm grip on his emotions. Somehow he was going to find a way to handle this crazy mess he'd drawn them both into.

He watched her shoulders slump, and a cloud of tenderness enveloped him. If he didn't even know what made him happy, how did he make someone else happy? Her fears were not unfounded. He'd offered her safety and he wouldn't renege on his bargain.

"It's all right," he soothed, stalling for time. "We don't have to make a decision this minute." He drew in a breath, then recalled her earlier complaint about his sighing. He expelled the air from his lungs slowly, quietly. What was she thinking? How did he fix the turmoil he'd set in motion? "We can talk more about this tonight."

Her eyes glistened. "Do you promise? Can we actually have a conversation for once?"

"Sure."

"I mean actually talk. Not about the weather or the cattle or the children, but really talk."

"We talk about other stuff every day."

She stamped her foot and made a noise that sounded suspiciously like a growl. "Sometimes I think you deliberately misunderstand me."

If that were actually true, this particular conversation might be easier. "I promise you, the only thing I'm trying to do is understand. You have to meet me halfway as well."

"All right. Tonight. I have to go," she declared abruptly. "The children are napping. I have to be back before they wake up."

Maybe he should try a different approach. "Tessa, wait."

She spun around. "What?"

He'd hurt her just now, and his heart wrenched at the thought. He burned to see beyond her mystified expression into the very heart of her. Maybe then he'd know what to say, what to do. Maybe then he'd know what she needed. He was a man who'd never had tenderness in his life, and he had no tenderness to give.

"It'll all work out one way or another," he hedged carefully. "You'll see."

He'd caused her pain because he was thinking only of himself. How did he become more than what he was? Was that even possible?

"Sure," she said, her reply decidedly lacking in conviction. "See you tonight. Don't be late. We're having potted chicken."

He definitely enjoyed her cooking and eagerly anticipated dinner each night. Sometimes the ingredients were a touch imaginative for his taste, but he couldn't fault her effort. "You cook really well. I like that thing you made the other night. You know, with the potatoes that were sliced and there was a kind of a sauce."

She tossed him a look tinged with suspicion. "Those are called potatoes in the German style, according to Bartleby."

"I liked those."

"Then I'll make them tonight."

He looked forward to the potatoes even though he was developing a definite annoyance with constant mention of Bartleby's name. He wished he'd burned the book when he'd had the chance. The man was everywhere. In the laundry, in the household cleaning, in the cooking. If he didn't know better, he'd think he was jealous of the man. The only thing Bartleby needed was a chapter on the care and nurturing of wives.

"That book seems really useful," he said, wondering if he sounded as inane as he felt. "Maybe I could borrow it sometime?"

"If you ever make potatoes in the German style, I penciled some notes about the recipe in the margin." She flashed him a cheeky grin. "Bartleby uses too much salt."

"I didn't know Bartleby made mistakes. I thought he was infallible."

"Everyone makes mistakes."

You're not a mistake, Shane.

Was she haunted by her own words? "Tonight, then."

"Tonight."

Despite her attempt at lightening the mood, she was still annoyed with him. He felt her lingering ire in the stiff set of her shoulders as she marched in the direction of the house. He ached to bang his head against something hard and unyielding. He'd failed miserably in his first marriage, and the same uncertainty returned. Each time he felt the faint stirrings of something more, a door slammed in his face. Instead of repeating the old mistakes, he was simply creating all sorts of new mistakes.

As if that weren't bad enough, he took three steps and ran into Wheeler, who didn't appear happy to see him.

Normally ready with a joke or a sly remark, Wheeler's dark face was set in a grim mask of annoyance. "When you hired me, you hired me as a free man, right?"

"Yes," Shane cautiously replied. He didn't know much about Wheeler's past, and he'd never asked. Sometimes details slipped out in conversation. Wheeler's parents were dead, and he had a brother who'd fought and died for the Union Army. Other than that, the man was a mystery. "You can come and go as you please. You know that."

"Do you have any complaints with my work?"

"None."

"Then as a free man, my free time is mine to do with as I please." Wheeler crossed his arms over his chest. "Or have things changed? I'm helping Tessa learn to stitch. Nothing more."

"Nothing has changed. I don't want you to feel obligated toward Tessa because she's my wife."

"When have I ever felt obligated to do something?"

"Never." Shane scraped a hand down his face. "I've been short-tempered, I know. I'm sorry. I'm figuring things out."

"You better figure things out faster, or you're going to lose that little lady." Wheeler's white teeth flashed against his dark skin, and he relaxed his defensive stance. "We've been through a lot together. I've never seen you tied up in knots like this."

He was making Tessa miserable, driving her away. And he didn't know how to stop. Shane absently rubbed a hand across his chest. "What if I make a mistake, Wheeler, and I can't fix it?"

Wheeler threw back his head and roared with laughter. "You made a mistake, all right."

"What's funny about that?" Shane demanded.

"You'll figure it out."

With that oblique response, Wheeler turned his back and set off for the barn. Nettled, Shane adjusted his hat low on his head. He was a man who acted with methodical precision. He'd never been one for introspection. He mostly trusted his gut. He'd built this ranch on a solid foundation of hard work and perseverance. From the be-

ginning, he'd surrounded himself with people he trusted.
No matter how hard he worked or how much he gained,
something had always been missing.

The children had changed him. He'd seen a glimpse
of something more. They were innocent, and seeing the
world through their eyes, he'd seen a chance at a different
future. For them, for himself. He'd desperately wanted to
share that vision with Abby, and she'd shunned it. Owen
and Alyce were not his by blood, and yet they were a
part of him. They'd shattered his defenses and left him
exposed.

He wanted to share his vision with Tessa, but something held him back. The moment was never right. It was
always too soon or too late. The lingering doubt that he
was the wrong man held him in check. He'd rushed things
before. Made assumptions. Not this time.

Except the gulf between him and Tessa was widen-
ing. He should apologize. He *would* apologize. He'd give
her time first, let her cool down. Her apprehension had
brought a renewed sense of clarity. He'd promised her
safety, and he'd left her feeling as though he might turn
her out at any moment. Sometimes he felt as though she
was testing him, seeing how far he'd let her go. Yet that
made no sense either. She was terrified of being out on
her own again. Why push him in that direction?

She was bored by him, and he had to change. If he
kept doing what he'd always done, he'd get what he'd
always got.

A nagging thought held him back. What if he changed,
and he still wasn't good enough?

Tessa stomped across the clearing. A freeze and thaw
had left the ground slippery, slowing her progress. She'd

thought the men genuinely liked her. How naive she'd been. A loyal worker mustn't refuse the boss's wife. Then again, if her husband ever strung more than two words together in a sentence, she wouldn't need their help all the time.

Why hadn't she seen the obvious sooner? As she recalled the number of times she'd asked the men for help over the past days, her humiliation came rushing back. They must have been simmering with annoyance.

Her steps slowed. She *had* been a pest. Shane had warned her against the loneliness and isolation, but she'd been arrogant once again, assuming the children might ease her transition. They had—to a point. Except she'd been naive in assuming they'd make up for true companionship. She'd thrown herself into their care, creating what she hoped was the perfect home for them. They loved her and she loved them, but they didn't fill the lonely void inside her. She'd turned toward the workers to fill the empty space.

Though she'd agreed to a partnership, she'd expected something more from her marriage. Not a grand passion, certainly—she wasn't a complete fool. She'd bullied Shane into the wedding because she'd expected companionship, warmth, the faint stirrings of friendship. Instead she'd got the same monosyllabic replies to her practiced questions.

How was your day?

Fine.

How was your dinner?

Good.

Who could blame her for going a touch batty? Instead of dealing with each other, they showered their attention on Owen and Alyce. The children, the very thing that had brought them together, stood between them as a shield.

She halted in the clearing and planted her hands on her hips. What had she expected? They were strangers. He was a widower. She'd never been a very patient person. If there was a problem, she searched out an answer and didn't quit until she discovered a solution. Maybe if she started asking different questions, he'd give her different answers. What did she have to lose in trying?

Upon reaching the house, she recalled the point of her errand with a sinking feeling in the pit of her stomach. As she doubled back, apprehension snaked down her spine. The potatoes were stored in the root cellar, and she'd put off going into the dank space long enough. She avoided the chore, making the trip last. There was always a part of her that feared pulling a jar off the shelf and discovering a nest full of spiders.

Yanking open the lean-to door, she braced the prop stick into place, then tromped down the stairs. Her boot heel skidded on a patch of ice slicked over the wooden tread. In a sickening flash her feet went out from beneath her.

Pitching backward, she seized the only solid thing available, the prop stick. For a tantalizing moment her hold remained solid. The next instant the stick fractured in two. A vicious blow cracked the back of her head.

Her shoulder slammed into the wall and suddenly she was falling. The door crashed shut, plunging her into darkness. As she plummeted down the remaining distance, a scream tore from her throat.

She sprawled at the base of the stairs, her consciousness ebbing and flowing in nauseating waves. Every part of her body throbbed. She pushed off and yelped at the stinging in her wrist. Agony pulsated behind her eyes.

Moaning softly, she slowly reached behind her head and felt the sticky warmth of blood.

Even in the darkness, her world pitched and tumbled, her vision spinning. She closed her eyes, longing for the peaceful numbness of unconsciousness. A thousand hammers beat against her head. The loamy scent of musty earth sent her gagging. There were spiders down here. She felt them already, skittering across her arms.

The children.

How long before someone noticed she was missing? What if they woke and found her gone? She narrowed her thoughts on them, staving off the shadows. Her strength sapped away with sickening speed, and she crawled toward the stairs. Despite her best efforts, darkness swirled around her, sucking her inexorably down. Tears wet her cheeks.

She'd rest for a moment. Gather her strength. Dinner was two hours away. Two hours until Shane returned. Alyce and Owen would never make it that long without going hungry or getting hurt. Children shouldn't be alone. Being alone was frightening.

A thought edged at her consciousness before the comfort of engulfing blackness descended over her. Here she thought the Fulton gang would be the end of her, and she'd been lain low by a sheet of ice.

Shane was going to be so annoyed.

Chapter Thirteen

Shane lingered in the south pasture over an easy repair to the fence line, and yet the answers he sought eluded him. He'd finished all his tasks and even invented more, finding excuses to stay away. He fisted his hand on his leg and stared at the muddy ground. The time had come to face Tessa and apologize.

As he reined his horse around, a rider coming in hot caught his attention.

Wheeler galloped toward him and stopped just short, the horse's hooves kicking up mud clods. Shane caught the animal's bridle, and his nerves thrummed. Wheeler was never rattled, yet raw emotion pinched his face.

"We got a problem." Wheeler spoke without preamble. "Mrs. McCoy is missing."

Shane's heart slammed against his ribs. "What do you mean she's missing?"

"Parker went to drop off some supplies, and the kids were alone. He waited awhile and she never came back. The boys are putting together a search party."

"What do you mean he waited?" A wave of pure terror swept over Shane. "You should have fetched me sooner."

"Took a while to find you." A note of censure crept into the other man's voice. "You left off without telling anybody where you were going."

A thousand different scenarios crowded Shane's thoughts. Tessa might have left him, he'd given her no reason to remain, but she'd never put the children in danger. "Tessa doesn't ride very well. She must have left on foot."

"She wouldn't leave those kids alone," Wheeler said with a negative motion of his head. "Not unless something bad happened."

Shane caught Wheeler's charged glance and was certain his own expression reflected the same stark fear.

"We'll find her." Wheeler spoke harshly. "She can't have gone far."

Shane marshaled his thoughts. There'd be time for self-recriminations and blame later. "The sooner we get back, the sooner we can start the search."

They took off at a gallop. Shane's horse was the fresher of the pair, and he reached the ranch first. The animal's sides were flecked with foam by the time he arrived. The men were already saddled and mustering in the corral behind the barn.

He swung off and led his horse into the center of the gathering. "What do we know?"

Parker shook his head. "Everything's locked up tight. She's not in the house or the barn. We checked the rest of the outbuildings. She hasn't been around the bunkhouse since this morning."

"No horses missing?"

"Nothing."

"No sign of strangers? Indians?"

Finch stepped forward. "I took a look around the perimeter. There's no fresh tracks leading to or from the road. The last time anyone saw her, she was heading toward the house."

"You checked all the outbuildings?"

"Like I said." Milt paced before the others. "Everything's shut up tight."

A fission of apprehension raised the hair on the back of Shane's neck. Tessa didn't like being alone.

"Let's take another look before we fan out. How long has she been missing?"

"Since four," Wheeler said.

His stomach knotted. She'd disappeared after their argument. "That's over an hour ago."

"About that."

"Probably she took a walk and got turned around," he declared, the words sounding unconvincing to his own ears. Fear threatened to consume him. The thought of her frightened and alone, maybe hurt, sent waves of terror crashing over him. He forced down his panic and fought for concentration. He wouldn't do her any good if he lost focus.

Shane looped the reins around his fist. "The temperature is dropping and the wind is picking up. We don't have much time until dark. Everyone keep your eyes sharp."

If she was injured, she'd never survive the weather overnight. The prairie didn't offer much protection from the frigid chill. Not to mention the search was fraught with challenges. Even in winter, tall grasses reached his waist. If she was down, they'd have to be right on top of her before they'd see her.

"Finch," he called. "You're the best tracker. Take the outer north edge. The rest of us will fan out and work our way in a circle." He glanced around for the missing man. "Is Parker with the kids?"

"He's keeping them busy."

"Good." A part of Shane wanted to gather the people he loved close, assure himself of their safety, yet he couldn't afford to lose any time. "Let's roll out."

The boys set off in opposite directions, but something held him back. Wheeler was right—she wouldn't have gone far. She was fiercely protective of the children. He coiled the reins around the top rail of the corral and set off on foot.

His head bent, he searched the ground. Tracks crisscrossed the area. Each thaw and freeze left a new layer, destroying any chance of singling out a set of footprints. Every door in the place was shut tight. Though it seemed unlikely someone would accidentally close up behind her, he was taking the search methodically.

He crossed to the meat hut and swung up the heavy bar, then heaved open the door. The solitary carcass hung from its hook. Guilt kicked him in the gut. He'd shown her the carcass that first day without thinking how she might react. He'd been raised on a farm, and he often forgot that others weren't as seasoned. Another failure on his part.

Next he set off in the direction of the root cellar. Just as Milt said, the opening hadn't been propped. She'd have never shut the door behind her, and yet he was drawn inexorably forward. As with the meat hut, he wasn't taking any chances. He swung open the door and peered into the darkness. Nothing. He'd almost released the handle when he heard a faint stirring. He threw the door wide and searched for the prop stick that held it open.

The pole was missing.

His heart leaped into his throat and he descended the first few steps. His heel slipped and he caught his balance against the wall. A faint moan snagged his attention. His pulse jerked and he leaped down the remaining stairs. A flash of white petticoat caught a sliver of light.

Tessa wasn't moving.

Emotion clogging his throat, he collapsed beside her. She groaned and her head lolled to one side. Touching her wrist, he felt the weak thread of her pulse beneath his fingers. Her skin was ice-cold and he whipped off his coat, draping the heavy material over her huddled form.

"Tessa, talk to me," he urged. "Where are you hurt?"

She groaned and her eyes fluttered open. "My head."

How long had she been in this dank, musty space? She needed light and warmth, but he was afraid of moving her until he sorted out her injuries lest he harm her further. Gently feeling around her scalp, his hand came away wet. He wiped the blood on his pant legs and gently searched for other wounds. She winced when he touched her left ankle.

He propped her head on his bent knee and brushed the hair from her forehead. "You're going to be all right. The boys are out searching for you. I have to leave you for a moment and holler for help."

The stairs were too narrow to carry her up himself.

She rested a weak hand on his sleeve. "Don't leave me alone."

Murmuring softly, he pressed her cold fingers between his warmer hands. "I won't leave you."

"I don't like it when you leave at night."

Tilting his head, he studied her face in the dim light. Her eyes were glazed, and he had the uneasy sensation she wasn't really seeing him. "I'm calling the boys. This might be loud."

Leaning away from her, he placed two fingers in his mouth and blew out a shrill whistle.

Tessa flinched and recoiled.

"I'm sorry. No more noise. I promise."

He pressed the backs of his fingers against her forehead. "Stay with me."

Her eyes fluttered open. "The children. I left the children."

"They're all right," he soothed. "Parker found them right off. He's with them now."

The tension in her body eased. Voices sounded outside. Finch and Parker arrived first, Red close on their heels.

Shane glanced up at their faces framed in the narrow opening of the door. "Fetch Doc Johnsen. She's hit her head and maybe broken her ankle."

"Right away, boss," Finch replied quickly.

Red motioned with his arm. "Hand her up."

Shane carefully stood and scooped her into his arms. She hissed a breath. "My leg."

"I know. I'm sorry." She was strong, he reminded himself. She'd fight through this. "Don't worry. We'll get you back to the house and warm."

"I'm not c-c-old."

A sure sign of potentially fatal chills. Anxiety sharpened his focus. He braced his foot on the bottom stair and Red reached down. Shane loathed letting her go, even for a moment. With Wheeler's help they lifted her from the root cellar, and he followed close behind, avoiding the ice-covered tread. The moment he stood on solid ground, Red handed her back and he set off for the house.

Tessa clutched his collar. "Why didn't you send a telegram?"

He and Red exchanged a confused glance. "Why would I send a telegram?"

"To show me you care."

"I care, Tessa."

He must have said the right thing, because her fingers loosened.

"Parker can take the kids back to the bunkhouse," Red said. "We'll keep an eye on them until you get things sorted out."

He held open the door and Shane ducked inside. Alyce and Owen dashed toward them, but their faces fell when they saw Tessa's still form. They might be children, but they sensed the gravity of the situation. The two slowed, toddling over, then clutched his pant leg and reached for Tessa.

"Papa, Papa."

"Tess-Tess."

He offered a weak smile. "Tessa isn't feeling well. Finch has gone to fetch the doctor. Doc Johnsen will fix her right up."

Parker and Red took charge of the children, and with murmured assurances and a promise of sweets, they were bustled away.

Shane rested Tessa on the bed and quickly divested her of her damp coat and tucked the quilt around her. Gathering every blanket he could find, he piled them over her small form. Her teeth chattered and violent trembling racked her body.

Milt hovered in the doorway. "Is there anything I can do?"

"Fire up the stove as hot as you can and put on a pot of coffee. It's going to be a long night."

"Sure thing, boss." He paused. "I looked. Truly, I did. I didn't see her."

"I know. I didn't see her at first either. It's not your fault."

Milt nodded, his throat working, then quietly turned away.

Tessa reached for Shane, her gaze unfocused. "I'm sorry."

"You had an accident. Nothing to be sorry for."

"You'll have to eat supper in the bunkhouse."

"Never mind supper. How's your head?"

He fumbled for a towel and wet it in the basin of water beside the bed. Working his hands through her hair, he discovered an enormous lump behind one ear. Blood darkened her hair and he wiped away as much as he could. She winced at his ministrations.

"I fell down the stairs," she said.

"You hit your head pretty hard."

"Emmett always said I was hardheaded anyway." Her voice quivered. "I miss him."

He still found it odd the way she talked about her father by his first name, but now wasn't the time for questions.

"Just rest. The doctor will be here soon."

"My leg hurts, too."

"I know." He caught her hand. "Why don't you close your eyes and rest?"

"Will you stay with me? I don't want to be alone." Her words were growing slurred and drowsy. "Keep the light on. I don't like the dark."

Though the setting sun brightened the room, he lit a lamp with a practiced scratch of flint and steel. He adjusted the wick, then replaced the chimney. "I won't leave you."

He pressed her ice-cold fingers between his much warmer hands and she calmed. After kicking off his boots, he perched on the bed beside her. Like a cat, she curled into the warmth of his body.

The quiet lasted only a moment before she began thrashing about. She groaned and clawed at her hair. "I can feel them."

"Feel what?"

"The spiders. The spiders are crawling in my hair."

He threaded his fingers through the silken mass, dislodging the few remaining hairpins. "There are no spiders, see?"

The rhythmic brush of his fingers quieted her, and her eyes drifted shut once more. He ran the pad of his thumb along her closed eyelid, brushing away a spot of dirt. She trembled in his embrace and he tightened his arm around her. She clung to him, her face buried against his chest. Fear and guilt were all mixed together with a fierce desire to protect and comfort her, cherish her.

Though he hadn't admitted the realization to himself, in only a few weeks she'd become a vital part of his existence. His day centered on catching a glimpse of her. She grew more exquisitely beautiful each time he saw her. His footsteps naturally quickened as the evenings approached, his eager anticipation of their time together obvious. Each day he marveled at the good fortune that had dropped her into his path.

After an eternity, the doc arrived, his cheeks chapped from the cold, his bag clutched in his hand. "I heard you had some excitement."

Doc Johnsen was a young Norwegian with straw-colored hair and bright blue eyes. He had an unflappable comportment and astonishing endurance. After the twins were born, he'd stayed the weekend, then visited each day, sometimes twice a day, until they'd thrived. The doc delivered both good and bad news with forthright directness, and Shane appreciated his honesty.

Easing away from her, Shane feathered his touch along her jaw. "She took a bad fall. Bumped her head. She's sprained her wrist and her ankle. Nothing feels broken."

Tessa reached for him and he circled around to the opposite side of the bed. The doc took his place, dipping the mattress as he adjusted his stethoscope over his ears. As the doc examined her, her eyes fluttered open. She mumbled Shane's name and he stroked the back of her hand.

The doc straightened with a frown. "That's a nasty bump you've got, Mrs. McCoy." He lifted each lid and checked her eyes once more, then turned toward Shane. "Has she been lucid since the accident? Speaking?"

"Some. She's talked a little. She didn't always make sense. She thought there were spiders in her hair."

The doc's expression turned grim. "Judging by her eyes, she's got some swelling on the brain. That combined with the cold may bring about some hallucinations."

Shane wasn't a demonstrative man, less so when other folks were around. Heedless of the doctor's presence, he slid his arm beneath Tessa's shoulder and pressed his cheek against hers. She didn't recoil from him, and he relaxed some. Her skin was cool and soft, her body weak. She'd been through a rough time today, and he wanted to infuse her strength with some of his own.

Memories of Abby's illness came rushing back. She'd been laid up so often after the twins' birth, none of them

had given much heed when the fever first struck. In a
blink everything had changed. The doc's face had taken
on that same grim expression. In the final hours, Abby
had gone still. Her breathing had turned shallow and
uneven and eventually she'd slipped away. The interval
between life and death had been sudden and irrevoca-
ble. He'd just stood there in mute shock and grief until
someone had urged him away.

He didn't think he could survive that kind of pain
again.

The doc checked her for other injuries. When he
touched her side, she flinched.

"Mrs. McCoy," the doc said. "Does it hurt to breathe?"

She shook her head weakly from side to side, her hair
brushing against Shane's jaw.

"Probably just a bruised rib." The doc frowned over
her leg where purpling marks circled her ankle. "It's not
broken, but it's a bad sprain. She'll be laid up for at least
a week or two."

Shane hated the pain she must be enduring. What a
punishment she'd taken. He loathed thinking about her
lying there, waiting for someone to find her, while he'd
been wasting time in the pasture.

The doc wrapped her leg tightly and she struggled
away.

Shane held her hand and she squeezed his fingers.
"Doc Johnsen is the best. You let him do his work."

Her eyes opened a slit and she flashed him a mutinous
glare. "I hurt all over."

"I know you do."

She flashed a weak look of triumph at his admission.
"At least we agree about something."

"We're going to be fine, you and me."

For years his only aim had been making the ranch a success. He'd fought against nature and himself, pushing himself and his men until they dropped. Every obstacle in his path had been crushed or removed. If he couldn't fix something, he discarded it in favor of something else. There was no use wasting time on something that didn't fit his plans. He was set in his ways. Because once he'd found something that worked, there was no use changing things.

People were not as easily tamed.

Abby had mostly ignored him. He'd tried creating the life he'd imagined in his youth, and when that hadn't worked, he'd abandoned the effort. With Tessa, he hadn't even tried. He hadn't tried because he assumed the outcome would be the same. Except remaining indifferent to Tessa had proved impossible.

He'd made up his mind about how things were going to be, and Tessa hadn't gone along with his plans. She'd unsettled his rigid control since the moment he'd seen her in Wichita, and all he'd thought about since then was wrestling back that control.

The doc uncapped a bottle of laudanum and measured a dose. "This will help her sleep during the worst of the pain."

"Don't talk about me like I'm not here." Straining half-heartedly away from him, she grimaced. "That smells foul."

Shane tipped the glass to her lips. "Drink. Please."

She flung out her hand and thumped his chest. "Just this once. Because you said 'please.'"

Once she'd taken the dose, he rested her against the pillows, then pulled the covers over her shoulders.

"Close your eyes." He laid his mouth against hers

in a gentle pressure, wanting only to offer reassurance. "You need rest."

She breathed a sigh and her fingers unfurled against his chest as she relaxed into sleep. Aware that he needed to reassure the children and check on the men, he reluctantly eased away from her side. Careful not to disturb her, he arranged the counterpane around her shoulders once more and dropped a kiss on her forehead.

The doc stood and motioned for Shane. "We should speak outside."

Milt was pacing the floorboards and his head shot up. "How's she doing? She all right?"

"She's resting now," Shane said grimly. "Will you sit with her while the doc and I talk?"

"Sure thing, boss." Milt hoisted a chair and carried it over the threshold.

Shane lingered as Milt took up vigil, his lips moving in a silent prayer.

The doc laid a heavy hand on Shane's shoulder. "You need some air."

The moment they stepped outside, Shane staggered a few steps away and became violently ill. The doc waited until the worst had passed, then handed over his handkerchief, easing him back and forcing him to sit on one of the risers.

Shane hung his head in his hands. "It's bad, isn't it?"

"Yes," Doc Johnsen replied bluntly. "The bumps and bruises will heal. It's her head I'm worried about. If there's too much swelling or bleeding on the brain, there's not much I can do."

"How will we know? When will we know?"

He couldn't go through this again. But he'd have to.

The children needed him to be strong. Tessa needed his strength as well.

The doc removed his stethoscope and coiled the loops in his hand. "Her pupils are uneven, and that's an indication of swelling. I'll stay through the night."

"Why is this happening?"

The two men weren't friends. They barely knew one another. And yet they were inexorably bound by tragedy. Their shared experiences had been both joyful and heartrending.

The doc gripped Shane's shoulder. "This isn't your fault any more than what happened with Abby."

"Everything feels the same."

"No. There's a difference. Tessa is different. I'm a doctor. I know a fighter when I see one."

She'd fight for Owen and Alyce. He pictured the three of them darting around the ranch, the twins trailing after her with rapt attention. She appeared just as fascinated with them, examining each rock and twig they plucked from the ground. She listened to their gibberish and told them silly stories. She was the best thing that had ever happened to him. She deserved some happiness in return.

The doc cleared his throat. "Is there family we should contact? She'll be laid up for a while."

"No. No brothers and sisters. Her parents are gone." He'd taken his own family for granted. Tessa was unbearably alone. She selflessly cared for all of them, with no one to care for her. "She only has us."

"Having the McCoys around is something. She's got more family than she'll ever need by marrying you."

Shane rested his elbows on his bent knees and clutched his head. He'd protected himself and driven her away in the process. Why had he spoken to her that way earlier? He'd been thoughtless and jealous. Ignorant, too.

The doc crouched beside him. "Stop beating yourself up. I've never seen a man quite as bent on being hard on himself. That little lady in there clearly adores you. I have eyes. You deserve someone like that in your life."

"No one deserves anything." Tessa didn't adore him. She was scared and alone and searching for comfort. He might have been anyone. "What happens now?"

"We wait." The doc pressed a hand into the small of his back and stretched, then blew out a breath. "I think you should send for your family. The next few days aren't going to be easy. You'll need help."

Tessa might be different, but everything about this accident was too familiar. The doc was here and Shane was sending for his family because his wife was ill. Everything was playing out the same as before.

"I'll have one of the boys fetch my aunt Edith," Shane declared.

"She's a good choice."

"She hasn't even met Tessa yet."

The weather had been good enough for a visit. Out of respect for the newlyweds, his aunt and uncle wouldn't come calling until he'd visited first. He'd thought about making the trip, but something had always held him back. Some minor repair or a horse that needed tending. Excuses. All of them. Aunt Edith was too perceptive. He'd feared she'd see his growing affection and call him on his feelings. Feelings he wasn't ready to acknowledge. Instead of facing his fears, he'd avoided the meeting. She'd know soon enough how he felt about Tessa.

The door opened behind him and Milt leaned out.

"Mrs. McCoy is asking for you, boss. She's not looking so good."

Shane's stomach folded in two and he followed the doc back into the house. Tessa thrashed about, a sheen of sweat coating her forehead. He perched on the bed and held her hand, murmuring soothing nonsense words. When she finally fell into an exhausted slumber, he stood, wiped his damp palms against his pant legs and backed away. Doc Johnsen had kept vigil as well.

Shane fisted his hand against his mouth and cleared his throat. "I should tend the children. Make sure they're okay."

"I'll check on them." The doc leaned against the door frame, barring his path. "You should stay, Shane. Clearly you're the best medicine for your wife right now."

His wife. At least he finally had something to tell Milt. He knew what made him happy. Seeing Tessa happy made him happy.

Chapter Fourteen

The next few days passed in a murky haze for Tessa. Voices abounded and her head ached. First she was on fire and then she was chilled to the bone. Blankets were fetched, and then ice was packed around her body. She heard the children's voices, but they were beyond her reach. Once she thought Emmett was there. He'd come to take her away. At first she'd wanted to go with him. Then she realized he was taking her to the Hensons and she fought against him.

"Don't leave me here. I hate it here."

A cool hand brushed against her forehead. "I won't leave you."

She grasped Emmett's hand, clinging to him. "I'll be good. I promise. You won't even know I'm there. I promise not to bother you or make a racket. I'll play quiet as a mouse."

"You can make noise," he said. "Little girls should always make lots of noise."

She dozed fitfully, and the next time she woke, Emmett was annoyed. He paced and scowled. "You nearly got us caught."

"It's only a game to you. I don't want to play the game anymore."

"This is how I earn my living, Tessa. Can't you see that?"

At long last a peaceful slumber overtook her, and she was floating on a gentle sea.

A long time later she woke to the scent of frying bacon. People shuffled around the room and she heard a voice speak.

"I appreciate you coming out, Anna," the woman said.

A sense of familiarity teased her senses. The voice belonged to JoBeth, Shane's cousin. Tessa struggled against the lethargy tugging her down. Her throat was dry and her body felt bruised as though she'd been beaten. A curious weakness had invaded her limbs, keeping her paralyzed.

"You should have called me sooner," the second woman said.

What had Jo just called her? Anna. That was her name.

"The whole point of the women's salon is avoiding situations like this," Anna continued.

"They're grown adults," Jo replied. "They'd already made the decision when they came to me."

"You might have at least offered her a different choice."

"You're right," Jo said, resignation in her voice. "I'll admit that you're right. But you weren't here. You didn't see Shane. He was like a man returned from the dead. How could that be bad?"

"But what about this poor woman," Anna grumbled. "Either way, I'm here now. Between the two of us, perhaps we can unravel this tangle."

Tessa made a noise and the speaking ceased. Why

were they talking about her as though she wasn't there? A niggling anger brought life back into her limbs. She wasn't "the poor woman." And what tangle needed unraveling?

Forcing open her eyes, Tessa searched the room and found Jo. The second woman approached the bed. Anna was a stunning brunette with brilliant blue eyes dressed in a splendid blue crepe suit. Something about Anna tugged at her memory. Where had she heard that name before?

JoBeth approached the bed, then squeezed her hand before resting her knuckles against Tessa's cheek. "She's awake."

Anna's forehead wrinkled with worry. "How are you feeling?"

"Awful. Thirsty. What happened?"

Jo grasped a pitcher of water from the side table and filled a glass before approaching the bed. "You fell down some stairs and landed a nasty crack on your head."

As Tessa gulped down the water, memories came rushing back. The dank scent of moldy earth, the skitter of tiny rodent feet, the sticky touch of spiderwebs. A shudder racked her body. "I remember now. Shane found me."

The mattress dipped as Anna perched at her side. "We haven't met yet. My name is Anna McCoy. I'm married to your husband's cousin Caleb."

Tessa finally recalled the name. "You're the mayor."

"Yes, I'm the mayor." Anna touched Jo's sleeve. "She's definitely come around this time. You'd best fetch Shane."

Following Jo's hasty exit from the room, Anna's expression grew somber. "I wasn't here when you arrived in town because of the work I do around the country. I have a charity that helps women who've found themselves in difficult situations. I wonder if you might be in a difficult situation. I gather your marriage was rather hasty. If you're unhappy, if things aren't working out as you supposed, I can help. You don't have to stay here if you don't want to."

"Shane." Tessa pushed upright and winced, cradling her sore wrist in her opposite hand. "Did Shane say something? Does he want me to go?"

"I haven't spoken with Shane." Anna straightened. "I'm speaking with you. I want you to know that marriage isn't the only option."

"But it's too late."

"We can have the marriage annulled."

Tessa glanced away.

"I thought so," Anna replied sagely. "I don't know Shane as well as some of the other McCoys, but the rest of the family speaks highly of him. Whatever the case may be, I want you to know that you have options."

A shiver of panic chased over Tessa's skin. "What if I want to stay here?"

"Is that what you truly want?" Anna's wide blue eyes shimmered with compassion. "Please know that you may confide in me. There's nothing I haven't heard."

This was all too much. Tessa's head throbbed and her body ached. She wasn't ready for a discussion of her marriage with a stranger. "Thank you for your offer, but I'm quite all right. I don't need to confide anything to anyone."

Her expression unreadable, Anna stood. "I'll go now. Shane will want some time alone with you. It was all we could do to pry him away from your side. He barely slept and ate even less. If you're up for a talk later, I'd enjoy telling you about the women's salon we've opened in town. It's a wonderful way to meet other ladies in the area."

Tessa's hackles lowered. Anna had only been trying to help. "I'd like that."

Shane appeared in the doorway and Tessa's heartbeat tripped ahead. He appeared haggard and almost gaunt. Dark circles showed beneath his eyes, and his hair was badly mussed and shaggy. A dark growth of beard shadowed his chin. Her eyes widened. She'd never seen him disheveled. He was normally meticulous about his grooming.

He exchanged a greeting with Anna as she exited the room.

Catching Tessa's gaze on his hair, he jerked one hand up and smoothed it back into place. "How are you feeling?"

"As awful as you look."

He scrubbed his fingers down the growth of beard on his face. "That bad."

She offered a weak nod. "Gracious, what happened to you?"

"It's been busy around here. You've been ill for three days."

"Three days?" Everything was a flurry of confusion. It seemed as though only hours had passed, not days. Her eyes widened in horror. "Oh no. Alyce and Owen. I left them alone. They were napping."

"They're fine. They didn't even notice you were gone. Parker came by with some fresh eggs just as they were waking and realized you were missing. He sent up the search warning."

Tessa pressed her fingers against her lips. "Something awful might have happened."

"But it didn't."

She sat up and brought her feet around, her legs tangled in the blankets, her hair hanging limply down her back.

Shane was at her side in an instant. "Don't move too quickly."

"It feels good being upright again." She patted a spot beside her. "Will you sit? I think I have a crook in my neck from being in bed too long."

He lowered himself beside her and clasped his hands. "Can I get you anything?"

"I'm fine."

"Jo made bacon this morning."

While she suspected she'd have a raging hunger later, her stomach wasn't quite ready for food just yet. "Maybe in a while."

Feeling sadly fragile, she tipped sideways and rested the side of her head against his shoulder. "How are Alyce and Owen?"

He wrapped one arm around her shoulders, his touch featherlight. "They're no worse for wear. They're missing you, of course."

A twinge pinched her side but she ignored the pain. She was afraid if she showed any sign of discomfort, he'd move away.

She liked having him near, liked feeling his solid muscles against her cheek. "Can I see them?"

"Finch has taken them for a ride in the wagon. I'll bring them by as soon as he returns."

She swiped at her eyes with the back of her hand, both exhausted and relieved. "I'd like that."

"When you're ready to eat, let me know. Can I get you anything else? Water?"

"Water sounds lovely." She touched her throat. "I'm parched."

He was warm and solid and he moved away far too quickly. While she'd have preferred avoiding a fall down a flight of stairs, she enjoyed the intimacy. She liked seeing this softer side of him. While he was always affectionate with the children, he'd never been the same with her.

He refilled her glass and she drank greedily, feeling as though she'd never be sated.

Sitting beside her once more, he ran his index finger lightly over the bruise behind her ear. His knuckles brushed the nape of her neck, stirring her senses.

"Does it still hurt?"

Behind his raw expression she sensed a tense vulnerability, and she was overwhelmed with the need to absolve him of any guilt. "Not anymore."

She smiled up at him and absently rubbed her cheek against his hand. They stared at each other for a long moment. Then he leaned away, appearing at a loss.

Her hopes faltered a bit at his withdrawal. "I'm glad you found me. I never doubted."

"You took years off my life." He rubbed the back of his neck. "I can't keep track of anything these days. Not the children. Not you."

"Everyone should have someone who minds when they're lost."

"I minded very much. Not to mention I never got my potatoes in the German style," he said, his tone light, his boyish half grin fully in place. "Promise me you'll never disappear again."

"I will do my very best."

Shameless gratitude rushed through her. She believed

he was genuinely concerned for her well-being, though she suspected his interest was due to his honorable character rather than any real attachment to her personally. As she'd recently discovered, a casual sort of concern was better than nothing at all.

He rubbed his eyes with a thumb and forefinger. "I'll fetch the children. They'll be anxious to see for themselves that you're well."

Their easy camaraderie had fled just as suddenly as it had arrived. Once again they were two strangers dancing awkwardly around each other.

Her head began to throb once more. "I'd like that. I'd like that very much."

With the children as a buffer between them, there'd be no more awkwardness.

He glanced through the open door, then returned to her side, his hand hovering near her shoulder.

At long last he touched her forehead, soothing the rough pad of his calloused thumb over the scratch at her temple. "I'm glad you're back with us. The house isn't the same without you."

As though embarrassed by his admission, he was gone in a flash. The man had her tied up in knots. A voracious curiosity about his past overtook her. How long would he mourn his first wife? She'd asked a few questions about Abby in the beginning, but his answers had been terse. She'd stopped asking after that.

She considered asking Jo and Anna, then balked. The questions were too revealing of her own insecurity, too personal.

Jo returned with lunch, interrupting Tessa's troubled thoughts, then excused herself when Anna called for assistance with the temperamental cooktop. They promised a batch of bread once they'd mastered the stove, and Tessa was grateful for their thoughtfulness.

She stared at the door for a while before boredom set in. She plucked the worn Bible from her side table and flipped to a random page. The children had discovered the book earlier, and she'd tucked it away for safekeeping. It looked to be old and well-read at one time, though a fine layer of dust now coated the stiff cover.

The insatiable curiosity had taken root. She wanted every scrap of paper, every clue that might give her insight into what drove Shane. She didn't care if it was snooping. Tiny bits of the puzzle didn't fit. He was open and honest about most things, but shuttered and silent about his late wife. Even a simple comment about the twins' blond coloring had silenced him. Family Bibles often held lists of family members and life events, and she desperately wanted information.

She thumbed through the pages and discovered several daguerreotypes tucked in the back. Lifting the photos revealed a list of important dates in the McCoy family. There were marriages and christenings recorded, along with births and deaths. She traced a path to the last two entries and discovered the date of Shane's marriage to Abby. She recognized his bold script. Below, in the same handwriting, was the date of the children's birth, five months later.

Five months.

Was there a picture of Abby in the stack? Something, anything more? Tessa thumbed through the photos and discovered a young woman with light hair and lively eyes. The woman was looking at someone on her right, though the picture had been cut, leaving only the gentleman's hand visible on the arm of the lady's chair. Squinting,

Tessa peered closer. The man in the photo was missing part of his index finger. She read the name scrawled across the back: *Abigail.*

Tessa pictured the children with their blond hair and blue eyes, and the truth knocked the breath from her lungs.

What had Abby's sister said that day? *Abby always did have a way of leaving her problems on someone else's doorstep.*

Owen and Alyce were not Shane's children.

While their coloring might not be irrefutable proof, she knew Shane. She knew what kind of man he was. If a friend had come to him in trouble, he'd do the honorable thing. That was why he'd married Tessa, after all, a stranger. He'd married a stranger because he was honorable and he thought he'd put her in danger.

Searching her memory, she scrambled for the scraps of information she'd learned about Abby. They were both from town, which meant she and Shane would have known each other as children. Had the father of the babies died? If Abby had been widowed, why hadn't Shane admitted the truth?

Unless he was keeping Abby's secret. Which meant there must be a good reason Abby hadn't wanted anybody to know the real father's identity.

Tessa slammed shut the book and stared at the half-open door. She was keeping this bit of information to herself. Shane was caring for the children and he loved them dearly. As long as he wasn't concerned about their real father, then it was none of her business either.

The depth of his devotion sent her heart aching. How many men would give their hearts that freely? How many would shoulder the burden with such steadfast affection?

Even as she savored the memory of his brief touch, another thought shattered her brief bubble of hope.

Shane had written the date of his mother's death, the date of his marriage to Abby and the date of Alyce and Owen's birth.

Her eyes burned.

He hadn't bothered with their wedding date.

Shane braced his elbows on the porch railing and clasped his hands before him. Anna joined him soon after. She didn't say anything right off. She let him gather his thoughts, and he appreciated her consideration. He liked her, though he didn't know her as well as Jo and Garrett.

Anna had a forthright manner and sharp, crystal-blue eyes. She was a tireless suffragette, and her efforts to gain the vote for women had achieved national attention. She'd even been shot during a rally, arriving in Cimarron Springs to recuperate and eventually marry his cousin.

She was one tough lady—he'd give her that.

Shane pressed his forehead against his knuckles. "Take Tessa back into town. I know you have people, connections. She doesn't belong here. Once she's well enough for travel, I'll send word."

"No."

The single word reverberated like cannon fire.

Shane straightened and gaped at her. "What do you mean? I thought you'd be happy."

"She doesn't want to leave." Anna turned and tucked her hands behind her, holding the railing as she leaned back. "She wants to stay here."

"She can't. Not after what happened. You must see that."

"Her fall was an accident. Accidents can happen in town as well, you know."

"We argued. I was jealous." He stuffed his hands in his pockets and avoided her curious stare. While he might want to hide the truth, she was sharp enough to guess his true feelings. "Tessa was spending too much time with the men."

Anna raised her eyebrows. "You thought she was stepping out with one of them? Tessa doesn't seem the type."

"Absolutely not. I was…" He was out of his depth. He was terrified of becoming attached to someone who might leave him. "I was jealous of how easily they all got along together. I felt like the outsider."

Anna's expression reflected sympathy. "If I married someone I hardly knew, I'd probably get to know the people around him first. That sounds far safer."

"That doesn't make sense."

How was speaking with Finch or Wheeler safer than speaking with him? They spent every evening together. They talked. She always inquired about his day. She was solicitous and curious.

He shook his head. "I don't follow."

"For a man who's been married, you don't know a lot about women, do you?"

What sort of answers had he given her? Safe answers. Guarded answers.

Shane snorted. "You don't know the half of it. I have a singular talent for landing in impossible situations."

"A trait of all the McCoy men, as far as I can tell." She offered an indulgent grin. "I'm curious. What drew you to Tessa in the first place? You hardly knew each other and yet you married. There must have been something."

"She dealt well with the children. They adore her and she them."

What a liar he was. In truth, he'd noticed her beauty first. He was a man, after all, a man with excellent vision. As maudlin as it sounded, she'd taken his breath away. Even after he'd realized Owen was safe, he'd drawn out the encounter, reluctant to let her go. She was smart and funny and kind. More than anything else, he'd been drawn in by her compassion.

"She likes your children. Very practical," Anna said. "And yet it sounds as though you regret your decision."

"Of course I don't. Except she's miserable out here. I can't make her stay. Especially after what's happened."

"Despite your overzealous feelings of guilt, her accident was not your fault. I gave Tessa every opportunity to confide in me. I offered her my protection. I offered her a way out of the marriage. She declined." Anna cocked her head. "Rather firmly, I might add."

A band of emotion tightened around his chest. "She did?"

"And yet you'd like me to take her away. Rather odd, don't you think?"

"It's not that." He hesitated. The answer was too personal. Too revealing. "I should have given her more time to change her mind."

"From what Jo said, Tessa didn't want that time."

"I should have been stronger, for both of us."

"Hmm." Anna pushed off from the porch railing. "I know this is personal, and you don't have to answer, but have you ever actually courted a girl?"

There was no use denying the obvious. "You and I both know the answer to that question."

She drummed her fingers on the porch rail and studied his face. "I have an intriguing idea for you. Christmas is a few weeks away. Edith has offered to come by each day and help out with the children. Just until Tessa is fully recovered. You'd be wise to take advantage of her assistance and get to know your wife a little better."

Why were women always presenting half of a suggestion and assuming a fellow knew the rest? "I don't follow."

"Spend some time alone with Tessa. Without the children between you. Just the two of you. I have my own little one, you know. I realize how distracting they can be."

Fear pounded like hoof strikes down his back. "I already know her."

"Really? If that were true, then I doubt you'd have been so surprised that Tessa positively panicked when she thought I might insist she leave." Anna crossed her arms. "You'll both benefit from the time together. There's nothing wrong with courting your wife."

His stomach dipped. He'd bore her to death in an instant. All he knew of life was hard work, horses and cattle. He'd traveled plenty, but always for work. He rarely even left the hotel when he visited another city, preferring his solitude.

Nothing in his life had prepared him for courting a woman. He'd humiliate himself if he admitted his ignorance.

Then again, Tessa was worth a little humiliation. "How do you court someone? I don't know the first thing."

Anna didn't laugh or scorn him, and for that he was grateful.

"That is an excellent question, Shane," she said. "Since I'm usually counseling the woman in these matters, I have excellent insight into these sorts of things. It's all very simple. Take Tessa for a walk. Show her around the town. Learn about her likes and dislikes. For example, do you know her favorite color?"

"Why does her favorite color matter?"

"It matters because it's a part of getting to know her. If her favorite color is blue, then buy her a nice blue ribbon the next time you're in town. Get to know each other. I have a feeling you two have more in common than you realize. Women aren't nearly as complicated as men often believe. Everyone wants to know that someone treasures them."

"But what if I buy her the wrong ribbon? What if she doesn't like that particular shade of blue?"

"Don't be difficult. This isn't about ribbons. It's about showing someone that you think of them when you're apart. It's why she mends your socks and cooks your favorite dinner when you've had a bad day. Love is shown in all sorts of ways other than words and gifts."

Love. The word gave him a jolt. "I can't do those things."

"Of course you can. If by Christmas you decide you don't suit, I'll talk with the reverend about an annulment."

He didn't even like thinking about that possibility. Even though letting her go had been his idea, the realization left him hollow. "There'll be a scandal."

"You let me worry about that. I have a few tricks up my sleeve as well, Shane McCoy. Don't underestimate me."

"I wouldn't dare."

The idea terrified him. He'd rather face a pack of hungry wolves than play at being the charming suitor. That was why he'd insisted on a marriage of practicality. Unbidden, he recalled Tessa's ashen face and her cries the evening of the accident. She'd been terrified of being left alone.

Somehow he'd imagined her life much like his, nothing very dramatic. Her desperate ramblings during her illness had hinted at a troubling past. "What if she decides to leave anyway?"

The more time he spent with Tessa, the more he recognized that he could easily fall in love with her. That he was already falling in love with her. What if she never returned his feelings?

Anna shrugged. "If she leaves you, then you're no worse off than you are now." She paused. "Courted by Christmas. That's my idea. Take it or leave it."

Her kind expression belied the harsh edge of her words. She was trying to help. They all were. He simply didn't know if he was the sort of person who could be helped. "I can see why we voted you mayor."

"Thank you."

"Courted by Christmas," he repeated.

Either this was the best idea or the very worst. Only time would tell. At least he finally had an idea where to start.

Chapter Fifteen

"Keep your eyes shut," Shane ordered gently.

A week following her accident, Tessa waited expectantly for Shane's next instruction. The weather had been unseasonably mild and his aunt, Edith McCoy, had been coming by each afternoon, affording Tessa a chance to rest and recuperate.

Her bumps and bruises were healing quickly, and she felt only a slight twinge in her ankle. Her wrist still gave her a jolt now and again, but even that was improving. Doc Johnsen was set to visit that afternoon, and she was certain he'd give her a clean bill of health.

Tessa took a cautious step toward the door, her injured arm crossed over her stomach and held immobile in a sling. "They're closed."

"Wait there," Shane ordered.

"I'm waiting."

Hinges squeaked and a cold breeze ruffled her hair. Something brushed her hand and she leaped, then laughed.

"You scared me," she admonished.

"Sorry." He touched her elbow and his breath whispered against her ear. "I'll lead you a few more steps, but you must keep your eyes closed."

"I will."

"Promise."

"Yes." She sent a playful swat in his direction. "Show me your surprise before I freeze."

He placed her hand in the bend of his elbow and covered her fingers. "Just a few more steps."

Keeping her eyes tightly closed, she trustingly followed his lead. A soft snort sounded and she automatically turned toward the noise.

"Almost there," Shane said.

Hoofbeats sounded and something else as well. The rustle of fabric, the squeak of leather. Anxious now, she fidgeted beneath his hold. "Can I look yet?"

"Almost."

He moved behind her and placed his hands over her eyes. The heat of his body surrounded her along with his distinctive scent—an enticing blend of leather, horse and the outdoors. Turning her head ever so slightly, she inhaled the enticing aroma.

He'd fetched her this afternoon after Edith's arrival, promising a surprise and appearing as giddy as a schoolboy.

His hands fell away.

"You can look now," he said.

She sucked in a fortifying breath and opened her eyes. A man stood at the bottom of the porch stairs holding the reins of a beautiful bay mare.

Tessa turned toward Shane. "I don't understand."

His grin widened at her confusion. "I promised you a horse, remember?"

Tessa's eyes widened and her lips parted. "For me?"

"Yes!" He clasped her hand and gently tugged her forward. "This is John Elder. He lives down the road a piece."

The man holding the reins tipped his hat with a generous smile. He was tall and solidly built with thick dark hair visible beneath the brim of his hat, his eyes shaded from view.

"Pleasure to meet you, Mrs. McCoy."

"Tessa," she replied automatically. "Call me Tessa."

"Come down and meet her." He motioned with one hand. "She's a sweetheart. I trained her myself."

Drawn forward by his easy manner, she cautiously traversed the last few steps with Shane keeping a protective hold on her elbow.

After the last step, he released her and stepped back a pace. She extended her trembling fingers and the beautiful horse nosed her hand. A sprig of holly had been tucked into the mare's bridle. Feeling giddy, she stroked the white stripe on the horse's muzzle.

"She's beautiful," Tessa breathed. "Does she have a name?"

"Bluebell," Mr. Elder replied.

"What a romantic name."

The man flushed beneath her amused gaze. "My daughter, Hazel, names all the animals. She has a rather vivid imagination. You can call her whatever you please."

"I wouldn't change a thing. Bluebell is the perfect name for this lovely animal."

The horse pawed the ground and shook its head up and down. Shane moved beside her and rubbed his hand down the black hair of its mane. "John raises the finest horses in the county."

She playfully elbowed him in the side. "I thought you did."

"John raises the finest riding horses. I raise the finest dray horses. We're not in competition with one another."

"I'm glad to hear that," she replied with a smile.

There was something different about Shane this morning, a lightness in his attitude. He was almost flirtatious and his mood was contagious.

She pressed her forehead against Bluebell's muzzle and rubbed her skin against the soft fur. "You're a pretty lady, aren't you?"

She'd never owned a horse. She'd never owned a pet of any kind. When she was younger, her mother didn't abide animals. Her life with Emmett had been far too nomadic for a pet.

Mr. Elder patted the horse's flank. "She's got a gait like a well-sprung carriage. She's smart, too. I put her through all the paces."

He snapped his fingers and Bluebell's ears pricked in his direction. Tessa trailed her fingers along the animal's side and rubbed her withers. "She's simply beautiful."

"Horse," a small voice called.

Owen toddled outside, Alyce close on his heels. They negotiated the steps, turning backward and crawling feet-first. They held hands and tipped back their heads, gazing up. They tended to cluster together when they were uncertain.

"This is Bluebell," Tessa explained. "Isn't she beautiful?"

"Horse," Owen stubbornly asserted.

"Bluebell is a bit of a mouthful, I know," she said. "We can call her 'horse' for now."

"Ba-bell," Alyce declared, casting a triumphant look toward her brother.

"Horse." Owen scowled.

Tessa gazed at the animal in wonder. She'd never owned anything this fine, this, well, this expensive. "I don't ride very well. I'm not certain I'll do your excellent training justice, Mr. Elder."

"Call me John. My wife was anxious to meet you, but Moira is a little under the weather."

Tessa frowned. "Nothing serious, I hope."

"Not at all." He grinned from ear to ear. "We're expecting another child come spring."

An aching need inside her unfurled. "Congratulations."

How lucky for Moira. Though challenging, Tessa had discovered she loved children. She adored Alyce and Owen. Hearing John Elder speak about his impending child with such pride in his voice, she realized she wanted more. She wanted a whole houseful of little ones.

John Elder fairly beamed. "Our seventh."

"Oh my."

He must have started his family young to have all those children.

Shane chuckled. "The Elders are a generous family. They've never turned away a lost soul."

"Some of our children come to us as infants," Mr. Elder said. "And some of them come to us a little older. My wife was an orphan and she's never turned away a child in need. No matter how they come to us, all of them are ours in heart." He squinted at the sky. "Looks like the sun is setting soon. I should be getting back."

Shane slapped him on the shoulder. "Thanks for coming out. You could have sent someone."

"When my closest neighbor asks to buy my best mount, I figure that calls for a personal delivery." Mr. Eider winked at Tessa. "And I got to meet the new bride as well. Welcome to Cimarron Springs. If you need anything, we're just down the road and across the creek."

"You're very kind." Everyone had been so warm and welcoming. Each day the ranch felt more and more like home. With Shane softening toward her as well, she had hope for their future. "Give your wife my regards."

"I will."

Distracted by their conversation, she'd taken her attention off the children. Owen brushed past her legs and toddled directly beneath the horse's hooves. Tessa's heart leaped into her throat and she lunged. John Elder snapped his fingers. Bluebell instantly stilled, standing stiff-legged with only a gentle twitch of her tail.

Tessa reached beneath the horse's belly and hugged the boy against her side with her uninjured arm. "Owen McCoy, you're going to turn my hair gray."

Shane shooed him toward where Alyce sat on the steps, as prim and proper as a porcelain doll.

"Up you go," Shane ordered. "You've frightened Tessa enough for one day."

Alyce scooted away. "Bad."

Owen socked her arm. "You bad."

Alyce sobbed and shoved him back.

Shane quickly intervened and broke up the tussle with a sigh.

Tessa glanced between the two children, their features highlighted in the rosy glow of the setting sun, and her thoughts drifted to the dates written in the Bible. Judging by the picture of Abby, the children's father must have been quite fair as well. She shook away her musing in frustration. Why did the identity of their father matter? Except she'd always had more than her fair share of curiosity.

Edith appeared on the porch, her hands firmly planted on her hips. "Come along, you two. We're making maple syrup crackle."

The idea of candy was far more interesting than the horse, and the twins shoved at each other in their race back inside.

"There was another reason I came in person," John Elder said, jarring her from her musings. "You may have squatters on your land."

Shane's gaze sharpened. "What have you seen?"

"Smoke. Late in the evening. I checked it out this morning and found a carcass. One of your cattle, I presume. The remnants of a fire as well. I followed the footprints. One man for certain, probably more."

"Indians?"

Tessa's breath caught. She'd never considered that danger.

"No," Mr. Elder replied. "These folks wasted a full three-quarters of the beast."

"Nope. That's not Indians." Shane caught her worried gaze and wrapped his arm around her shoulders, giving her a comforting squeeze. "Don't worry. We've never had problems this far north."

If not Indians, then who? *The Fultons.*

Busy with her new life, she'd forgotten all about them. The danger remained. She doubted they'd forgotten about her. Despite Shane's assurances, tiny shards of fear pricked her spine. Her legs shook beneath her, threatening to give way.

Shane tucked her against his side. "Have you informed Garrett?"

Nodding, Mr. Elder said, "I sent someone into town first thing. Garrett isn't there. Called out on a land dispute. Could be a week before he's back. David, his deputy, is taking a look."

"David is good, but I'd prefer the marshal. Tessa and I had a run-in with a man in Wichita. A member of the Fulton Gang." She stiffened and Shane soothed her upper arm in rhythmic circles. "I doubt it's them, but let's not take any chances."

John Elder rubbed his chin. "Can't say that I've heard of that bunch."

"They usually stick around Kansas City. Keep a sharp eye out, just in case."

"I will." Mr. Elder extended the reins to Tessa. "She's all yours."

Shane held out a restraining hand. "Are you certain you're up to it?"

"Indulge me," Tessa implored. "I've never owned anything this beautiful, and I'm not letting go just yet."

"All right. But don't tax yourself."

"Thank you." Even with Mr. Elder looking on, she stood on her tiptoes and pressed a kiss against his cheek. "She's perfect."

A flush crept up his neck.

His generosity humbled her and her guilt flared. She'd been lulled into a sense of complacency. In truth, nothing had changed. Emmett was missing. The Fultons were a threat. The men John Elder had seen might be beggars or tramps. Or they might not. The horse nudged her hip and she playfully skipped ahead. She enjoyed her new life.

She loved the children and she believed she was doing good for them. Shane was coming around.

And yet a deep sense of unease chased away her brief contentment. She gazed at the prairie, the undulating grasses visible above the scattered patches of snow. As long as the Fultons were out there, she'd always be in danger.

If she'd put this family in danger as well, she'd never forgive herself.

For the next few days Shane and the men scoured the fields, searching for any sign of the men who'd slaughtered his cattle. Despite their efforts, their search met with frustration. Shane didn't know whether to be relieved or worried. The unknown nagged at him, and Tessa's lingering fear was more than worrisome. There was something more going on between her and the outlaw, and he needed her trust. Unless she confided in him, he was helpless.

In anticipation of his first evening of officially courting his wife, he'd donned his best coat, and with a fresh shave and a touch of the cologne Wheeler kept in his shaving kit, he nervously approached the door to the ranch house. He'd already made arrangements with Edith, but he'd forgotten to inform Tessa of his plans. Probably he should have done that.

Shane slicked back his hair and lifted his knuckles toward the door. Should he knock? It felt as if he should knock. Yet knocking at his own house seemed odd as well. As he pondered the correct behavior, the door swung open.

Tessa smiled. "I thought I heard something out here."

"I was going to knock," he said dumbly.

"It's your house. I'm your wife. You don't have to knock."

He raked his fingers through his hair again. "I wasn't sure."

"Come inside." She snagged his arm and dragged him off the porch. "You're letting in the cold."

Once inside, she waved him toward the table. He sat and clasped his hands on the table. "How are you feeling?"

She took the chair to his right. "I'm feeling wonderful. Fit as a fiddle. Edith says you're guilty about my accident."

"Edith talks too much."

She covered his hands with her own. "What happened was an accident."

"I said I'd keep you safe."

"Now you're being silly. You can't prevent all the icy patches in the world."

"I—"

She placed two fingers over his lips. "I won't hear another word. We're supposed to be courting. If I don't have something to tell JoBeth when she brings the children around, she'll have my hide."

He splayed his fingers on the table and collapsed forward. "Then you know about the courting? Good. I was going to mention it…"

"Don't worry. Edith filled me in. I hope they didn't browbeat you too much. We can go through the motions, make everyone happy. It'll be our little secret."

"Good. Sure. I have the wagon hitched. How about dinner in town tonight? Just the two of us?"

"That sounds lovely," she replied, and he knew immediately that Edith had also informed her of his plans for the evening. "Let me fetch my coat."

A short time later they were settled on the buckboard of the wagon, two blankets tucked around Tessa's legs and her feet propped on a warm brick. She wore her ridiculous emerald green hat, muffler and mittens, managing to look silly and charming at the same time.

He slapped the reins against the horses' backs and cast her a sidelong glance. "Anna said we should ask each other questions. So, um, what's your favorite color?"

"Peach. I guess. My favorite shade is during the sunset, when the sky turns kind of a peachy pink. How about you? What's your favorite color?"

"Green." He searched for a descriptor. Did he like the green of an evergreen? Or grass? After a moment he said, "Just green."

Not as exciting as a sunset, but it was the best he had.

"When Edith insisted I wear my best dress before she took the children off to her house, I admit I was a little nervous."

"Me, too."

"I've never courted anyone before."

"Me neither." They both grinned and he added, "We're a pair, aren't we?"

The air was crisp and the sky cloudless. He couldn't have picked a better day for their new beginning. Earlier he and the boys had tossed around questions he might ask, and he searched his memory. "This will give us a chance to know each other better. Where were you raised?"

"I was born in Chicago. We lived in an apartment on the third floor of a tenement. I remember my mother hanging laundry between the buildings. My dresses smelled of wood smoke and pipe tobacco."

"But you didn't stay? What happened after your mother died?"

She puffed a breath of warm air into her mittens and warmed her nose. "After my mother died I stayed with some relatives. Some months later, my father, Emmett, took me with him."

Something in her closed expression had him searching for a different question, less personal questions. He'd circle back to her family later.

The next twenty minutes passed in much the same way. With the help of the questions he'd compiled earlier, he pushed and prodded the conversation, cajoling and parrying with her. Yet no matter how carefully he broached the subject of her past and her family, she deftly turned the conversation back on him.

He knew her favorite color, food and time of day, yet frustratingly, infuriatingly, he didn't feel he was any closer to actually knowing the heart of *her*.

"What of your father?" she asked. "What was he like?"

Shane's hands tightened on the reins. "Gone."

She murmured a noncommittal response, and he recalled her previous criticism of his suppertime conversation. He finally understood what she'd meant. He'd been talking, but never really opening up about himself. No wonder she'd been unsatisfied.

Since he'd been pushing her to open up to him, he owed her the same in return. "My father left when I was thirteen. It was just my mother and me after that."

She leaned nearer and hugged his arm. "I'm sorry.

That must have been very difficult for both you and your mother."

"We had good times and bad. I heard he died some years back."

He'd always admired Tessa's affection with the children. Recently he'd noticed that affection had been extended to him. She was incredibly demonstrative, touching his bent knee as she scooted past, brushing her fingers along his sleeve, laying a hand on his shoulder as she served him at the dinner table. He'd never considered himself the kind of man who enjoyed that sort of thing. Not anymore. He yearned for her slightest touch.

She straightened once more. "Maybe that's why we're so awkward with each other. Neither of us has ever seen a proper marriage. We have nothing to go by."

"It doesn't have to be that way. There's no reason we can't change things."

"You're uncharacteristically optimistic this evening."

He started. "I didn't realize I was pessimistic."

"Hmm, perhaps not. You're more of a realist, I suppose." She plucked at the red tartan blanket covering her legs. "Have you caught any sight of the men Mr. Elder saw?"

"Nothing," he bit out in frustration. "I'd have liked to settle the thing at least and discover their identities."

As the town appeared in the distance, they lapsed into silence. He hitched the wagon before the hotel and assisted Tessa down, letting his fingers linger around her waist a touch longer than necessary.

They stepped into the warmth of the restaurant, and he surveyed the crowd. Several tables were occupied but there was plenty of seating.

He turned toward Tessa and caught her shocked expression. He followed her gaze toward a dark-haired gentleman rising from his seat.

Tessa abandoned his side and wove through the tables, then launched herself at the gentleman, who caught her against his chest.

"Emmett!' she exclaimed.

Shane's heartbeat thudded against his ribs. This was Tessa's father?

Everything Tessa had said had led him to believe that Emmett Spencer was dead. Yet here he was. Very much alive.

"Emmett!" Tessa squealed again, too shocked to do anything but stare.

Stumbling back, he lifted her off her feet in a bone-crushing hug, then set her away from him. Tall and lean, Emmett's bandit-dark hair had only just started graying at the temples. He kept both his thick hair and beard neatly clipped and his expensive clothes tailored and spotless. Any passerby who didn't know him would think he was a respectable fellow and not a seasoned outlaw who'd spent a lifetime skating in and out of trouble.

"You look as pretty as a peach." His eyes glistened. "I've missed you."

She stepped away and blinked back tears. "Where have you been? I was worried."

She had plenty to say to him but this was not the time or the place. These past weeks had taught her the value of family, and she'd try to remember that when they spoke alone later. He didn't appear any worse for wear, and while she was thankful for his good health, her resentment lingered.

How like Emmett to simply appear unannounced, throwing everything into an uproar.

"I had to go underground. You know that."

Despite her curiosity, there were too many other people around.

Tessa realized they'd drawn the curious stares of the other patrons. She dragged Emmett back through the jumble of tables toward the vestibule. Shane was still standing in the spot where she'd left him, an unreadable expression on his face.

She ducked her head against her own guilt. She'd led him to believe Emmett was dead. No doubt he was curious about her father's sudden reappearance.

"Shane, this is my dad, Emmett Spencer." She sucked in a fortifying breath. "Emmett, this is my husband, Shane McCoy."

"You can't be serious. I'm gone for a few weeks and you up and marry."

"I haven't seen you since last September."

"It can't be that long." He paused, as though mentally gauging the time passed. "Is this why you made all that fuss in Wichita?"

"No. I hadn't even met Shane yet."

Emmett snatched her hand and studied her fingers. "You're not even wearing a ring."

Trust her dad to pick out that one small detail.

Tessa tucked her hands into the folds of her skirt. "It's a long story. We got married rather suddenly. There wasn't time for a ring."

The men exchanged a brief handshake. Both of them wary and eyeing each other like a couple of roosters with their chests puffed out.

Shane hooked his thumbs into his belt loops. "Join us for dinner, Mr. Spencer?"

"Actually, I'd prefer a word alone with my daughter, Mr. McCoy. We haven't seen each other in a while." He looked Shane up and down. "Seems like we have some catching up to do."

Tessa silently pleaded with her husband and he gave an almost imperceptible nod of his head. "I'll wait at the table. There's a parlor in the back for guests. It's usually empty this time of day."

Tessa gripped his hand in a quick, grateful squeeze. He knew something was wrong. How could he not? How was she ever going to explain this?

Together she and Emmett found the tiny parlor with a fire crackling merrily in the hearth and two tufted wing-back chairs set before the warmth.

Emmett perched on the edge of one chair and she took the other.

"Who is he...that...that farmer?" Emmett demanded. "Did he take advantage of you?"

"He's a rancher and it's nothing like that. It's a long story." Her chest seized at a sudden thought. "The marshal. The town marshal has met you before. You'd best steer clear of him."

"Have a little faith in your old man. I checked on the local law enforcement before I settled into town. Marshal Cain is resolving a land dispute two towns away. I've got another day or two before he's back. I've been in town for two weeks. I'd given up hope of ever finding you. I nearly fainted when you waltzed in the door."

"You haven't answered my questions properly. Where have you been? Why didn't you answer my telegrams?

I've been worried." She chucked him on the arm. "You have some explaining to do."

There was no use scolding Emmett. He was impervious.

"Me?" He rubbed at his arm with an exaggerated grimace. "Why did you leave Wichita? How'd you end up here? This town is filled with nothing but churchgoers and salt-of-the-earth folks." He tugged on his collar. "Makes me nervous. I can't find a poker game to save my hide."

"Thank goodness for that. You leave these people alone. I'm living here now. I can't just pick up and run if you start a ruckus." She stared into the flames. "Is everything squared? Are we safe now?"

He adjusted his trousers over his knees, then clasped his hands before him. "About that. I need your help with a little project."

"No." She shook her head for emphasis. "Absolutely not."

Betrayal shot through her veins. He'd come only because he wanted something from her. Here she'd thought he'd actually discovered his conscious.

"Hear me out. You're the best locksmith west of the Mississippi. You're the best person for this job."

Tessa narrowed her gaze. Charming Emmett was back at his finest. First he'd begin with the flattery. If that didn't work, he'd move to guilt.

"No."

"It's one job," he pleaded. "And it's for a good cause. Me."

"No, no and no."

Emmett's mouth hardened and he stood halfway from his chair. "It's that farmer, isn't it? Has he got some sort of hold over you? I'll take care of him. I know people. Say the word and he'll be on the next steamship bound for the gulf."

"Don't you lay a finger on him. You hear me?" Tessa pressed her hands against his chest and shoved him into his seat once more. "It's nothing like that. I met him in Wichita. He has these two beautiful children. He's a good man. He doesn't know about you. What you do for a living. What *we* did for a living."

"You'll be bored to death in a year with that fellow. People like us don't change."

"I'm not like you. Why can't you see that?"

Emmett's scowl only deepened. "We're back on that again, are we? It's not bad for a man to make a living off his wits. If a fellow can't play a round of poker, then it's not my fault."

"It's not just the poker. You know that."

He crossed his arms over his chest. "Land grabbers don't deserve fair dealings. There's nothing wrong with cheating a cheat. That's the rule."

"It's not a rule. Not everyone thinks like you."

Emmett made a sound of disgust in his throat. "I don't understand. You never had a problem before that preacher got his teeth into you. You want to know the truth? That snake-oil salesman was no better than I am. He's worse, even. You think any of them folks are getting the salvation he promised? At least I'm up-front in my dealings. That preacher has no better chance getting through the pearly gates than me."

She pressed her hands against her cheeks. "I don't want to argue. I had to leave Wichita in a hurry because I spotted Dead Eye. He was looking for me."

That information snagged his attention. "Why didn't you tell me?"

"I tried to. Why haven't you answered my telegrams?"

"Because I can't go near any of my old haunts. Those Fultons have people everywhere." He settled back into his seat and pinched his forehead. "Glad I missed him when I went looking for you. The last place I knew you'd been was Wichita. I picked up the trail there."

"And you came looking for me for a job." She drew her brows together. "You were worried about me, too, right?"

"Sure, sure. Absolutely. But you're smart and capable," Emmett scoffed. "You know how to steer clear of them Fultons. They're not too bright. The delay has put me behind, though. We have to put this plan together lickety-split."

There was no use reasoning with him. Once Emmett got hold of a plan, he was obsessed. Never mind that his only daughter was married and he'd practically growled at her husband. Never mind that an outlaw was on the lookout for her, putting her new family at risk. There was a plan. Time for everyone to drop everything and go along with Emmett.

"Dead Eye Dan had my picture." She spoke through gritted teeth.

"He must have stolen it. I sure didn't give it to him. How can you even think that of your old pa?"

Not even ten minutes into their reunion and already her patience was thinning. "You haven't answered my question. What job are you working this time?"

"You're gonna love this." He held up a hand, silencing her protest. "I found the guy who set me up before. He was working as a teller in a bank in Wichita. Caught him up in Abilene living like a king. Turns out he and Dead

Eye Dan had the same particular friend. Dead Eye must have told her about his plan, and she double-crossed him with the teller. They turned us in. That's why there was a posse mustered before we could spit twice. It was a brilliant plan. While I was holed up under the floorboards waiting for dark, that teller was hauling out all the money. Who's gonna believe a bunch of outlaws when they say the money is already gone? Wish I'd have thought of it myself. The law thinks the Fultons have the money. The Fultons think I have the money. And those two got off scot-free. It's brilliant."

Tessa snickered. "Brilliant. Yes. And how do you propose to expose his guilt?"

"I steal the money back from him, give it to the Fultons, then clear my name."

"This teller is living like a king, you said. How much money does he have left? You really think the Fultons will settle for chump change after they'd had a chance at the whole prize?"

"It's better than nothing." Emmett started to rise, then caught himself and paused. "Help out your old man, one last time. If the Fultons put a bullet through my heart, you'll never forgive yourself for not helping."

There it was, the guilt. Right on time. Emmett was nothing if not predictable. "Don't start in on me. I didn't get you into this mess, and there's no way I can get you out."

All at once his face slackened, and he looked older and exhausted. Studying him closer, she realized he was thinner, his cheeks more gaunt than the last time she'd seen him. Guilt gnawed at her gut.

She touched his sleeve. "Pa, you know I can't help you. Especially now. I have a family to think about."

"Don't call me Pa. It's common."

"We are common. Or had you forgotten?"

"We're anything we want to be. I told you that. People believe what they see."

A rock settled in the pit of her stomach. "Things have changed for me."

She loved Emmett. She desperately wanted him safe. And yet having him here terrified her. She'd started over. She liked the person she was becoming. Emmett brought back the past just when she was creating a new future.

Things between her and Shane were finally changing for the better, but their relationship was fragile. She wasn't ready to share her past with him. A sharp pain throbbed in her chest. Emmett was her father. How could she ask him to leave? Especially with the Fultons still after him. He knew her too well. If something happened, she'd never forgive herself.

He wasn't likely to stay long anyway. Especially once the marshal returned. Emmett preferred a fresh audience for his trade, and the marshal was already aware of his proclivities. A little part of her, a hidden part of her, had known that settling in Cimarron Springs had changed their relationship for good. She'd chosen Shane and the future he offered over Emmett, and the decision tore at her.

Making the right decision didn't necessarily make the choice easy.

Emmett tugged on his ear. "What about this husband of yours? You gonna invite me for dinner? You said he had children."

Tessa stood and edged toward the door. How did she introduce Emmett without revealing too much of her past? She didn't want any more lies.

"My husband is a good man." She rested her hand on Emmett's sleeve. "Please don't ruin this for me."

He grinned, smoothing the creases of worry along his forehead into laugh lines. "When have I ever ruined anything?"

Chapter Sixteen

Shane sensed Tessa's unease the moment she stepped into the room. Emmett Spencer was tall and leanly built. He appeared at once affable and charming. His grin was wide and his teeth well cared for. He sported dark hair with a feathering of gray at the temples. Despite the difference in their coloring, there was a definite resemblance between the two.

Though Emmett was at least two decades older than Shane, he imagined Emmett still drew admiring glances from the ladies. Dressed in a deep brown suit, he had the easy, self-confident charm of a man used to getting his own way.

The rest of the dinner passed affably. Emmett regaled them with funny anecdotes from his travels. He assumed the air of a charming host, never letting the conversation lag for long, but never really saying anything personal. By the time the evening ended, Shane had developed a grudging admiration for the man.

Tessa was afraid of something, but her father was not the source of her fears.

All of the proper pleasantries were exchanged. Emmett was dutifully invited for supper on Sunday and Tessa promised she'd visit the following day. A perfectly ordinary meeting between a man and his father-in-law, and yet Shane had an uneasy feeling there was nothing ordinary about Emmett.

Despite the success of the evening, his unease grew. Emmett Spencer was very much alive, though Tessa had led him to believe otherwise.

The ride back in the wagon was far colder and quieter than the ride into town.

Shane stared at the top of Tessa's bent head. "We need to talk."

"I know. Let's wait until we're home and the children are asleep."

"Fair enough."

The rest of the ride passed in silence. The children took their time falling to sleep. Once they'd finally quieted, Tessa sat on the floor and gathered the wooden blocks he'd carved and painted for the children into a wire basket.

He lowered himself onto a chair behind her. "Leave that. I'll clean up later."

Instead of standing, she leaned back against his leg and rested her temple against his bent knee. "I'm sorry I lied about Emmett. I knew you thought he was dead."

His hand hovered above her hair. Some of the pieces had loosened from the neat bun at the nape of her neck and he longed to touch them. To feel the silky tresses. "Why didn't you want me to know about him?"

What are you afraid of? He held his tongue.

He wrapped a tendril of her hair gently around his finger, marveling at the brilliant color. She didn't flinch or pull away, and her acceptance emboldened him. He let his hand rest on her shoulder.

She rubbed her cheek against the back of his hand. "We all have secrets, don't we?"

"Yes."

"Tell me about Abby," she questioned, her voice soft. "She's the children's mother and I know nothing about her."

Had Tessa guessed about the children? He'd seen her looking between them more than once. Abby had been adamant that no one know he wasn't the children's father. She'd been protecting them against gossip.

He'd clung to the secret as penance for his own guilt. Time had mellowed him. Even if they'd got married that first time, he wouldn't have been able to save her. Abby had always flirted with destruction. She craved excitement. He wasn't going to save her because she couldn't even save herself.

If he let go of her secret, he let go of the idea that the past might have been different.

There was no need to protect them against Tessa. "Abby was already expecting when we married."

"But the children aren't yours."

"I didn't say that."

"You didn't have to." She turned her head and gazed up at him. The lamplight caught her lashes and cast shadows on her cheeks. "I know what kind of man you are."

If she knew what he was feeling now, she might not be as assured. "Abby and I knew each other when we were young."

If he wanted honesty from Tessa, then she deserved something from him. He laid out his story, telling her about his own father and the life he'd lived following his absence. He told her about how Abby had wanted them to marry when they were younger and how he'd refused her. He told Tessa about Abby's return, about how she claimed she'd made a mistake and she'd never stopped loving him. He revealed how he'd foolishly thought they'd go on as they had before.

Tessa listened without interrupting. When he'd finished his story, she was quiet for a moment before asking, "How did you feel about Abby?"

A question he'd avoiding asking himself. "She moved to town when she was eleven. There weren't many children at the schoolhouse, and we were the same age. We studied together, sat together. Seemed inevitable we'd pair up. Just worked out that way. We were friends," he said, recalling those days as though looking through someone else's eyes. It all seemed like a different time and place. "I loved her the way you love someone who's been a part of your life. But I was never in love with her. I didn't know the difference. I assumed we'd go on as we had before, with the same easy friendship. Marriage changed everything. I understood that too late."

Tessa folded her hands on his knee and rested her chin on her knuckles, gazing into the distance. His fingers had tangled deeper into her hair, and he marveled at the springy softness.

"Do you know the identity of their father?" Tessa asked.

"Abby never said."

"But you suspected."

"Yes and no." Tessa was far too perceptive. He'd considered and discarded several possibilities over the years. "Abby had a wild streak. She adored adventure. When we were kids, I'd often catch her too near the train tracks.

She'd stand close enough that she felt the wind as they streaked by. She needed danger. She once told me that everything changed when she discovered she was carrying Alyce and Owen. A part of her wanted them safe and secure, but the other part still craved that adventure. She wanted to do the right thing by them, but she was always fighting against herself. Eventually, we all lost."

"She and Emmett would have gotten along well." Tessa sighed. "Her struggles must have been very difficult for you to watch."

"Agony. There's nothing worse than seeing someone you love hurting, helpless against their suffering. I'd have taken her pain if I could have."

While the final days with Abby had been bleak and hopeless, in the beginning there'd been good times. Even after Owen and Alyce had been born, there'd been good days mixed with the bad. He sometimes got caught up in how things had ended and forgot how they'd begun. The further time slipped into the past, the easier it was to forgive. He missed her; he missed who she'd been before time and trouble had blighted the optimistic girl he'd once known.

"We can't change other people," Tessa said sadly.

He'd laid himself open, exposing all his secrets. The time had come for Tessa to answer his questions. "Why did you lie to me about Emmett?"

She braced her hands against his knee and stood, and he reluctantly withdrew his touch as she moved away. She disappeared into her room and returned again with a distinctive clothbound ledger. He'd seen her studying the book before and vaguely wondered about its contents. He'd assumed it was some sort of diary.

She scraped a chair nearer to his, creating a distance between them. "Are you certain you want to know?"

"I'm tired of secrets and lies, Tessa. They rarely do anyone any good. I'm ready for the truth."

Tessa gripped the book between her hands, her knuckles whitening. Shane had been honest with her. She owed him honesty in return. "Emmett makes his money gambling and swindling land grabbers."

There. She'd said it. Except she didn't feel the relief she'd expected. With the ledger clutched between her hands, the rest of her explanation locked in her throat. She didn't want to leave, and if he knew the whole truth about her past, she feared his reaction.

"Emmett is a good man," she continued. "Truly, he is. Kind and generous. But he and Abby had many traits in common. He enjoys living on the edge of a precipice. Emmett is at his happiest when he's closest to disaster. When I was growing up, he'd win us a fortune, then spend it all in an instant. He always needed a challenge. If there wasn't a challenge readily available, he created one."

Shane crossed his arms over his chest, his jaw tight. She missed the soothing touch of his fingers in her hair, the gentle warmth of his comfort.

"What about you?" he asked. "How did you get along?"

"Fine, really. I know that my childhood sounds terribly unconventional, but after what I'd been through, I didn't mind. When I was very young, all I knew of Emmett were the stories my mother told. He wasn't suited for domestic life. I believe my mother thought having a child might settle him down. Except that didn't work. Eventually, he looked at us as his jailers rather than his family. After my mother passed away, I lived with relatives." She paused, catching her breath. "They did not enjoy having me around. Emmett came for a visit and realized that I was—I was unhappy. He saved me from that miserable fate and I'm eternally grateful to him."

"Was this family called the Hensons?"

Tessa reared back. "How do you know their name?"

"You mentioned them when you were ill." He touched her hand. "I know they were unkind to you."

She tugged her hand from his reach and wrapped her arms around her body. She'd always been ashamed by their treatment. "They had other children. I was the outsider. Emmett saved me from all that. Don't you see? He did his best."

"He was your father, Tessa. It's his job to protect you. You don't owe him anything."

"I know that." She laughed hollowly. "He can't help himself. He tries. I know he tries. We argued last spring. I wanted him to settle down. I was so weary of moving around all the time. I wanted something permanent and lasting."

"Is Emmett mixed up with Dead Eye and the Fultons? Is that why the outlaw was looking for you?"

Her cheeks suffused with color. "It was all a misunderstanding. The Fultons blame him for something he didn't do. He's been trying to fix things, but it's complicated. It's difficult."

"Does your father realize the danger he put you in?"

"Of course! He loves me. Truly, he does. He's just, well, he's just Emmett. He does what he pleases. Everything always turns out right for Emmett."

Shane pushed off from his seat and turned from her. He braced his hands against the kitchen table, leaning forward.

A sudden chill settled over her. "What are you thinking?"

"Why didn't you ask for Emmett's help before? In Wichita."

"I couldn't find him. After his trouble with the Fultons, he disappeared. I wasn't certain if I'd ever see him again."

"Now he's back. In Cimarron Springs. Why?"

"To check on me, I suppose." The answer sounded false even to her own ears. "You must believe that he'd never do anything that might hurt me."

Shane's mood prevented her from saying anything more. She doubted he'd be pleased to hear Emmett had wanted her to help him rob someone.

"Like getting involved with a gang of thugs, then disappearing and sending them after his only daughter?"

She stood and laid a hand against the tense muscles of his back. "Please don't be angry. I thought he'd settle things. Emmett always has a way of slipping out of difficulty. I was certain this time would be the same. I'd have never put your family in danger if I had known he wouldn't resolve this."

"Our family. It's our family, Tessa. Don't you see that?"

She pressed against his back and wrapped her arms around his waist. He didn't understand and she didn't want him to. "Like it or not, Emmett is part of our family as well."

She'd been willing to walk away from Emmett forever all those weeks ago. Realizing she may never see him again had shocked her from her callous indifference. As long as Emmett was alive and near, there were always possibilities.

"He should have been there for you, Tessa."

"Don't be silly. I'm a grown woman. I can take care of myself." Shane didn't call her on the blatant lie, and she appreciated his tact. She'd done a dreadful job looking out for herself and they both knew it. "Please, don't let this stand between us. I know we can work things out."

He turned and they were standing only inches apart. He leaned forward and slid one large hand between her neck and the hair falling over her shoulder, tugged loose by his gentle touch earlier. Her heart began an erratic rhythm. The skin where his fingers touched tingled with the contact.

"If we…if I…" she mumbled, enthralled with the way his thumb stroked the line of her jaw. Fascinated by the rapid pulse beating in the hollow of his neck. His gentle touch set her nerves to attention. Smoothing her hands over his shoulders, she threaded her fingers behind his neck. Feeling emboldened, she raised on tiptoes and his mouth swooped, engaging hers with a swift eagerness. His lips were firm and resolute, yet silken and pleasing.

Long seconds later he lifted his head and studied her face. His eyes held an intense look. Her stomach fluttered. She hugged him close, feeling his rapid breathing. What a fraud she was, what a traitor. She'd happily divulged Emmett's secrets while keeping her own.

The ache of loneliness weighed on her chest. The girls from the Harvey House had welcomed her without reserve, but she'd always held back a part of herself, keeping the full truth hidden.

Her whole life she'd been hiding. As a child, her mother had hidden the truth of her father's activities, keeping up the appearance of respectability. Emmett, on the other hand, had treated each day as a new adventure.

He adored the new personas they created and relished starting over again and again. Tessa was weary of starting over. She craved security and permanence.

With Emmett in town, how long before Shane realized the extent of her involvement in his previous schemes? She was not without guilt. Even at eight years old she'd heard enough about Emmett from her mother to understand the choice she was making in leaving with Emmett rather than staying with her relatives.

The words stayed frozen in her throat. Once again she reflected on the precarious nature of their relationship. They were building trust with each other, yet she couldn't bring herself to reveal the truth about herself. She simply wanted to be held and comforted. His arms tightened around her and she imagined, just for a moment, that she was the person he thought her to be.

She'd tell him the truth. Soon. But first she wanted to savor the feeling of being cherished.

There'd be time enough for the truth later.

Chapter Seventeen

The following day, Edith arrived at her usual time. After exchanging pleasantries, the kindly woman shooed Tessa out the door. "Go on, now. I've got everything under control. Enjoy your time with Shane."

A blush tingeing her cheeks, Tessa met him on the porch. He was dressed in his work clothes today and her gaze was drawn to his mouth. She liked kissing him and he seemed to like kissing her as well. Their relationship had changed since last evening. The difference was slight, but encouraging. She glanced down and frowned. Though a bright afternoon, Shane held a kerosene lamp.

Her frown deepened. "Where are we going?"

His expression grew somber. "We need some peaches. Come to the root cellar with me."

Her heart tripped and she dug in her heels, violently shaking her head. "No. I'm not going back down there."

"Sooner or later you have to face your fears."

"No. I don't."

He reached for her hand. "I'll be right there with you the whole time."

As he talked, he drew her inexorably forward. She let

him lead her across the clearing even though she had no intention of accompanying him down those awful stairs.

She hadn't gone near the root cellar since the accident. The boys were always willing to fetch her anything she needed, and she repaid them in slices of pie for their trouble. The arrangement was working well for everyone.

Shane squeezed her fingers. "It's just a hole in the hillside with jars of peaches."

"And spiders. And mice. And snakes."

"They're more afraid of you than you are of them."

"Don't be so certain." She returned his good-humored grin with skepticism.

He paused his step, faced her and cupped the back of her neck. "I know you can do this."

Blood rushed in her ears. He was right. It was only a hole in the ground. Nothing to be afraid of.

"Promise me you won't leave." A shiver that had nothing to do with the cold shook through her. "That you'll be with me the whole time."

He reached for her hand once more and tugged her forward. "Absolutely."

As they reached the propped-open door, he faced her once more. "Are you okay? Are you ready for this?"

"Of course I'm not ready for this. I'm terrified." She squared her shoulders. "You go first."

"I'll go first."

Juggling the lantern in one hand, he descended a few steps. Tessa followed him and rested her hand on his shoulder. With his free hand, he crossed his arm over his chest and covered her fingers. The loamy scent of the damp dirt sent her heart racing.

She swayed and Shane paused.

He swiveled in the narrow space and caught her hand. "We can stop here."

She shook her head. "No. I want to go on. I want to go further."

He backed down the next step and she followed. Ever so slowly, they descended the last step. Lunging forward, she wrapped her arms around his middle and pressed her face against his chest. He held her that way for a long time, then crouched and set the lamp on the floor.

She opened her eyes a slit and glanced around.

He didn't say anything, letting her wrestle with her unease. There was nothing to be afraid of down here, and yet the disquiet remained. Memories came rushing back. Emmett often left in the evenings. *The best pickings are after midnight*, he'd say. *That's when the real men come out to play.* He'd douse the lamp and lock the door, thinking her asleep. She'd relight the lamp and stare at the ceiling. She'd listen for every thump, every footstep and every jiggle of the doorknob until he crept back home.

Her whole body trembled and Shane put space between them, gripping her forearms. "We'll go."

"No." She sniffled. "It's not that. I was thinking of something else. I didn't even realize until now how much I feared being left alone. When I was younger, Emmett often worked late into the night. He left me alone. There was no other way. I think…I think that's why being down here bothered me so much."

"Childhood fears don't always end with childhood."

"He told me not to be afraid, but I was." She flashed a watery smile. "You're right, though. I do feel a little better now."

She inhaled a deep breath and searched the brightly lit space. Everything had changed. She didn't enjoy being down here, but she wasn't terrified either. Facing her fear had blunted the force of the effect.

They spent the rest of their time together walking hand in hand along the frozen creek bed. Shane didn't ask about Emmett, and she didn't offer any more information. It was enough that they were together.

They returned to the house and Edith waved them inside. She handed Tessa an envelope.

"Almost forgot," Edith said. "Someone dropped this by the telegraph station for delivery, and I told Jo I'd bring it by."

Tessa recognized Emmett's flamboyant scrawl immediately. She tore open the envelope and scanned the contents.

Dear Tess,
    Please join me at the hotel tomorrow for lunch.
Noon. I have important news for you.
Emmett

She glanced up to where Shane was replacing the lantern on the shelf in the kitchen. "Everything all right?" he asked.

If she went tomorrow, she'd be walking straight into a trap. Emmett never called her Tess. Which meant he was sending her a message: *Don't come.*

Nothing would ever be all right again. "Fine. Emmett wants me to have lunch with him tomorrow."

He was warning her.

Edith tilted her head. "Who is Emmett?"

"My father. He's staying in town."

"Well, land's sake, child. Why didn't you say so? I'll

come by earlier tomorrow. There's nothing like family, is there?"

Tessa gave a distracted nod.

She folded the note and scored the seam with her thumb. "Thank you, Edith. I'd appreciate the time with him."

Since John Elder had spotted the abandoned campsite, she'd known things were bound to come to a head. Too many separate pieces were converging. Emmett had arrived and the Fultons were hot on his heels. Or maybe it was the other way around.

This thing had to end, one way or another. If the Fultons had caught up with Emmett, it was just as well. If they were setting a trap for her, that meant they wanted something. If they wanted something, she had leverage.

If they had Emmett, they knew by now he didn't have the money. There was even a chance Emmett had talked them into going after the bank teller. Either way, she'd never know unless she walked into their trap.

Once she'd paid Emmett's debt, they'd finally be free. Then she'd tell Shane the whole truth of her past. If he still wanted her as a wife, she'd put her heart into their family. If he chose to let her go, so be it.

Either way, she had to see this through. She'd already faced one fear this morning. It was high time she faced her other fears as well.

Something was wrong.

Just like the day Tessa had fallen down the stairs, Shane hadn't been able to shake the feeling all morning. John Elder had sent a messenger from his ranch over that morning. Seemed that some of Shane's cattle had wandered onto Elder land. He and the men had been riding the fence line searching for the break.

They'd searched for hours before finally discovering the breach. He knelt before the separated barbed wire and studied the neatly clipped ends.

Milt planted his elbow on his saddle horn and glanced over his shoulder. "What you got there, boss?"

"Someone did this on purpose."

"You think it's them rustlers John Elder saw the other day?"

"Maybe."

His nerves thrummed. "I don't like this. Let's go back to the house."

There was something wrong. All his instincts urged him to return to the house. He mounted his horse once more. "Did Tessa say when she'd be back?"

"According to Edith, she'll be back before supper-time."

Though Shane felt better knowing Red was keeping an eye on things at the ranch, worry gnawed at his gut. There were too many odd events coming together too quickly. First John Elder had spotted poachers on the land, then Tessa's dad had arrived, and now his fence had been cut.

Not to mention Tessa had taken for town, and he didn't entirely trust Emmett Spencer. Being with her father should have been the safest place for Tessa. She'd said he was harmless, and Emmett sure put on a good show. Cimarron Springs had seemed the securest place for the two to meet up. Everyone knew everyone else, and the poker games were tame since the marshal had cleaned up the town. Shane's unease remained. Considering the man's activities, he was a danger.

Even if it meant dealing with Tessa's anger later, Shane needed his own assurances.

He motioned for Milt. "I'm riding in. You okay with that repair?"

"I'll have it fixed in a lick. I'll follow the line, see if there's any more breaks. Check for strays."

"Wheeler will stay and help you finish up."

He kicked his horse into a lope and made it back home in the wag of a dog's tail. He slowed the animal to a walk the last hundred yards, cooling him. Red asked if he could remove the saddle and curry him down.

Shane shook his head in the negative. "I might make another run."

Everything in the house was in order. Edith didn't appear worried about Tessa's errand into town, and the children were distracted with a new set of animals the boys had carved. Restless, Shane crossed the threshold into Tessa's room.

As he turned to leave, Tessa's ledger caught his attention. She'd brought it out the previous evening when she'd told him about Spencer, but she'd never explained why. He hadn't realized the oversight until now.

He flipped open the cover and paused. This was personal. He shouldn't be looking. As he closed the book, the columns of neatly written lists caught his attention. This wasn't a diary; this was a list. A quick skimming revealed the truth of Tessa's ledger. An item caught his attention and he ran his finger beneath the entry on the left across to the entry on the right.

Distracted shop owner while Emmett stole a hat.

In the opposite column she had written, *Returned lost toddler to his father.*

He recalled her coin trick with the children and the

way she'd easily overcome the lock at the hotel. Clearly she was atoning for past transgressions.

He flipped to the end of the entries and read the last line.

Married Shane McCoy.

The words blurred and he pinched his eyes with a thumb and forefinger.

He set down the book and left the bedroom. That was what he got for looking.

Edith frowned as he crossed the room. "Is something wrong? You look like you got bad news."

"It's nothing. When Tessa gets back, tell her I'll be busy for the rest of the evening. Someone's been cutting fence and we've got miles of barbed wire to search."

Edith harrumphed. "Cattle rustlers. It's bad enough they gotta take the cattle, but they leave work behind as well."

The children, accustomed to his comings and goings, didn't raise a fuss when he left.

Tessa had married him because he was a charity. He was nothing more than a chance at atonement. At least he finally understood why she'd married a lonely widower with two children. What a sacrifice she'd made.

What had she said all those weeks ago? *I've lived everywhere. I just want to live somewhere.*

He glanced up and realized he was standing in the barn. He sat on a bale of hay and clutched his head in his hands. What was the difference? He'd known she wasn't marrying him out of love or affection.

He liked feeling as though he'd offered safety and shelter. He didn't like thinking she only felt sorry for him. The poor, lonely widower with two children. Compensation for a lifetime of stolen hats and picked locks.

Was he any better? He'd set out as the benevolent protector. He recalled their time together, how she'd kissed him with sweet tenderness. Did she feel anything between them?

Parker came around the corner and paused. "Everything all right, boss?"

"Just thinking."

"About what?"

"Tessa."

Parker chuckled. "I have to admit, the boys and I were a mite worried when you brought home a wife. Never can tell how things are going to turn out, you know? But she's a real find. Things are different around here. In a good way. She's brought new life to the place. I've never seen the little ones so happy."

Shane steadied his hands on his knees. What did it matter why they'd come together? Parker was right. She loved those children. They were the whole reason they'd met, the whole reason the two of them were together. Charity or not, they were married. He wasn't giving up on his marriage.

As Tessa's husband, he was going to have a man-to-man with Emmett. Until Tessa's father cleared things with the Fultons, he was endangering Tessa. As her husband, Shane was putting a stop to that. Emmett was always welcome, he was her father, but not until he'd cleared up his own troubles.

If Tessa's father wasn't going to look out for her, then Shane would take on the task. He pushed off into a stand. "I'm going into town."

He'd have the talk now, with Tessa present. That way she'd understand. Then he'd ask her back home. On the return trip, he'd clear up a few things about her riding off without an escort.

The moment Shane reached town, his cousin JoBeth dashed out of the marshal's office and caught the bridle of Shane's horse.

"You'd best come inside," she said. "The marshal needs to see you."

Shane had known something wasn't right. He should have never left Tessa alone. He glanced down and realized his hands were trembling.

Chapter Eighteen

Tessa stepped into the small parlor where'd she'd spoken with Emmett before. No fire had been lit and the two chairs had been turned toward the entrance. Dead Eye Dan sat in one; Emmett occupied the other.

He caught sight of her and shot out of his chair as though he'd been sprung from a cannon. "Tessa!"

"I got your note," she said easily.

"Then why?" The anguish in his voice gave her pause. "You knew what I meant. Why do this?"

"For you." She steeled her resolve. "It's time this is finished. Everyone else has profited. Why not us?"

Dead Eye chortled. "Your daughter here is the smart one of the two, isn't she?"

Emmett hung his head. "She's here now, Dan. I've made some mistakes in my life, but you're about the worst. We might as well get this over with. Why don't you tell me what you want?"

Dead Eye smacked his lips together. "We're going to rob the bank in town."

"I told you already," Emmett said with a sigh. "The lock on the safe in town is too sophisticated for me."

"I know." Dead Eye rubbed his hands on his pant legs. "Don't worry. I took care of that clerk who messed up the job in Abilene." At Emmett's look of surprise, his grin widened. "You think I didn't know? That fellow was two-timing me with my best sporting girl. She decided they'd rob the bank and pin it on us. Didn't take me long to track her down. Went after that clerk next. Things are all wrapped up on that account—don't you worry."

Emmett shook his head. "Then why come after me? Why come after Tessa?"

"You got it all wrong, fellow. I was never after you. It was always about this little lady here."

Tessa gasped. "Me?"

"Everybody thought Emmett was the lock man. He's good, but you're the real prize, aren't you? Once I got double-crossed, I figured out the flaw in my plan. Too many folks knew ahead of time. I know all about your little talent. Emmett wasn't good for nothing but two-bit gambling after you were gone. Didn't take much to figure out who really had the talent in the family. You're getting us into that bank tonight. Then you're going to open that safe."

Nearly five years before Emmett had befriended a locksmith. Tessa had discovered she had a knack for locks, and she and the locksmith had made a sport out of challenging safe locks. She didn't know if she still had the touch or if the locking mechanisms had changed since that time.

"Tessa." Emmett lifted his pleading gaze. "You've got talent. I know you can do this."

"Yeah," Dead Eye agreed. "You can do this. Because if you don't, I'm gonna kill you."

"What happens after?" she demanded.

As though she had to ask. She'd go the way of the bank teller and the saloon girl.

"You'll get your cut. Do whatever you want after that. I'm not too worried about you turning us in, am I? Because if I go to jail, so do you. No one is going to believe that Emmett Spencer's daughter didn't go along willingly."

"You're just going to let us walk away?" Emmett gave a slight shake of his head. "That'll be the day."

Dan pressed a hand against his chest and assumed an expression of mock outrage. "I'm hurt. After all we've been through together, and you don't trust me. That cuts me to the quick."

Emmett snorted. "What's your plan?"

"It's real simple. The marshal is away, which leaves the deputy. It gets better. The deputy lives on the outskirts of town and has a whole passel of children. We could ride up and down Main Street and fire our weapons and he probably wouldn't notice. Which means the bank is ripe for the picking. This whole town is filled with idiots. We wait until after dark. Tessa here will get us inside and open the safe. After that, we split the money and go our separate ways. Nothing to it. No double crosses. Just the money."

Tessa scrambled for a stall. "I need equipment."

"What do you need?"

"A stethoscope."

Dan snapped his fingers and another man stepped from behind the curtain leading to the back rooms.

"I saw a sign for a doc in town," Dan said. "Why don't you pay him a visit? Real quiet like. We'll be needing his stethoscope."

The man turned and left without offering a reply.

"What else?" Dead Eye demanded.

"I'll need darker clothing. Even if the deputy isn't on duty, someone might see me. I'll pick up something at the mercantile."

"You think I'm an idiot? I'm not letting you out of my sight."

Tessa shrugged. It was worth a try.

"You can come along." She tossed her head. "You don't have to worry about me. I'm ready to get out of this stupid town. Robbing a bank suits me just fine. Right, Emmett?"

Emmett looked between the two and nodded. "Uh, sure. Right. We're up for the job. It's been ages since I ran a good con." He sat up straighter and caught her gaze. "Feels good to have the team back together again."

His smile didn't quite reach his eyes. There was a difference about him. A difference she understood all too well. For the first time in his life, Emmett found himself in a situation he couldn't talk himself out of. Dead Eye wasn't going to be satisfied with glib answers and false promises.

If they were going to outwit the outlaw, Emmett couldn't skate out of making the hard choices. While she'd miss his playful innocence, they all had to grow up sometime.

Dead Eye considered her with a slow nod. "Good."

Tessa exchanged a quick look with Emmett. "It's hours until midnight. As you said before, everyone in this town is stupid. I say we enjoy ourselves. Eat a good meal. Visit the mercantile. Have a little fun before we rob them blind."

She sure hoped her acting skills had improved since Shane had called her out in Wichita.

Shane. Her whole chest ached. He'd hate her once he discovered what she'd done.

How long did she have until he discovered she was missing and sent up the alarm? What happened then? As long as the Fultons believed they were safe, she and Emmett had a chance of escaping. They were dead after they robbed the bank. Dead Eye was only toying with them. Once he had what he wanted, she and Emmett were liabilities.

She'd taken a risk when she'd left. She'd known there might not be any way out. She'd taken the chance at death for a chance at a future. Tessa thought of Shane, then pictured Owen and Alyce, and blinked her eyes rapidly. After tonight, either she'd be dead or she'd be a wanted bank robber. Either way, she'd never see them again.

There was no way to get word to Shane without exposing her plan.

As long as Dead Eye and his gang thought they were merely hiding out in the town, everyone else was safe. No matter what happened, it had to stay that way. She'd take her chances with the gang if it meant keeping Shane and the children safe.

She loved Emmett but he'd known what might happen. The rest of the townspeople were unwilling participants, and she owed them their safety.

She'd take her chances for her family. They were her life. They were worth dying for.

Shane paced the marshal's office. "What do you mean relax? That outlaw has my wife. Why didn't David pick him up right off?"

"I'm sorry, Shane." Garrett shoved his forearm into Shane's chest. "It was my call. I wanted the whole gang. Once Dead Eye settled into the hotel, I knew the others weren't far behind. We have the element of surprise.

As long as they think no one is watching them, they'll stay relaxed."

"Then pick them up now."

"If we go in with our guns drawn, who knows what will happen. We're still missing one. If I pick up three out of four, we're asking for trouble. The last one will come back for the others."

Shane punched his palm with his opposite fist. "So you're just going to sit here and do nothing?"

"No. I've got half the town watching out for them. We have to wait until the right moment. We've got bad guys and civilians having dinner together in the hotel. Your wife is right in the middle of that hornet's nest. This isn't the best time to stir things up. We need to separate the Fultons before we make our move."

"I'll stir things up."

Why had he decided to ignore his instincts this time? He'd known Tessa's father was trouble no matter how many times she'd claimed he was harmless.

"Listen, those boys think we're idiots. They're holed up in that hotel as big as you please. They're not even trying to hide. They think we're all a bunch of yokels. As long as we let them believe no one is watching, they'll keep their guard down. That's how we want them. Relaxed."

A door slammed and David burst into the office from the back. "I waited like you said and I heard everything."

The marshal grinned and slapped Shane on the back. "Just what I was waiting for. It's good having a deputy who grew up in town. He knows all the hiding places."

David brushed a coating of dust from his hair. "There's a grate over the parlor that vents into the room above. My brothers and I used to eavesdrop on the adults when we were supposed to be in bed. Mr. Edwards moved a dresser over the spot when he bought the hotel. Didn't take much to move it out of the way again. Mrs. Edwards has been watching their every move. She picked up a few things as well. She says they're a bunch of slobs with bad table manners."

"I don't exactly care if they used the right fork," the marshal urged. "What did you hear?"

The deputy relayed the plan and the marshal's expression turned grim. "What do you think, Shane?"

"If she robs the safe, there's a good chance they'll send her into the bank alone. We can rescue her then."

"They wanted her all along. I did some asking around. Your wife has quite the reputation as a locksmith. How well do you know her? Can she manage?"

"She'll keep her cool. She's smart. She's got courage." Shane recalled her trick with the coin and the way she'd picked the lock at the hotel. "It's Tessa they wanted. Emmett was the trap. It was always Tessa."

How long had she known they were coming for her? Why hadn't she trusted him?

"Then let's put our own person in the bank. We'll catch them in the act."

David nodded. "Sounds like a plan."

They all had it tied up in a bow, but Shane wasn't playing. "I don't like it. There are too many unknowns. What if they don't send her in alone? They won't let her leave alone, that's for certain. They'll have a plan to get rid of both her and Emmett."

"I'll keep an eye on her," David said. "Mrs. Edwards has the whole staff on duty. They can't sneeze without someone taking note. Those boys think they're invisible. They don't see us as a threat. That gives us the advantage. They're not going to do anything to risk their plan for tonight."

"On one condition." The only person he trusted to keep an eye on Tessa was himself. "Let's get word to her."

"She may not want your help. There's a chance she's right where she wants to be. You know what David heard."

"Not a chance."

"I had to ask. You know her best."

He did know her. There wasn't any doubt in his mind. She was doing her best to keep them all safe. Emmett's arrival had forced her into a Solomon Judgment. Since she couldn't save everyone, she was going to sacrifice herself.

He wasn't going to let her make that sacrifice. "I have an idea."

The marshal reached for his gun belt. "Don't get me wrong—I need your help. Just remember, the last time we had a showdown in town, my wife shot me. Here's hoping things go better for you."

"I'll take the risk."

"I had a feeling you'd say that. Now let's hear this plan of yours. Just keep in mind my wife's family will never forgive me if something happens to either one of you."

The three men made a plan and split up. The marshal was tasked with setting up his part at the bank, David returned to the hotel and resumed his position, and Shane made his way to the mercantile. According to David, Tessa had made arrangements with the outlaws to buy some darker clothing for the evening's escapades.

Not knowing how long he'd have to wait before her arrival, Shane approached the counter and studied the display beneath the glass. Never one to pass up an opportunity for a sale, Mrs. Stuart sauntered over and followed his gaze.

"Hello, Mr. McCoy. What brings you in today? A little something for the missus?"

"Just looking." A glint of silver nestled in a black velvet pillow snagged his attention. "I'll come back later."

She caught the direction of his gaze and lifted a key from the dangling ring at her waist and unlocked the case, then slid out the velvet-lined box. "We've a fine selection of wedding rings, but you put the cart before the horse again this time, didn't you?"

She flashed a sly wink.

She'd always been his biggest critic. Then again, she was everyone's critic. At least he was in good company.

The overhead bell indicated the arrival of a customer. Shane glanced around and caught sight of Tessa's pale face, the outlaw clutching her elbow. His good intentions fled and he took an involuntary step toward her. He halted when he caught a flash of the gun barrel strapped against the outlaw's thigh.

This wasn't the time for playing the hero. Not yet, anyway.

Gritting his teeth, he resumed his task. "Mrs. Stuart, I'll give you the biggest piece of gossip Cimarron Springs has ever heard, but you have to do one thing for me."

Her eyes widened. "I don't gossip."

"Of course not."

"What would you like me to do?"

"For the next ten minutes, act as though you don't know me."

Emotions flitted across her face. She was curious, yet uncertain. Her innate nosiness finally won out. "You better not be fooling me."

"No fooling. You'll have the best story at the quilting bee this Wednesday."

"Then would you like to see a ring, Mr.—?" She flourished her hand with a broad wink.

Shane glanced over his shoulder. The outlaw and Tessa were studying the ready-made clothes near the back of the store.

"Wait." He held up his index finger. "Hand me that whiskey bottle."

Her expression skeptical, Mrs. Stuart reluctantly reached behind her and retrieved a bottle. After accepting the whiskey, Shane unscrewed the cap and splashed the liquid over his shirt.

"I don't care how good of a story I get out of this stunt." Mrs. Stuart scowled. "That's going on your tab."

"I know." He held his index finger over his lips and hushed her. "Remember what I said."

She jerked her head in a curt nod. "This better beat the time Mabel saw JoBeth shoot her husband."

"Nothing can beat that."

Yanking his hat low over his eyes, he stumbled through the store. As he made his way toward Tessa and the outlaw, he bumped every display he passed, making a point of creating a commotion. Dishes rattled and cans trembled.

As he neared Tessa, he swayed on his feet and knocked into her shoulder. She dropped the shirtwaist she held with a yelp. Her eyes widened in recognition.

He swayed on his feet and grasped her shoulders, as though steadying himself. "Hey there, little mishy," he slurred. "You're jusht the lady I need."

She waved her hand before her face. "I don't think so. Go away, you drunken oaf."

He teetered back then rocked forward. "Aw, please. Jusht for a minute."

She kept her grip on his upper arms, her eyes imploring him to leave.

The outlaw slammed an arm against his chest. "She's with me, mister."

Shane stared into the man's eyes and realized he'd come face-to-face with Dead Eye Dan. One of his eyes was focused sharply on Shane's face; the other was slightly askew.

Shane lifted his hand, his finger waving unsteadily in the air. Then he pressed his index finger against the man's forehead. "You gotta funny eye, mishter."

Dead Eye growled and snatched Shane's lapels.

Tessa threw herself between them and caught Dead Eye's gaze. "Why don't we humor the man? He's obviously drunk. If he causes a brawl, the proprietor will summon the law. We'd hate for anyone to get in trouble, wouldn't we?"

Dead Eye hesitated, then threw Shane off with a hard shove. "What do you want, fool?"

"Rings." Shane snatched Tessa's hand and dragged her toward the counter, the outlaw close behind. Her feet slipped and he instinctively wrapped an arm around her waist and steadied her. She caught his gaze, her eyes wild and frightened. Though she gave a slight shake of her head, she didn't push his hand away.

Upon reaching his destination, he rested his hip against the glass case and made a show of leaning heavily against the counter. He raised her hand until her fingers were an inch away from his eyes. A pulse beat wildly in the base of her neck. If he knew Tessa, she was more worried about his safety than her own.

"Your fingers are about the size of my wif-wif-wife's. Which ring would you like? You know, if you were my wif-wife?"

Tessa strained away. "If this is your usual state, then I would buy her something extremely expensive as an apology."

He studied the case. After making a selection, he slid a gold circle around her ring finger. "Too big."

He yanked off the ring and tossed the circle onto the counter. "There's gotta be something pretty in all this junk."

"Well, I never!" As he pawed through the other selections, Mrs. Stuart glared. "Those are valuable. Do be careful."

He found another ring featuring braided filigree. "Don't you worry about my wife, little missy. She's got the whole town looking after her. The marshal and everything." He slid the ring onto Tessa's finger. "Someone is always watching out for her."

"They shouldn't." Her voice broke. "You should just go home."

"Not until I'm finished." He lurched forward and spoke near her ear. "I'll be near."

He splayed his fingers, giving her a glimpse of the paper in his palm. Her expression flickered.

She shook her head, waving him off, but he wasn't giving her a choice. He slid his hand closer.

Tessa met his unyielding gaze, her eyes registering her reluctant acquiescence. Tears glistened on her lashes. "Your wife sounds like a very fortunate woman."

"I don't care about her past. I only care about her future."

Dead Eye guffawed. "Who'd wanna come home to this drunk?"

Shane stumbled, shielding his hands from the outlaw, and slid the note into her opposite palm. With a deft flick of her wrist, the paper disappeared up her sleeve.

Distracted by the display of liquor bottles, Dead Eye engaged Mrs. Stuart in a haggle over the prices.

Shane lifted Tessa's hand once more. Her fingers were chilled and he chafed them gently.

He should have bought her a ring weeks ago. Her fingers trembled as he slid the gold circle over her knuckles. He rubbed the delicate feathering of veins along her wrist.

Fearful of attracting the attention of the outlaw, he released her. "There, this one fits perfect."

Holding her arm aloft, Tessa admired the ring. "Your wife will like this very much."

"I'll be waiting for her tonight. She'll know where. She's gonna be so happy to see me, she might even give me a kiss."

Tessa smiled a touch sadly. "I bet she will."

Dead Eye shoved him away. "All right already. That's enough. Move along, you old drunk. You've had your fun."

The outlaw caught Tessa around the upper arm and dragged her toward the clothing once more. She glanced over her shoulder and he fisted his hands. He took a step and someone gripped his upper arm. Whipping around, he nearly socked David before he recognized the deputy.

"Everything is going according to plan," David said. "Don't get riled."

"How would you feel if that was your wife?"

"Just like you do. Nothing is going to go wrong."

"It better not."

Shane understood the marshal's reasons for leaving Tessa with the outlaw, but Dead Eye was going to pay for his rough treatment of her. He'd never have agreed except they had Emmett as well. There was no way she was leaving her father alone. If the outlaws wanted Emmett's cooperation, they couldn't harm Tessa. If they wanted Tessa's cooperation, they couldn't harm Emmett. Either way, they had to bide their time.

Mrs. Stuart grunted. "All right, I did my part. You owe me for the whiskey and the ring. She was still wearing it when she left."

Shane smiled grimly. "I know."

She belonged to him, and she'd wear his ring. Now and forever.

Chapter Nineteen

Emmett paced the locked room while Tessa stared at the ring on her finger. He knew. Shane knew. The marshal knew. They were all watching out for her.

Muttering beneath his breath, Emmett yanked on the window, but it held firm. One of the Fultons had nailed it shut. "As soon as we're out in the open, I want you to run. I'll distract the rest of the gang."

She motioned him over and spoke near his ear. "The marshal knows the plan. He'll be waiting for us in the bank."

Emmett blinked. "How does he know?"

"He just does. I'm fairly certain everyone in town is in on the plan."

"You're joshing me?"

"I'm not."

The door flew open and Dead Eye's brother Randall stood on the threshold. "As long as you two don't give us any trouble, we're eating in the dining room."

Tessa raised her eyebrows. "Very civilized."

"Well, we're all just a bunch of friends here, aren't we? Wouldn't want these folks getting suspicious or anything." He glared. "Just remember, one wrong move, and I put a hole in your daughter. Got that, Mr. Spencer?"

Tessa smirked. They weren't all that concerned about her getting away. Excellent.

Emmett waved his arms with a flourish and she preceded him through the door. They made their way to the dining room and Tessa paused.

Over half of the tables were filled, and she immediately recognized most of the patrons. The entire dining room was filled with McCoys. She spotted Edith and Eli McCoy sitting with Jo and another boy she didn't recognize.

Cheerful lengths of evergreen looped from the arches, and a sprig of holly dangled from the center.

The Reverend Miller occupied a table with a younger, dark-haired man. She didn't see the marshal, Garrett, but she figured he wasn't far away considering all the others. As she searched the room, her gaze landed on a very familiar hat.

Shane sat alone.

Her heart swelled. He wasn't letting her out of his sight. None of them were. Even though she was surrounded by outlaws and preparing to rob a bank, she'd never felt safer.

She took her seat and Randall and Dead Eye sat opposite her and Emmett. Mrs. Edwards took their order and Tessa complimented her on her bright yellow crocheted collar.

"Thank you." Mrs. Edwards touched the edge. "I sell all sorts of pieces over at the mercantile. Hats and scarves and mittens. For gentlemen, too," she added.

Emmett flashed his most charming grin. "If they're as pretty as you are, I just might take a look."

Mrs. Edwards giggled.

Randall glowered. "Shut it. We're here to eat."

"How rude." Mrs. Edwards huffed, then turned and flounced toward the kitchen.

The conversation ground to a halt after that. When Mrs. Edwards finally returned, Tessa reached for a plate, but the proprietress held the meal out of reach.

She set it before Randall with more force than necessary. "Enjoy your meal, sir."

The second dish she slid gently before Tessa. "This one is yours, ma'am," Mrs. Edwards said with wink.

Tessa suppressed a grin. She didn't know what Mrs. Edwards had done to Randall's food, and she didn't want to find out.

The rest of the meal passed in silence and they returned to their room once more.

Randall peered in. "We leave at midnight. Be ready."

The door shut and the key turned.

Tessa snorted. "Bold as brass, aren't they? Eating in the dining room, staying at the hotel. Where do you suppose the other two are hiding? There's four of them, aren't there?"

"They're doing this on purpose," Emmett declared with a huff. "Don't you see? They want us to be seen with them. One way or another, they're going to pin that bank robbery on you and me. We'll be hanging from a tree before the weekend, mark my words."

Tessa pictured all the familiar faces in the dining room. "I told you, we're fine."

"We'll see," Emmett muttered.

With nothing else to occupy the time, she rested on top of the duvet, dozing off and on. Despite her precarious situation, she sensed Shane was near.

Emmett shook her awake a few hours later. She stretched and yawned, then stumbled behind the screen and changed into her dark clothing.

Once they'd unlocked the door, she stepped into the corridor and met with Randall and Dead Eye. Dead Eye took her by the arm and Randall planted his hand in the center of Emmett's chest.

"You're staying," Randall declared.

"No!" Tessa spun around. "I need his, uh, I need his help."

"Nope." Randall muffled Emmett's protests with a gag. He unfurled a rope and secured Emmett's hands, then shoved him onto a chair. "Your pa is our insurance. Just in case you get any ideas."

Tessa's heart wrenched. "I'm not leaving him."

With languid ease, Randall took his gun from his holster, cocked the trigger and aimed the barrel at Emmett's temple. "Go. Or I kill him."

"I'm going."

He didn't have to tell her twice.

Tessa scurried after Dead Eye. She crept through the corridor and slid into the chilled evening air. Keeping a sharp eye on her, Dead Eye led her behind the row of buildings. Everything was silent. Not even a whisper of wind stirred the air. A sliver of moon illuminated the remaining snow and lent enough light to traverse the streets.

They reached the bank's service entrance and Dead Eye scouted the perimeter. "All's clear."

Tessa removed her hairpin and carefully worked the lock. Her fingers grew stiff with the cold. Beside her, Dead Eye fidgeted and held his hands to his nose, puffing cold air onto his fingers.

Tessa smirked. "Maybe you should have gotten some of Mrs. Edwards's mittens."

"Shut up." He smacked the side of her head. "Stop dawdling."

Tessa worked the lock, breathing a sigh of relief when the mechanism sprang free. "It's open."

She turned the knob and stepped inside. The outlaw shut the door behind him. "Dumbest town I ever seen."

Once inside, she approached the cage surrounding the teller area leading to the back where the safe was kept. She quickly worked the much easier lock and swung open the barred door.

She cast a furtive glance over her shoulder, searching for the marshal. Once they reached the vault, Dan slid his hand into his coat and revealed a stethoscope.

She wiped her damp palms against her dark skirts. Where was the law? Had something happened? She was certain she'd read Shane's clues correctly. His note had said only that he'd be here.

With no other option, she knelt and donned the earpieces, then pressed the diaphragm against the cold metal. She spun the combination dial right and left, listening for the telltale click.

Dan shoved her shoulder. "Hurry up."

She brushed him aside. "Be quiet. This takes time."

Despite the cold air, a fine bead of sweat formed on her brow. She got the first number, then the second. Her brow knit in concentration, she heard the third number spring free. Holding her breath, she reached for the handle.

Dan leaned close, his hot breath stirring the hair on her neck.

Tessa twisted the handle.

The outlaw shrieked. Someone slammed against her. Though it was dark, she caught Shane's distinctive scent. He urged her behind the safe and shielded her with his body. The scuffle continued behind them.

"We got him," Garrett called. "It's safe."

Shane stood and lifted her upright. He sheltered her against his side and led her into the lobby, then lowered her onto a chair and knelt before her. "Are you all right?"

"Emmett. They've got Emmett."

"Don't worry. They won't get out of the hotel. The boys have the place surrounded."

Another man approached with a lantern. He held the light near her face. "I'm Caleb McCoy, ma'am. That's a nasty bruise on the side of your face."

She unconsciously touched the mark.

Shane made a sound like a growl. "Did Dead Eye do that?"

She smoothed her fingers across his forehead. "It doesn't hurt, I promise."

"Tessa, I—"

She pressed two fingers against his lips, preventing his answer. "No words. Before you read me the riot act, I need to know Emmett is safe."

The marshal stepped into the lobby, Dead Eye handcuffed beside him.

The next few moments passed in a blur. Dead Eye shoved against the marshal. Garrett lost his grip. Shane straightened. His arm swung around and his fist made contact with the man's jaw. A sickening crack sounded. Dead Eye crumpled.

Shane leaned over his prone body. "That's for hitting my wife."

As Tessa gaped, absorbing the sudden violence, Shane

knelt before her once more and smoothed the hair away from her face.

Behind him, Garrett chuckled. "Well, Shane, you made my work a little harder. How am I supposed to get him back to the jail?"

Shane clasped her hands and drew her to her feet. "That's your problem."

They stepped outside and Tessa started toward the hotel, but Shane held her back. "I'm not letting you out of my sight until we know it's safe. A man can only handle so much."

Main Street was lit up and crowded with people. Tessa stared. "Where did they all come from?"

"Word spread fast that we had a gang of bank robbers in town."

Someone broke through the crowd and dashed toward them. Emmett held out his hands. "Tessa!"

He caught her in his embrace and her insides melted.

After crushing her against him, he held her at arm's length. "You'll never guess what happened. Randall took one step out the door and Mrs. Edwards beaned him with a frying pan. Caught him right across the temple. He's out cold. I don't envy Mr. Edwards."

"Mrs. Edwards is a widow."

Emmett scratched his temple. "You don't say."

Main Street had taken on the feel of a winter fete. People milled around and an enterprising worker from the restaurant had set up a table where he was peddling hot coffee. The two outlaws captured near the livery were delivered to the deputy holding Randall. Garrett and Dead Eye came around and joined the group. All four outlaws were paraded down Main Street with much applause for the lawmen leading them away.

Navigating the festivities, Shane led her back to the hotel. As they wove their way through the crowds of people lining the boardwalk, Mrs. Stuart appeared from the mercantile.

"You owe me, Shane McCoy," she declared.

Tessa looked between the two.

Mrs. Stuart shrugged. "Never mind. Bring your little ones around soon. I've got some peppermint candy for them."

Shane's eyes widened. "Will do."

Tessa tugged on her ring. "I almost forgot. You'll be wanting this back, Mrs. Stuart."

Shaking her head, Mrs. Stuart grinned. "Oh no. That's all yours. Bought and paid for. Your husband has good taste, Mrs. McCoy."

"You'd best call me Tessa. There's too many Mrs. McCoys around here."

"Ain't that the truth?" She laughed. "Ain't that the truth."

They arrived back at the hotel where Doc Johnsen had been roused. He inspected her bruise and prescribed a compress of raw meat, which Tessa politely declined.

As he turned to leave, she called out, "I've got your stethoscope."

He rubbed the back of his neck. "I wondered why someone broke a window for that. Why do a bunch of outlaws need doctor's equipment?"

"To crack a safe."

"I had no idea." The doc shrugged. "All's well that ends well, I guess. Try and stay out of trouble, Mrs. McCoy. I don't think your husband's nerves can stand another incident."

Left alone with Shane, Tessa grew shy. "Thank you for looking out for me."

His expression was stern. "The doc is right. You're gonna be the death of me. Promise you'll never put yourself in danger like that again." He heaved one of his great, gusty sighs, and this time she didn't even mind.

Shane grasped her hand. "Why did you marry me?"

The marshal had urged honesty in the marriage, and it was high time she found her courage. "I noticed two things about you that day in Wichita. The second thing was how much your children loved you and how much you loved them. I knew right then I wanted to be a part of that love."

"What was the first thing you noticed?"

"I noticed how handsome you were. Alyce had mussed your jacket, your trouser leg was caught on your boot and your hat was set at an odd angle. I'd never seen a finer-looking gentleman in all my life. So there you have it, Shane. I married you for your striking good looks. Now you know the truth."

"And because you felt sorry for me. I saw your book, Tessa."

Her stomach dipped. "Then you know everything?"

"Yes."

She ducked her head. "I had this idea that if I made up for all the things I'd done, I'd be worthy of love from someone like you. But it doesn't work that way, does it? Now the whole town knows I can pick a lock and open a safe."

"That's where you're wrong. I love you. I love everything about you. Your past, your present and your future."

Her whole world burst into color. "Truly?"

"Truly." He squeezed her hands. "The hardest thing

a person can do is change. You're the bravest person I know, Tessa."

"I love you." Her voice caught and she tugged her hands free. "I love you, but I was afraid to tell you. I was afraid if you knew who I was and what I'd done, you'd hate me."

He reached for her but she strained away. "I endangered your life and the life of the children."

"You walked right into a trap for us." His eyes shimmered with emotion. "If that's not love, I don't know what is."

"I had to do something. As long as Emmett owed the Fultons, they'd never let us live in peace."

"You put your life in danger for us. For Emmett. Even though you knew you'd expose your secret?"

"Yes."

"That sounds like a very honorable thing to do. I love you, Tessa, and I don't love dishonorable people."

"But the children," she implored. "Who wants a former outlaw for a mother?"

"Outlaws make the best parents. You'll always know what they're up to. They'll be the most popular kids at school."

"And your family? What about the McCoys?"

"Did you see that restaurant this evening? Once word spread about what was happening, the whole town turned out."

"For you," she said.

"For us."

Someone knocked on the door frame and Jo peered around. "Now that the excitement is over, I thought you might want a little company. Edith has had her hands full with these two. They must have sensed something was wrong, because they wouldn't go to sleep."

Alyce and Owen toddled into the room in their pajamas. Tessa knelt on the floor and gathered them close, kissing each one in turn. She glanced up and caught sight of Emmett.

Tessa waved him forward. "Come and meet your grandchildren."

For the second time in her whole life, she caught the sheen of tears in Emmett's eyes. "And who is this little princess." He crooked his finger toward Alyce, who grinned in return. "Why, you're as pretty as a new penny."

"Aw-ice," she replied.

"Alyce," Shane corrected her.

Owen toddled nearer Tessa, who knelt by his side and smoothed his hair. "This is Owen."

Emmett stared at the boy, his expression faltering. He stooped and tilted his head, then scratched behind his ear. "Hello there, little Owen. You are the spitting image of a fellow I knew some years back."

"Don't be silly," Tessa scoffed. "He's a child."

Emmett tugged on his ear. "Oh, well. You're probably right. It's the coloring and the name. The other fellow's name was Owen, too, and he had the same eyes. That blond hair really stands out. You're nothing like that rascal, are you, little fellow? That other Owen was a real outlaw. Got himself hanged a couple years back." Emmett caught himself and grew solemn, crossing one arm across his chest. "Sorry. That's not fit talk around the children."

Shane had stilled, his expression frozen.

Emmett rubbed his chin. "Strangest outlaw I ever saw. He lost his trigger finger in an accident. Had to learn to shoot left-handed. He was never very good after that. Probably how he got himself caught."

Tessa gripped Shane's arm. He'd gone ashen.

There was little chance Emmett's observations were a coincidence. "I'm so sorry."

Shane sat back on his heels. Everything fell into place. Abby had always loved danger. She'd run off and disappeared. She'd never revealed the identity of the children's father. The one photo he had of her, the one he'd saved for the children, she'd cut out the man standing beside her.

The hand resting on the arm of the chair had been distinctive...

Tessa touched his shoulder. "If Abby had wanted them to know, she'd have given you the information. She had every opportunity."

"I think in the end she was trying to protect me."

"We'll never know for certain if he really was their father."

"No. Everyone who knew the truth is gone."

"It's strange, isn't it?" Tessa tilted her head. "How everything came together for us? What are the chances of us meeting on that platform?"

"What are you saying?"

"Maybe God was looking out for you all along." Tessa cupped his cheeks. "For you, for the children. Even for me."

"I'd like to think that," he replied.

Of all the people in Wichita, Owen had approached Tessa. What were the chances?

"Abby chose you," Tessa said. "You're their father in every way that counts."

"And you're their mother."

"No." She pressed a kiss against his cheek. "I'm their stepmother. Abby will always be their mother. She loved them. She did her best. I'll do my best as well."

"She was more troubled than I knew."

"She's at peace now. What about you, Shane? Are you at peace?"

He captured her lips and kissed her until she was breathless and sagging in his arms. "I'm moving back to the main house."

"You better. You know I don't like to be alone at night."

He nuzzled the sensitive skin at the nape of her neck. "Then I'll have to make sure you always have company."

Owen pushed his way between them and held up his arms. "Up. Up."

Tessa giggled. "I think someone is jealous."

Shane rolled his eyes. "I told myself I'd stay away from you until Christmas. I promised myself I'd give you the space to get used to me. To see if you liked me."

Tessa made a strangled sound in her throat. "I gave myself until Christmas to convince you that we suited. It's a wonder we had such trouble. We were working at cross-purposes."

"No more." He folded her in his embrace once again. "You're my wife."

"And you're my husband. You're the only man for me." Tessa drew the children in and they all hugged. "And we're a family."

Unheeding of who heard, Shane let out a whoop. He was finally the right man.

Epilogue

The top of the fir tree appeared in the door first. With much muttering and shuffling of feet, the rest of the enormous tree emerged into the ranch house. Emmett held the front and Shane anchored his arms around the cut trunk.

Tessa gasped. "I hadn't expected anything quite this, um, large."

Shane grimaced beneath the heavy weight. "An ice jam upstream changed the course of the creek. The roots were already rotted. Figured I might as well take something that was going to die anyway."

"All right." She waved him inside. "But I have no idea where you're going to put that thing."

The two men wrested the tree into place and adjusted the base around a device Wheeler and Finch had designed.

Tessa grinned at Emmett. "I was at the ladies' salon yesterday and Mrs. Edwards was asking about you."

His cheeks pinkened. "Probably wondering about the sale of the hotel."

The reward money for capturing the outlaws had been spread all over town. Tessa and Shane had refused their portion. Emmett had approached Mrs. Edwards about buying the hotel with his cut. Since her husband's passing, managing the restaurant and the hotel while keeping up with her knitting had proved too difficult.

Tessa studied her father's blush. "I heard her telling JoBeth that the new owner of the hotel was quite handsome."

Her father puffed up. "She did, did she?"

Emmett was still Emmett. The disaster with the Fultons had changed him, but she didn't know if the change was permanent. He was here now, and Tessa was going to enjoy his company and pray for the best.

"She did."

Shane caught her around the waist. "It's not a bad place to start. Tessa married me for my good looks."

"It's true," she replied. "That and some other stuff as well."

"Other stuff," he repeated with a grin.

While Tessa and Shane strung loops of berries and popcorn around the tree, Emmett sat on the floor and played with the children. He was even better with a coin than Tessa, and Alyce and Owen were delighted.

Since she'd been feeling more exhausted than usual lately, Tessa joined them. Owen toddled over and grasped the locket around Tessa's neck. She released the clasp and revealed the two tiny oval pictures.

She pointed at each one in turn. "That's my mama, and that's my dada."

Owen reverently touched each of the pictures. He pointed to Shane and said, "Dada." Without hesitating, he pointed to Tessa and said, "Mama."

The confusion was natural. She started to protest but

Shane interrupted her reply. "Yes, Owen. Mama and Dada."

Touching Shane's cheek, Tessa smiled tenderly. "Abby is always with us."

Shane covered her hand with his. "Yes. Always."

Owen held out his chubby hand. "Ball."

Tessa glanced upward. "Thank You."

She didn't know why they'd been brought together all those months ago, but she was eternally grateful.

She stood and strung another length of popcorn around the tree. "This is the first tree I've ever decorated. I'm glad it's such a fine one."

Shane knelt at her feet.

Tessa laughed. "What are you doing?"

He took her hand, his gaze solemn. "Tessa Spencer McCoy, I have officially asked your father for your hand in marriage."

Emmett glanced up and winked. "He did."

Shane beamed. "Emmett Spencer has enthusiastically agreed to my suit."

Her father grunted. "I don't know if *enthusiastic* is the word I'd use."

"With Emmett's *enthusiastic* permission," Shane continued, "I officially ask for your hand in marriage. To love and to honor, to laugh with, to cry with, to hold and to cherish. I promise that I will always build forts with you and help you hide from our children."

Her eyes misted. "We're already married."

His expression grew serious. "Someone once asked me what made me happy. I didn't have an answer. Now I know. You make me happy. I love your sharp wit, your ability to cook potatoes in the German style and your eccentric family."

Emmett grunted again.

Shane's throat worked. "I love that you brought joy into our house and peace into my soul."

Tessa knelt before him and cupped his face. "Merry Christmas, my darling. I love you more than Owen loves his ball."

"Merry Christmas."

She indicated the snow falling gently beyond the window. "If this weather keeps up, we may be snowed in after Emmett leaves."

Shane dropped a kiss on her forehead. "The weather has always been good to me where you're concerned."

In deference to the falling snow, Emmett left an hour later. The twins were exhausted from all the attention and collapsed into slumber soon after.

Shane took a chair before the Christmas tree. Tessa perched on his knee and gazed out the window.

He rested a hand on her hip. "Are you hungry? Thirsty? There's some spiced cider left."

Tessa wrinkled her nose. "No, thank you."

His grip tightened on her waist. "Are you feeling all right?" His voice vibrated with concern. "You didn't eat much dinner."

"My stomach has been bothering me lately."

Shane grew still. "Should we call Doc Johnsen?"

Tessa shook her head. "No. I feel fine otherwise. Just a little tired. And my stomach usually only bothers me in the morning."

Their gazes locked.

Shane's expression filled with wonder. "Do you think?"

"It's too soon." Tessa touched her stomach. "Far too soon."

Shane smiled. "I guess we'll know in the fall."

Filled with wonder and hope for the future, she leaned back and tucked her head into the crook of his neck. "Wouldn't that be wonderful?"

"Yes." Shane pressed his lips against her temple. "You know what would be even better?"

Tessa frowned. "No."

"Another set of twins."

She groaned. "Be careful what you hope for, Shane McCoy."

He kissed her then, long and sweet. "I hope we're snowed in for a week."

"Merry Christmas, my love," Tessa whispered.

"Merry Christmas, my love," he replied quietly.

Outside the window, moonlight sparked off the snow, and one star twinkled brighter than all the rest.

* * * * *

Dear Readers,

The book Tessa uses, *Bartleby's Book of Household Management*, was inspired by an actual book. In 1861, Mrs. Isabella Beeton published *Beeton's Book of Household Management*. The volume was a compilation of twenty-four installments in the *Englishwoman's Domestic Magazine*. By 1868, almost two million copies had been sold. I think it's fair to assume a few of those copies had made it across the pond by the late 1880s.

While the book consists mostly of recipes, many of them copied from other sources, Mrs. Beeton also included tips on household management. Though readers assumed Mrs. Beeton was an elderly woman with gray hair and a starched apron, she was only twenty-one when she started writing the book.

Beeton's Book of Household Management has been lauded as a glimpse into the history of Victorian England. I had fun comparing the rules and formalities of Victorian England to the rough-and-ready conditions of the Old West.

I hope you enjoyed Shane and Tessa's story. I love to hear from readers! If you're interested in learning more about the Prairie Courtship series, visit my website at SherriShackelford.com, or reach me at sherrishackelford@gmail.com, facebook/SherriShackelfordAuthor, Twitter @smshackelford, or regular old snail mail: PO Box 116, Elkhorn, NE 68022.

Thanks for reading!
Sherri Shackelford